THE PANIC

THE PANIC

WASHINGTON ST
PATH
PATH

Neil Kleid
Script & Letters

Andrea Mutti
Interiors & Cover

Edited by **Felix Stringer Horne** and **Mariah McCourt**

Created by **Neil Kleid** and **Andrea Mutti**

Dark Horse Books

MIGDAL COMICS

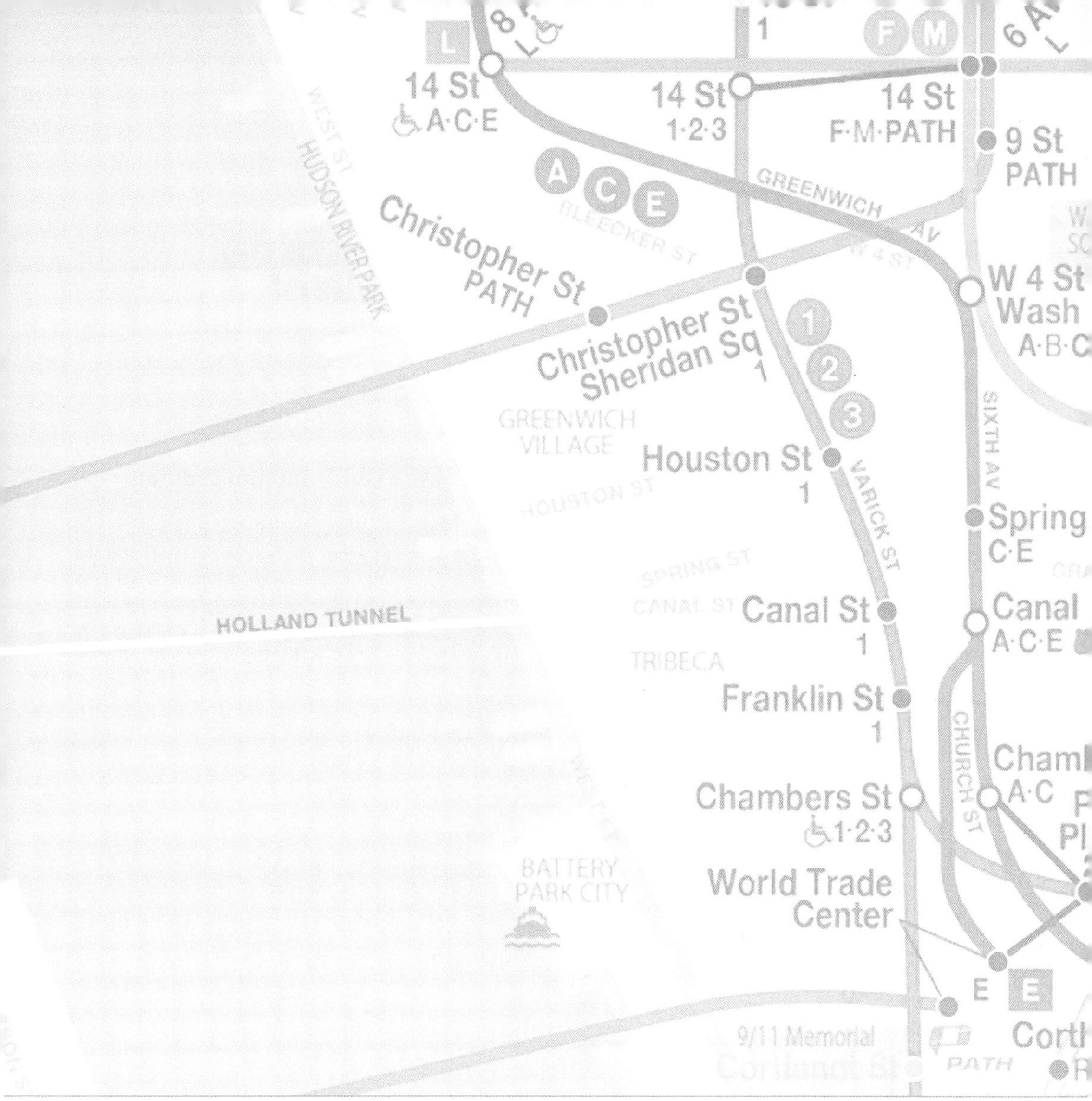
L
14 St
A·C·E
1
14 St
1·2·3
F
M
14 St
F·M·PATH
9 St
PATH
WEST ST
HUDSON RIVER PARK
A
C
E
GREENWICH AV
BLEECKER ST
W 4 ST
Christopher St
PATH
W 4 St
Christopher St
Sheridan Sq
1
1
2
3
GREENWICH VILLAGE
Houston St
1
HOUSTON ST
VARICK ST
SIXTH AV
Spring
C·E
SPRING ST
CANAL ST
Canal St
1
Canal
A·C·E
HOLLAND TUNNEL
TRIBECA
Franklin St
1
CHURCH ST
Chambers St
1·2·3
A·C
WEST ST
BATTERY PARK CITY
World Trade Center
E
E
9/11 Memorial
PATH

Andrea would like to thank **Aunt Ornella**.

Neil would like to thank **Laurie**, **Jack**, **Owen**, **Olivia**, and **Connor**.

The creative team would like to thank **Amanda Stevens**, diversity and inclusion consultant for *The Panic*, and also **Chip Mosher** and everyone at **Comixology** for believing in us.

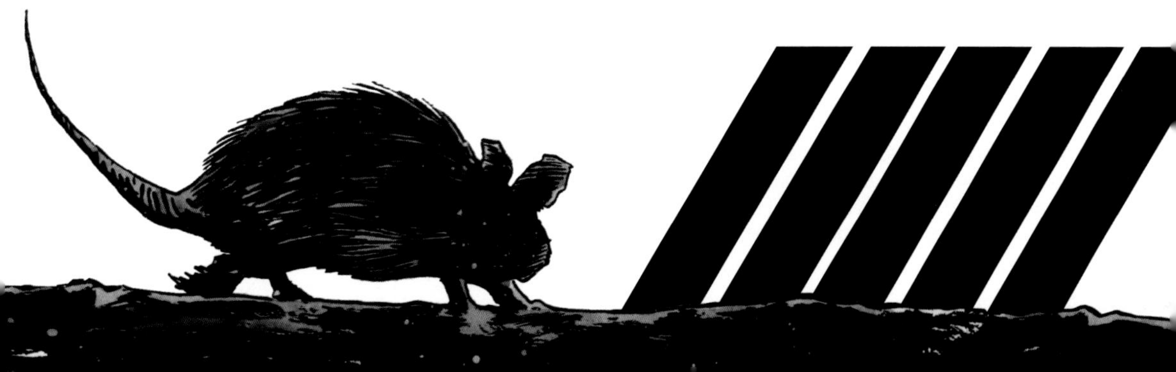

Dark Horse Team

President & Publisher
Mike Richardson

Editor
Daniel Chabon

Assistant Editors
Chuck Howitt-Lease & Misha Gehr

Designer
Lin Huang

Digital Art Technician
Jason Rickerd

Special thanks to Tom Ashley, Jeff DiBartolomeo, Bryce Gold, and Em Erdman.

Neil Hankerson Executive Vice President | Tom Weddle Chief Financial Officer | Dale LaFountain Chief Information Officer | Tim Wiesch Vice President of Licensing | Matt Parkinson Vice President of Marketing | Vanessa Todd-Holmes Vice President of Production and Scheduling | Mark Bernardi Vice President of Book Trade and Digital Sales | Randy Lahrman Vice President of Product Development | Ken Lizzi General Counsel | Dave Marshall Editor in Chief | Davey Estrada Editorial Director | Chris Warner Senior Books Editor | Cary Grazzini Director of Specialty Projects | Lia Ribacchi Art Director | Matt Dryer Director of Digital Art and Prepress | Michael Gombos Senior Director of Licensed Publications | Kari Yadro Director of Custom Programs | Kari Torson Director of International Licensing

Published by Dark Horse Books
A division of Dark Horse Comics LLC
10956 SE Main Street, Milwaukie, OR 97222

First edition: November 2022
Trade paperback ISBN 978-1-50672-807-0
Comic Shop Locator Service: comicshoplocator.com

10 9 8 7 6 5 4 3 2 1
Printed in China

THE PANIC
Contents © 2021, 2022 Neil Kleid and Andrea Mutti. All rights reserved. "Comixology" and the Comixology logos are registered trademarks of Comixology. Dark Horse Books® and the Dark Horse logo are registered trademarks of Dark Horse Comics LLC. All rights reserved. No portion of this publication may be reproduced or transmitted, in any form or by any means, without the express written permission of Neil Kleid and Andrea Mutti, Comixology, or Dark Horse Comics LLC. Names, characters, places, and incidents featured in this publication either are the product of the author's imagination or are used fictitiously. Any resemblance to actual persons (living or dead), events, institutions, or locales, without satiric intent, is coincidental.

Library of Congress Cataloging-in-Publication Data

Names: Kleid, Neil, author. | Mutti, Andrea, 1973- illustrator. | Stringer-Horne, Felix, editor. | McCourt, Mariah, editor.
Title: The panic / Neil Kleid, script & letters ; Andrea Mutti, interiors & cover ; edited by Felix Stringer Horne and Mariah McCourt
Description: First edition. | Milwaukie, OR : Dark Horse Books, 2022. | Summary: "Ten strangers, trapped beneath the Hudson River, are forced to depend on their fellow commuters in order to survive an apocalyptic event. Those left must fight their way through more than rubble to make it to safety. But the darkness is closing in, and with it their own individual fears and paranoia. It'll be a long road to the end of the tunnel . . . that is, if they don't kill each other before they get there."-- Provided by publisher.
Identifiers: LCCN 2022022083 | ISBN 9781506728070 (trade paperback)
Subjects: LCGFT: Apocalyptic comics. | Graphic novels.
Classification: LCC PN6727.K596 P36 2022 | DDC 741.5/973--dc23/eng/20220606
LC record available at https://lccn.loc.gov/2022022083

01
“Coffin”

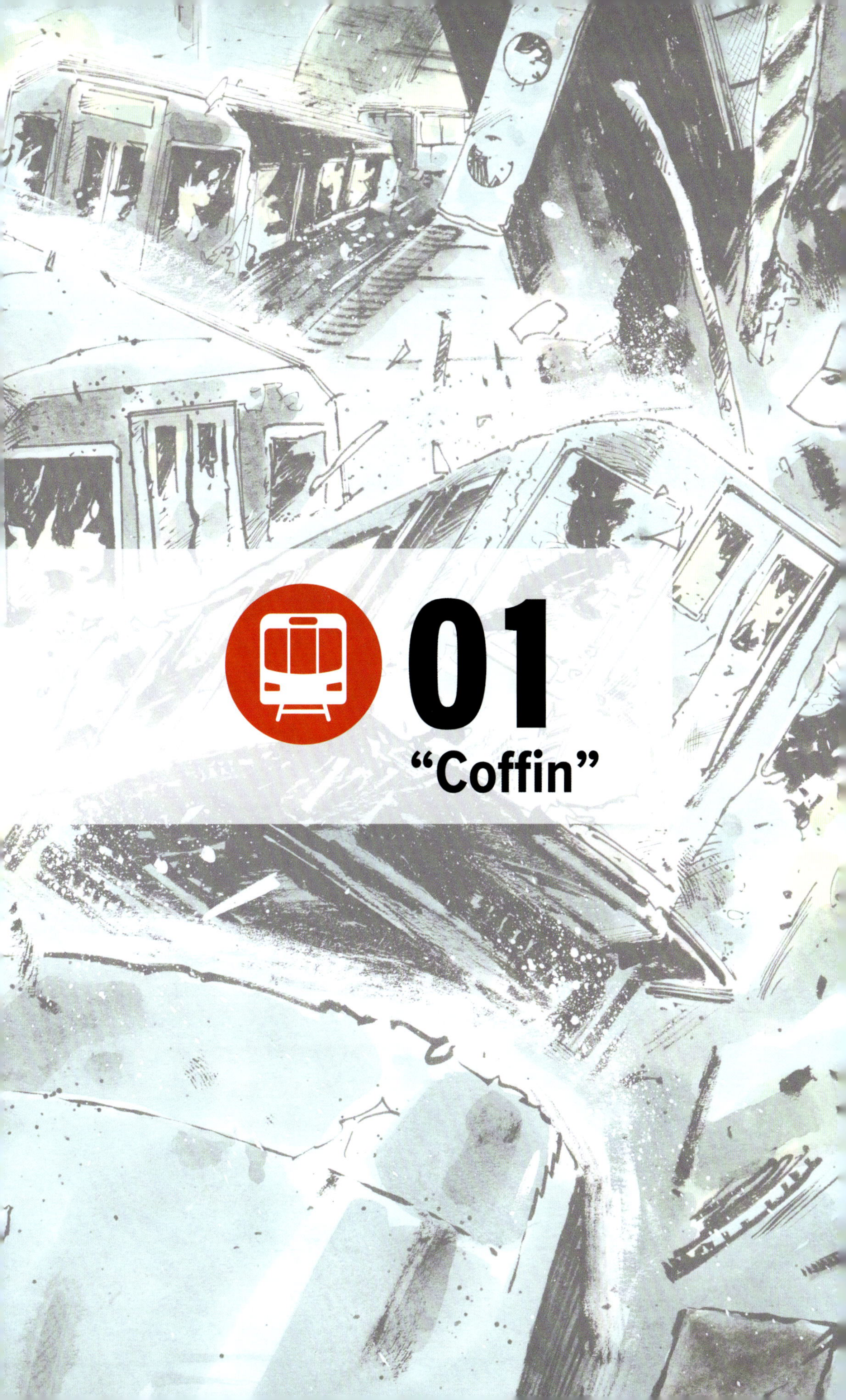

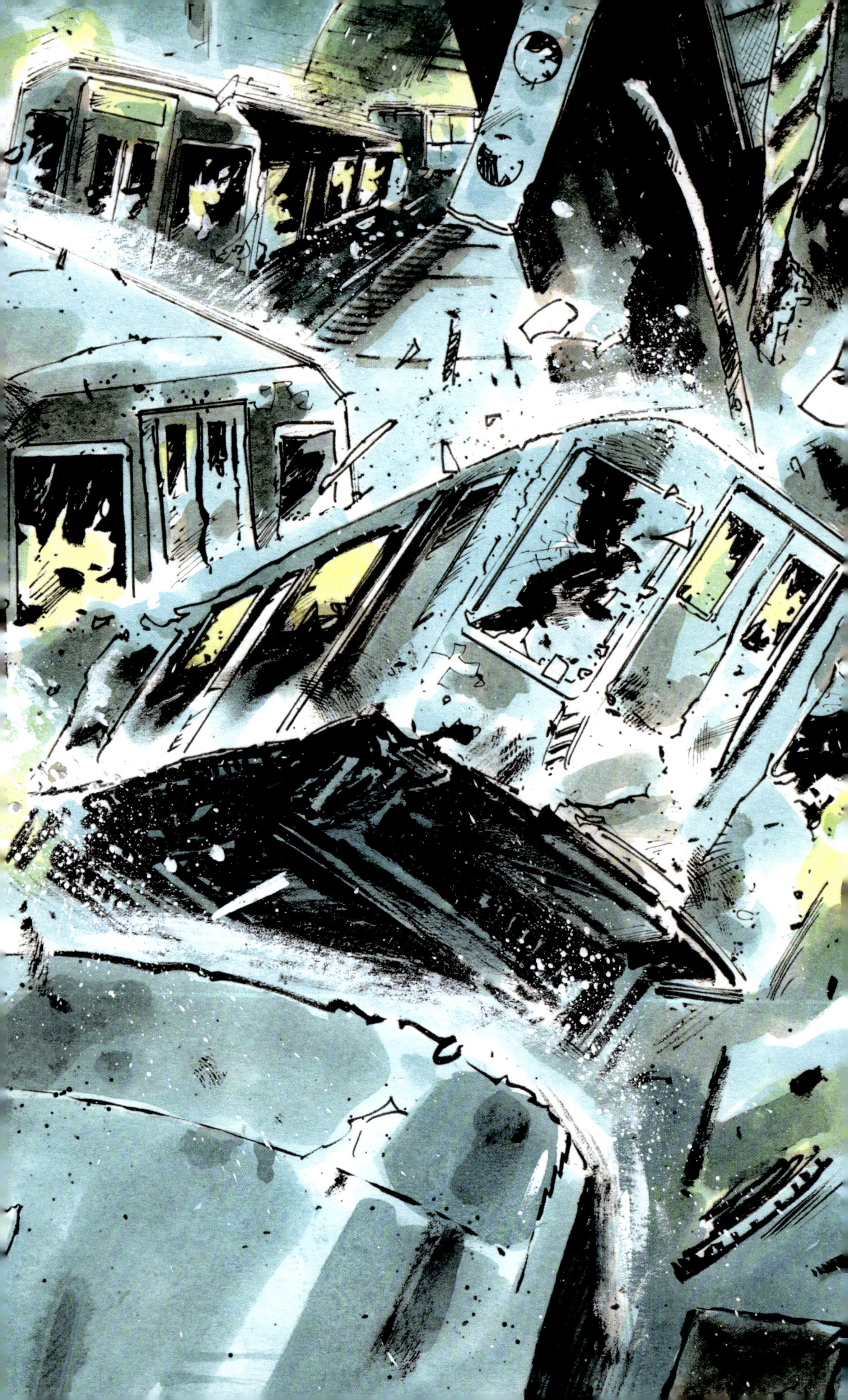

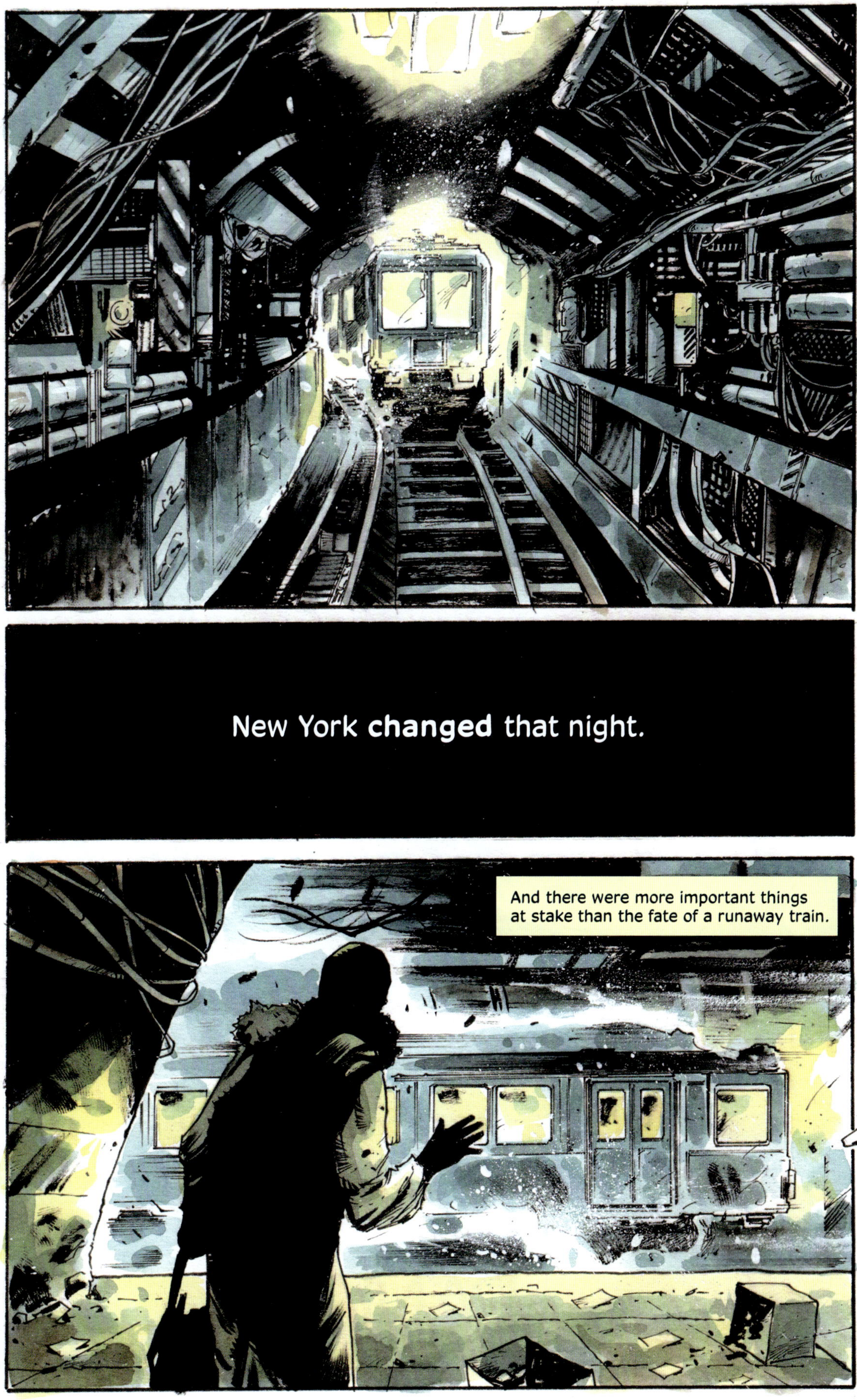
New York changed that night.
And there were more important things at stake than the fate of a runaway train.

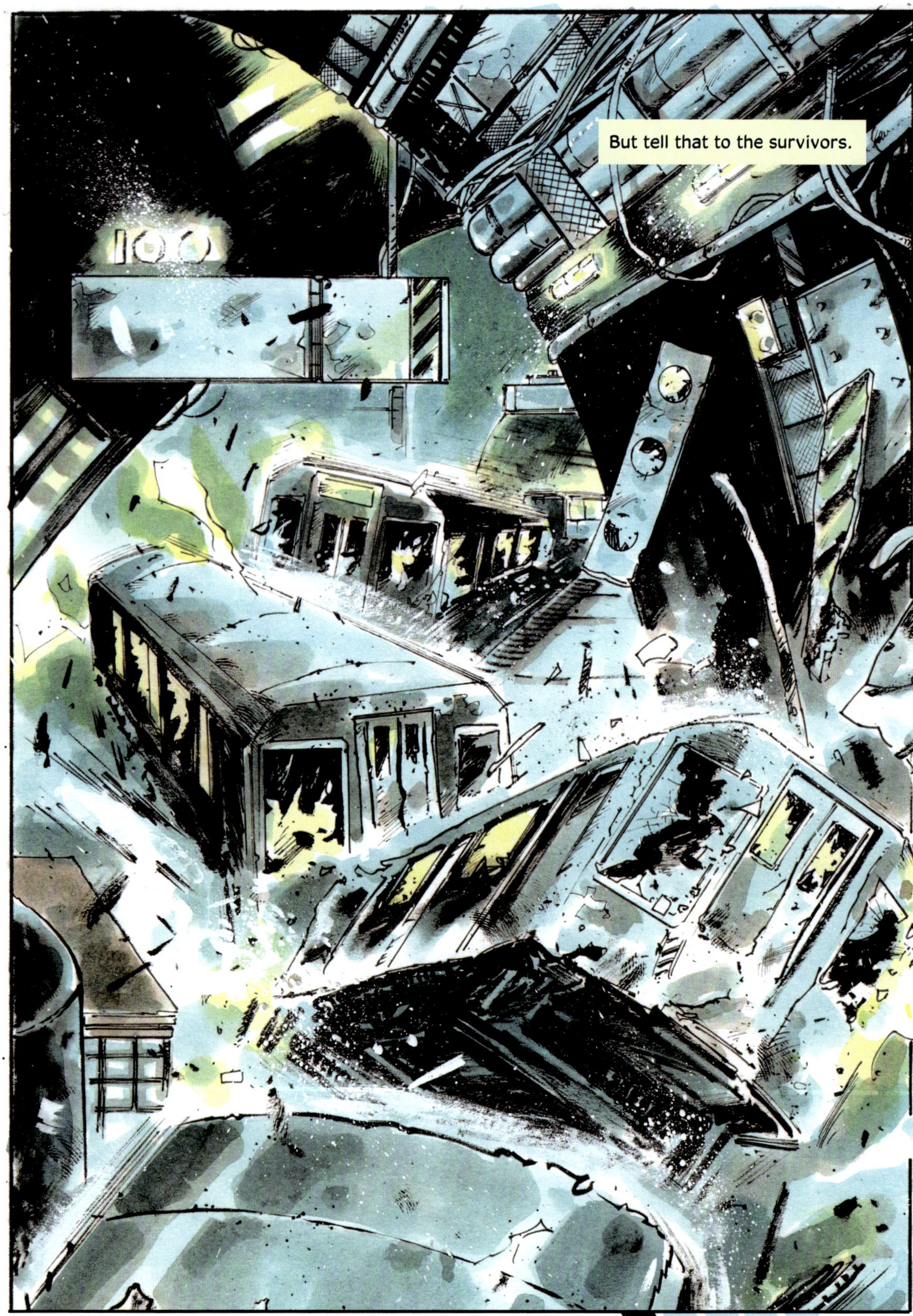
But tell that to the survivors.
100

the
PANIC
Chapter One: "Coffin"

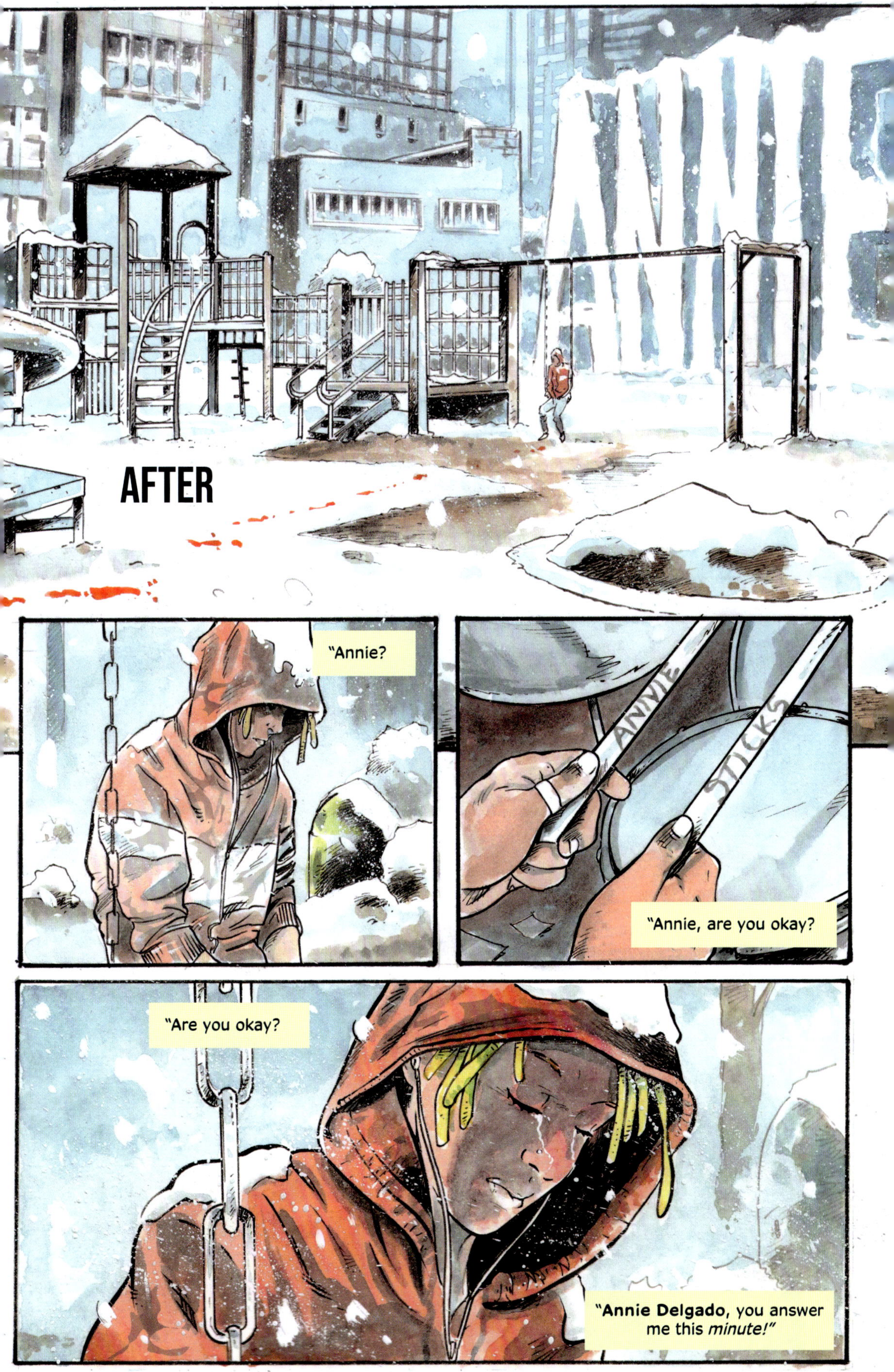
AFTER
"Annie?
ANNIE
STICKS
"Annie, are you okay?
"Are you okay?
"**Annie Delgado**, you answer me this *minute!*"

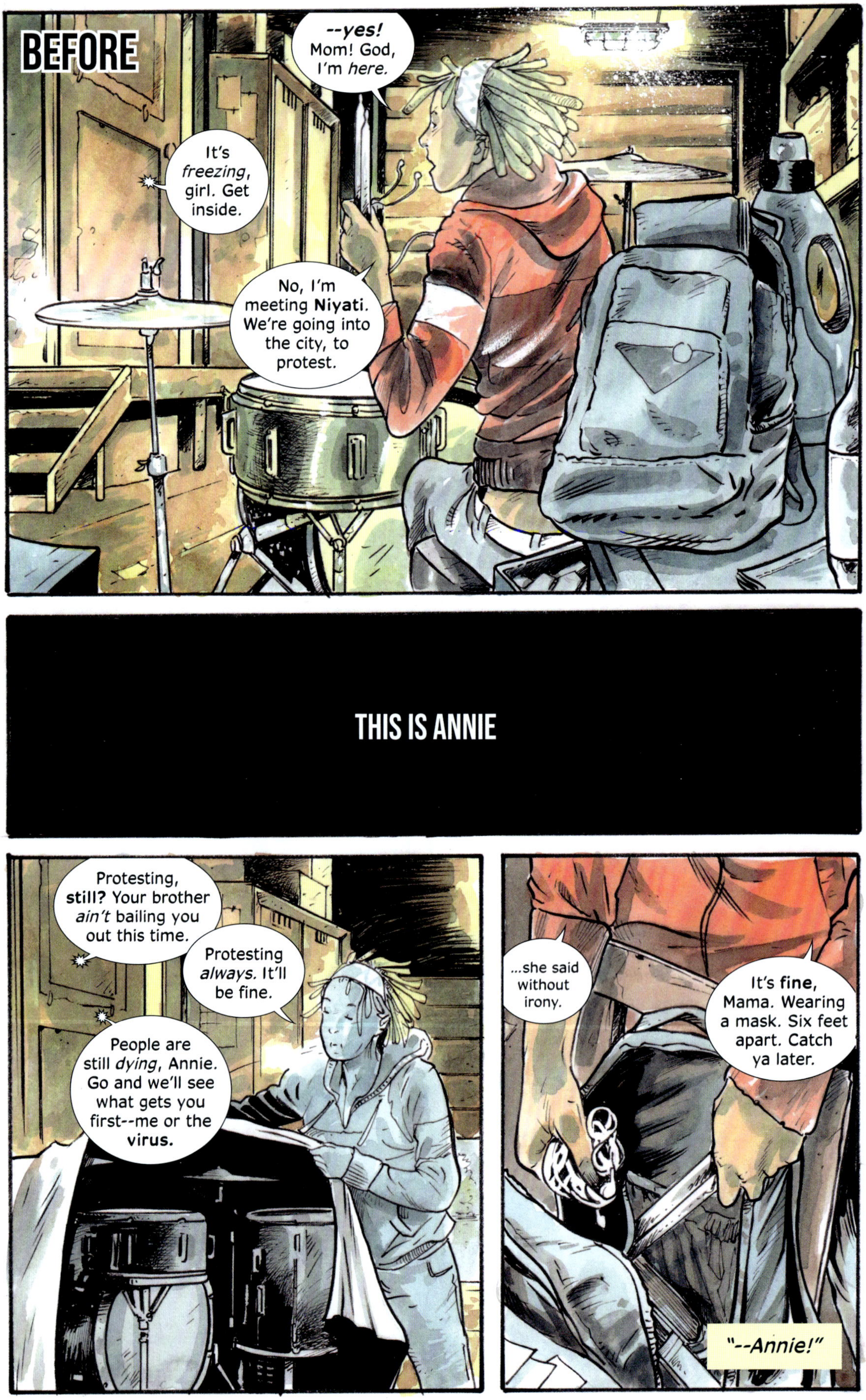
BEFORE
--*yes!* Mom! God, I'm *here.*
It's *freezing*, girl. Get inside.
No, I'm meeting **Niyati**. We're going into the city, to protest.
THIS IS ANNIE
Protesting, **still?** Your brother *ain't* bailing you out this time.
Protesting *always.* It'll be fine.
People are still *dying*, Annie. Go and we'll see what gets you first--me or the **virus.**
...she said without irony.
It's **fine,** Mama. Wearing a mask. Six feet apart. Catch ya later.
"--*Annie!*"

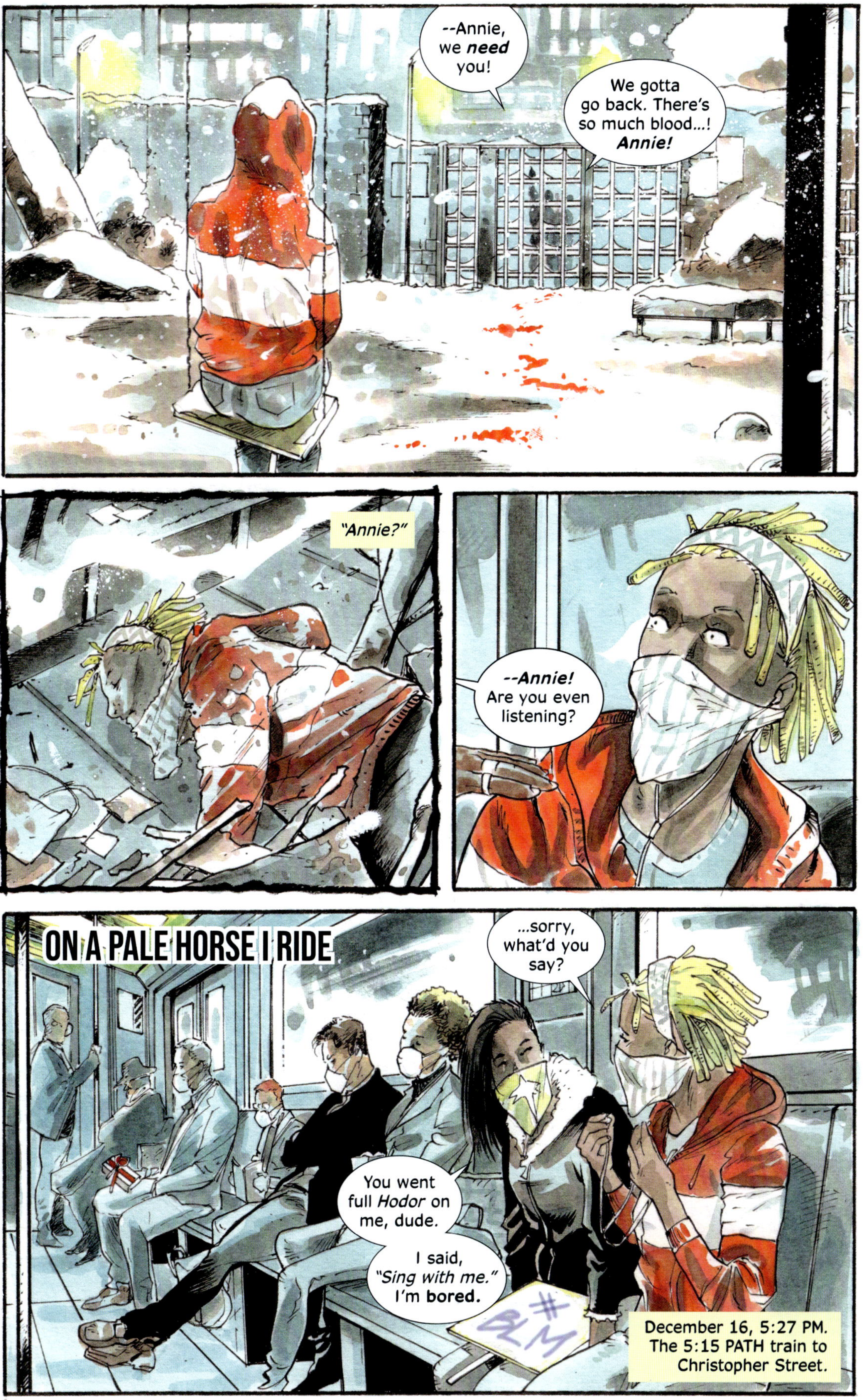
--Annie, we *need* you!
We gotta go back. There's so much blood...! ***Annie!***
"Annie?"
--Annie! Are you even listening?
ON A PALE HORSE I RIDE
...sorry, what'd you say?
You went full *Hodor* on me, dude.
I said, *"Sing with me."* I'm **bored.**
#BLM
December 16, 5:27 PM. The 5:15 PATH train to Christopher Street.

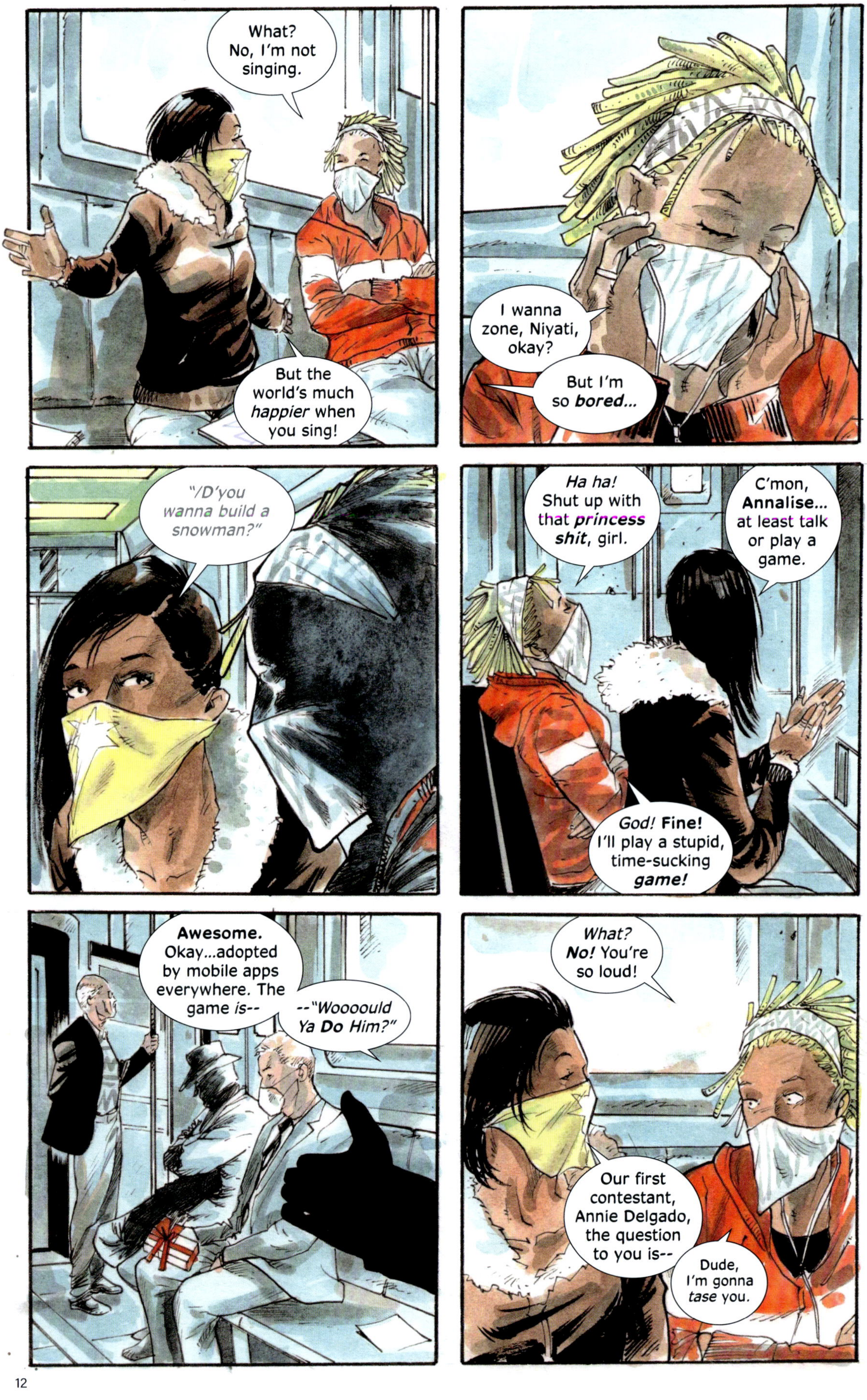
What? No, I'm not singing.
But the world's much *happier* when you sing!
I wanna zone, Niyati, okay?
But I'm so ***bored...***
"/D'you wanna build a snowman?"
Ha ha! Shut up with that ***princess shit***, girl.
C'mon, **Annalise...** at least talk or play a game.
God! **Fine!** I'll play a stupid, time-sucking ***game!***
Awesome. Okay...adopted by mobile apps everywhere. The game *is--*
--"Woooould Ya ***Do*** *Him?"*
What? ***No!*** You're so loud!
Our first contestant, Annie Delgado, the question to you is--
Dude, I'm gonna *tase* you.

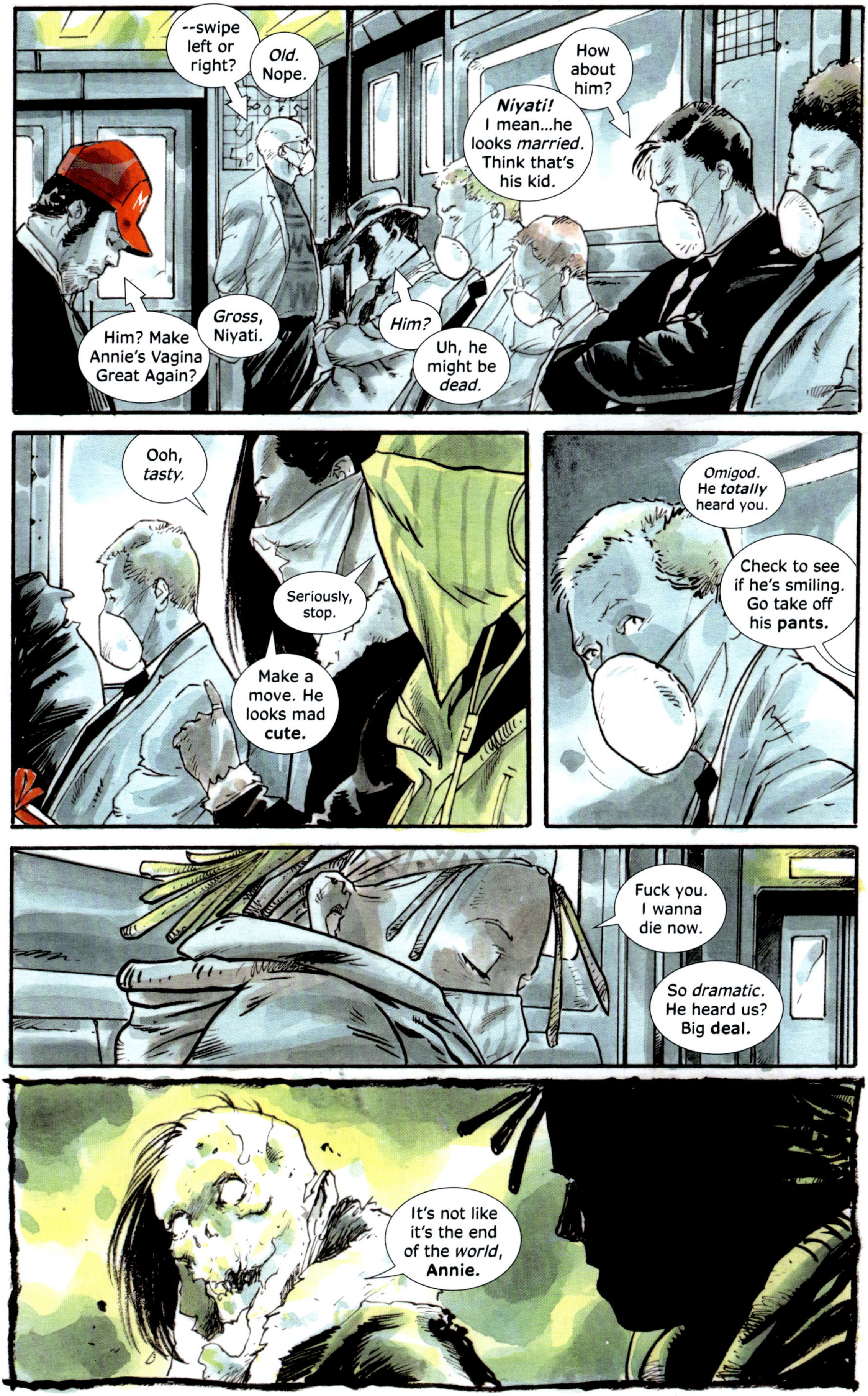
--swipe left or right?
Old. Nope.
How about him?
Niyati! I mean...he looks married. Think that's his kid.
Him? Make Annie's Vagina Great Again?
Gross, Niyati.
Him?
Uh, he might be dead.
Ooh, tasty.
Seriously, stop.
Make a move. He looks mad cute.
Omigod. He totally heard you.
Check to see if he's smiling. Go take off his pants.
Fuck you. I wanna die now.
So dramatic. He heard us? Big deal.
It's not like it's the end of the world, Annie.

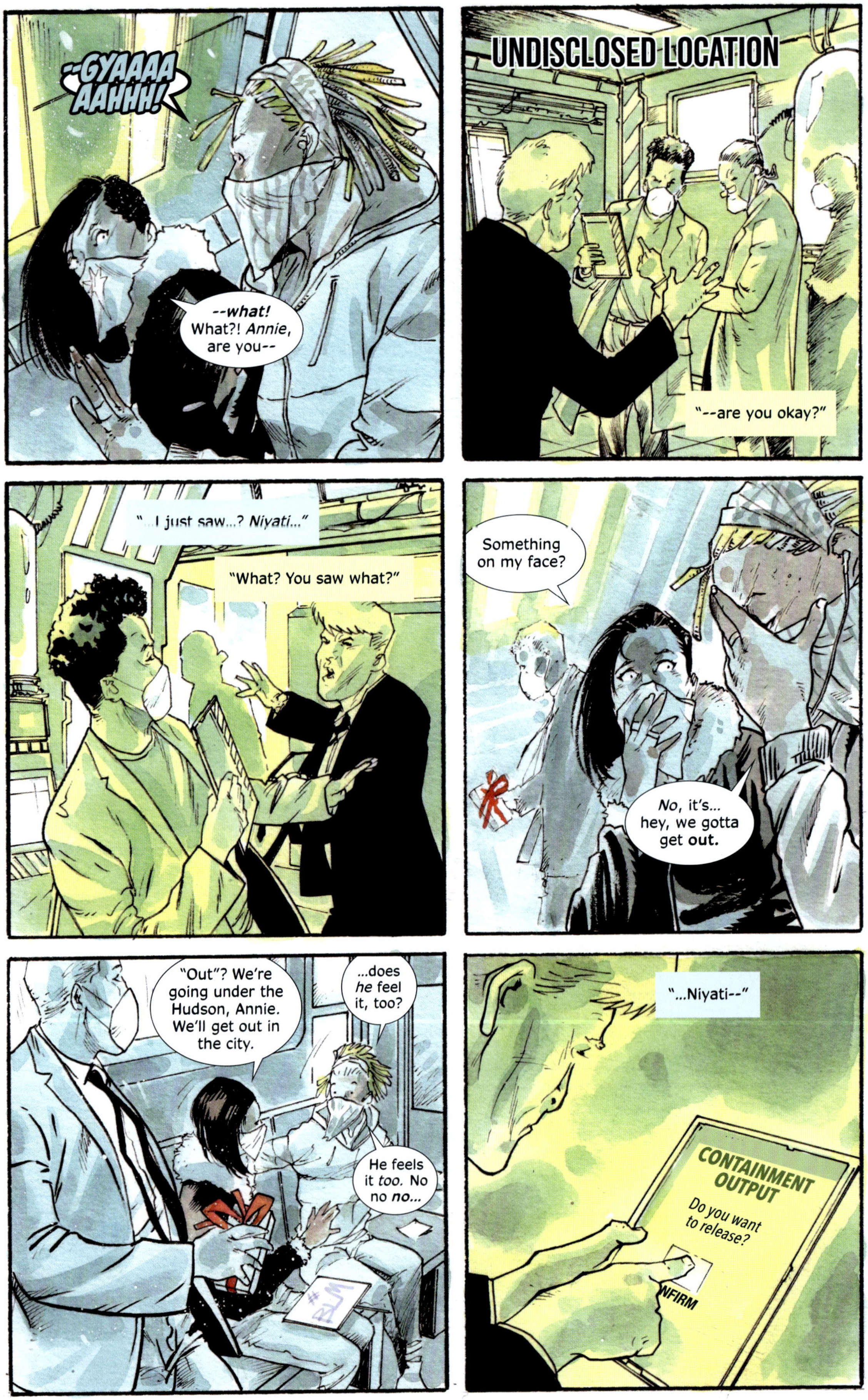

--GYAAAA AAHHH!
--what! What?! Annie, are you--
UNDISCLOSED LOCATION
"--are you okay?"
"...I just saw...? Niyati..."
"What? You saw what?"
Something on my face?
No, it's... hey, we gotta get out.
"Out"? We're going under the Hudson, Annie. We'll get out in the city.
...does he feel it, too?
He feels it too. No no no...
#BLM
"...Niyati--"
CONTAINMENT OUTPUT
Do you want to release?
NFIRM

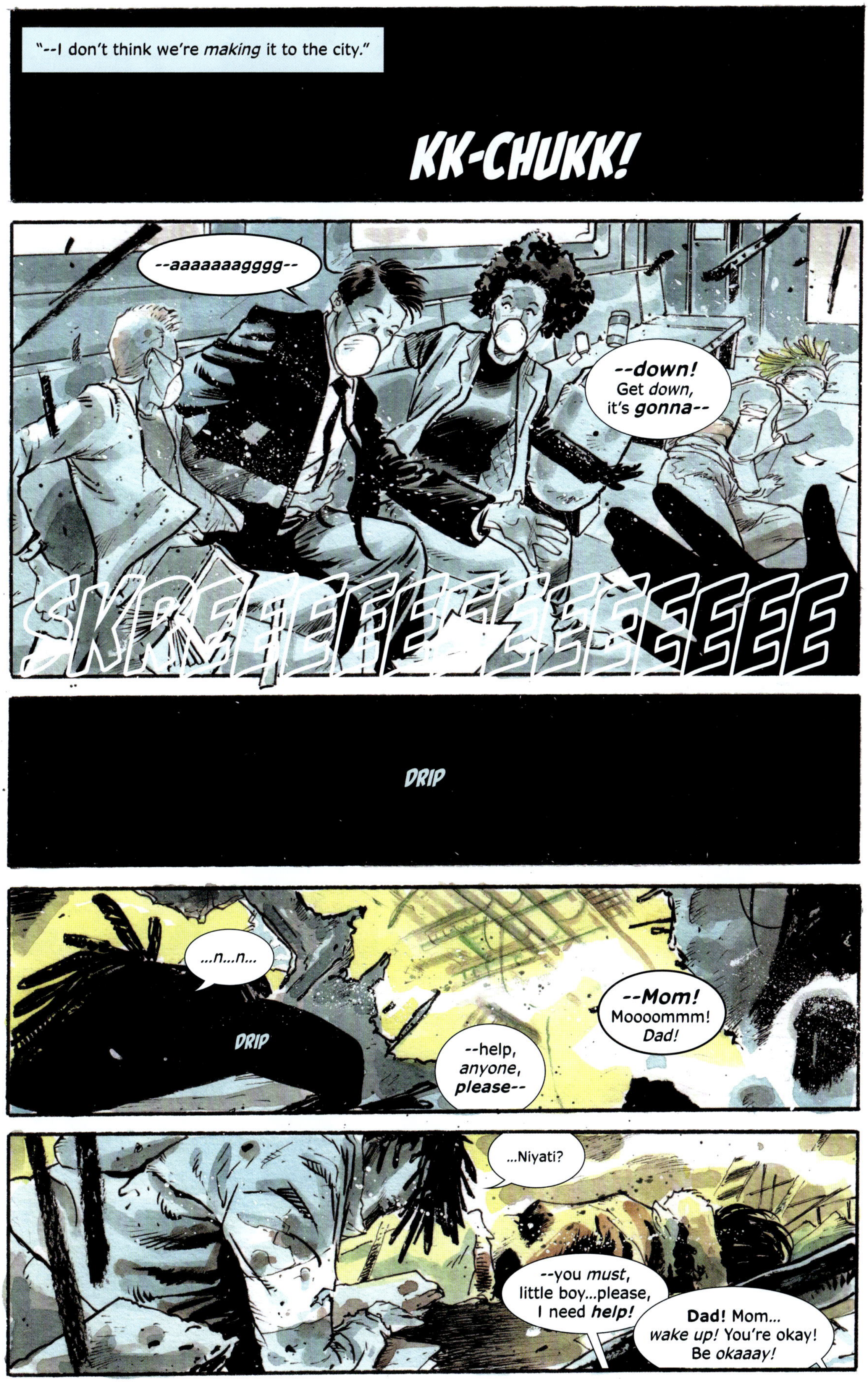
"--I don't think we're *making* it to the city."
KK-CHUKK!
--aaaaaaagggg--
--**down!** Get *down*, it's **gonna**--
SKREEEEEEEEEEEEEE
DRIP
...n...n...
DRIP
--help, *anyone*, **please**--
--**Mom!** Moooommm! *Dad!*
...Niyati?
--you *must*, little boy...please, I need **help!**
Dad! Mom... *wake up!* You're okay! Be *okaaay!*

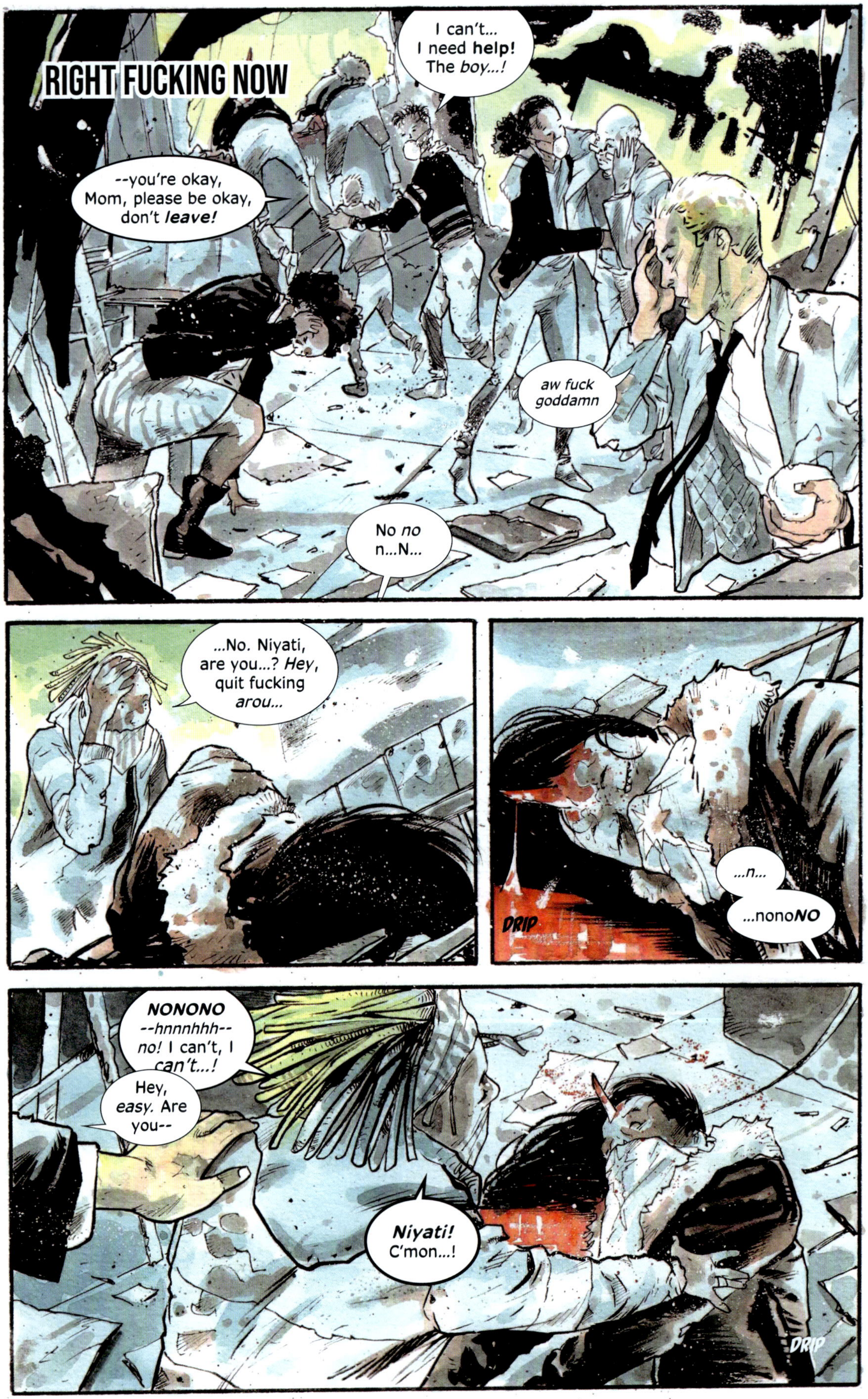
RIGHT FUCKING NOW
I can't... I need **help!** The *boy*...!
--you're okay, Mom, please be okay, don't ***leave!***
aw fuck goddamn
No *no* n...N...
...No. Niyati, are you...? *Hey*, quit fucking *arou...*
...n...
...nono***NO***
DRIP
NONONO *--hnnnhhh--* *no!* I can't, I *can't...!*
Hey, *easy.* Are you--
Niyati! C'mon...!
DRIP

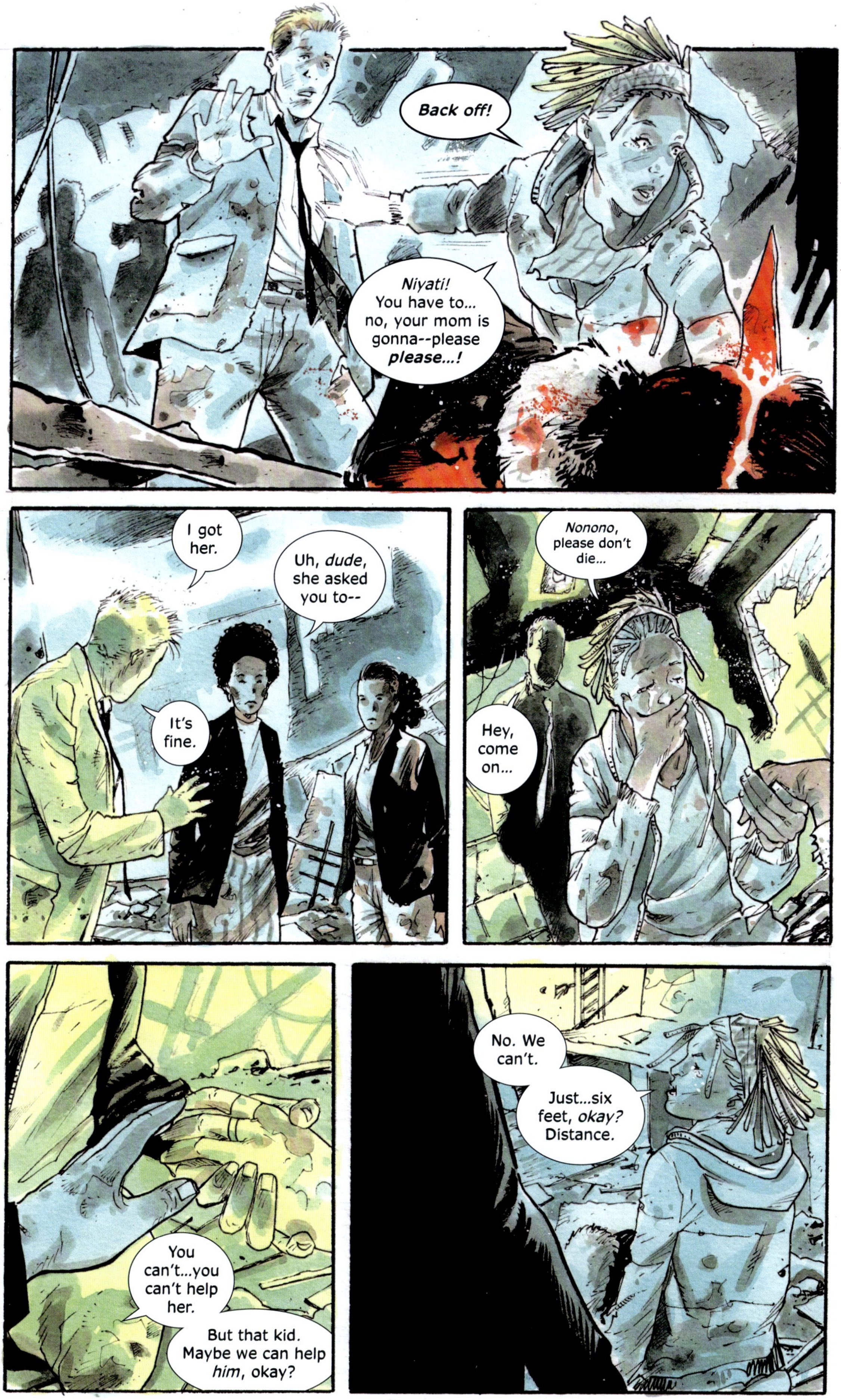
Back off!
Niyati! You have to... no, your mom is gonna--please please...!
I got her.
Uh, dude, she asked you to--
It's fine.
Nonono, please don't die...
Hey, come on...
You can't...you can't help her.
But that kid. Maybe we can help him, okay?
No. We can't.
Just...six feet, okay? Distance.

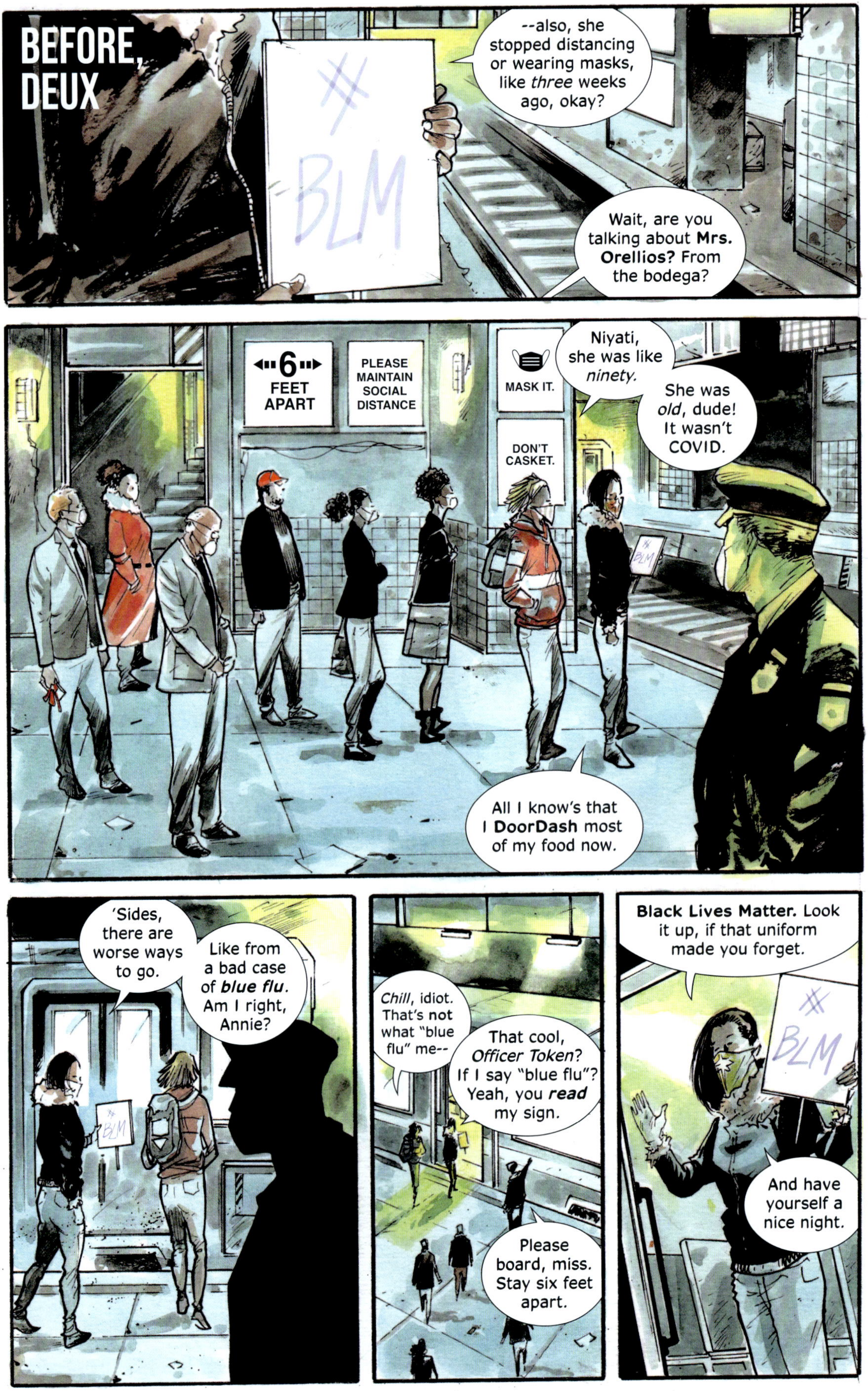
BEFORE, DEUX
--also, she stopped distancing or wearing masks, like three weeks ago, okay?
Wait, are you talking about Mrs. Orellios? From the bodega?
#BLM
6 FEET APART
PLEASE MAINTAIN SOCIAL DISTANCE
MASK IT.
DON'T CASKET.
Niyati, she was like ninety.
She was old, dude! It wasn't COVID.
All I know's that I DoorDash most of my food now.
'Sides, there are worse ways to go.
Like from a bad case of blue flu. Am I right, Annie?
Chill, idiot. That's not what "blue flu" me--
That cool, Officer Token? If I say "blue flu"? Yeah, you read my sign.
Please board, miss. Stay six feet apart.
Black Lives Matter. Look it up, if that uniform made you forget.
And have yourself a nice night.

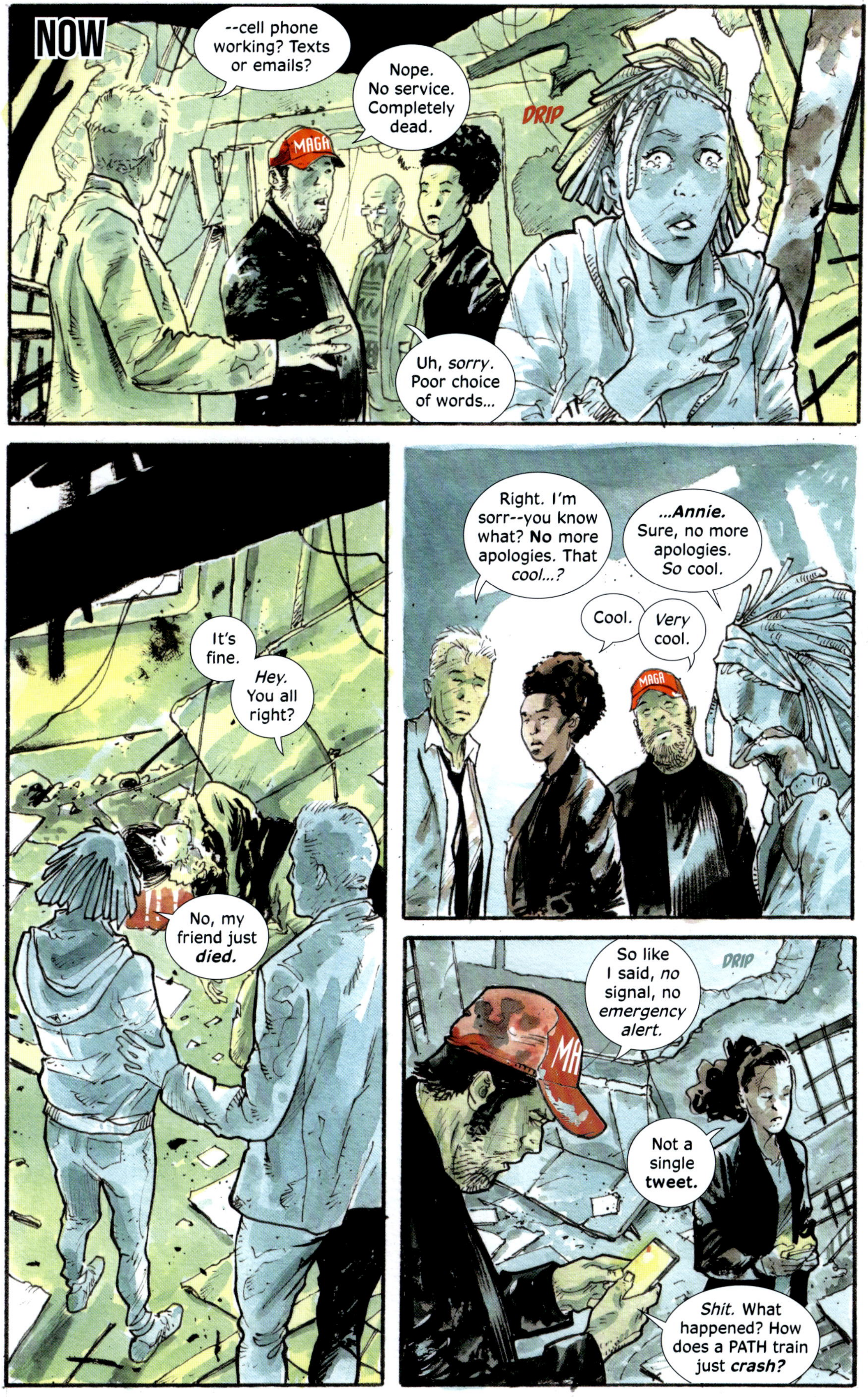
NOW
--cell phone working? Texts or emails?
Nope. No service. Completely dead.
DRIP
Uh, *sorry*. Poor choice of words...
It's fine.
Hey. You all right?
No, my friend just ***died.***
Right. I'm sorr--you know what? **No** more apologies. That *cool...?*
...Annie. Sure, no more apologies. *So* cool.
Cool.
Very cool.
So like I said, *no* signal, no *emergency alert.*
DRIP
Not a single **tweet.**
Shit. What happened? How does a PATH train just ***crash?***

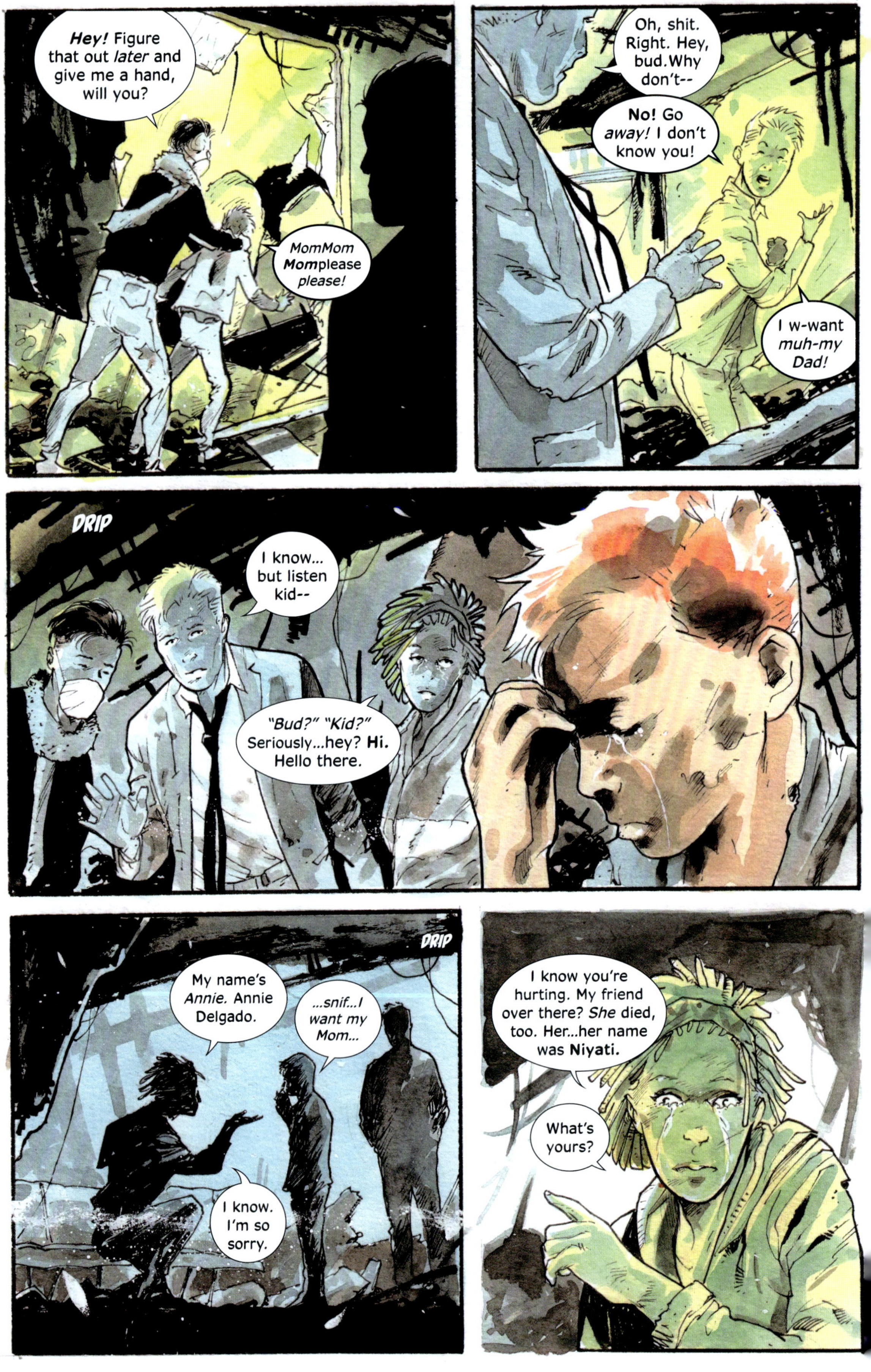
Hey! Figure that out later and give me a hand, will you?
MomMom Momplease please!
Oh, shit. Right. Hey, bud. Why don't--
No! Go away! I don't know you!
I w-want muh-my Dad!
DRIP
I know... but listen kid--
"Bud?" "Kid?" Seriously...hey? Hi. Hello there.
DRIP
My name's Annie. Annie Delgado.
...snif...I want my Mom...
I know. I'm so sorry.
I know you're hurting. My friend over there? She died, too. Her...her name was Niyati.
What's yours?

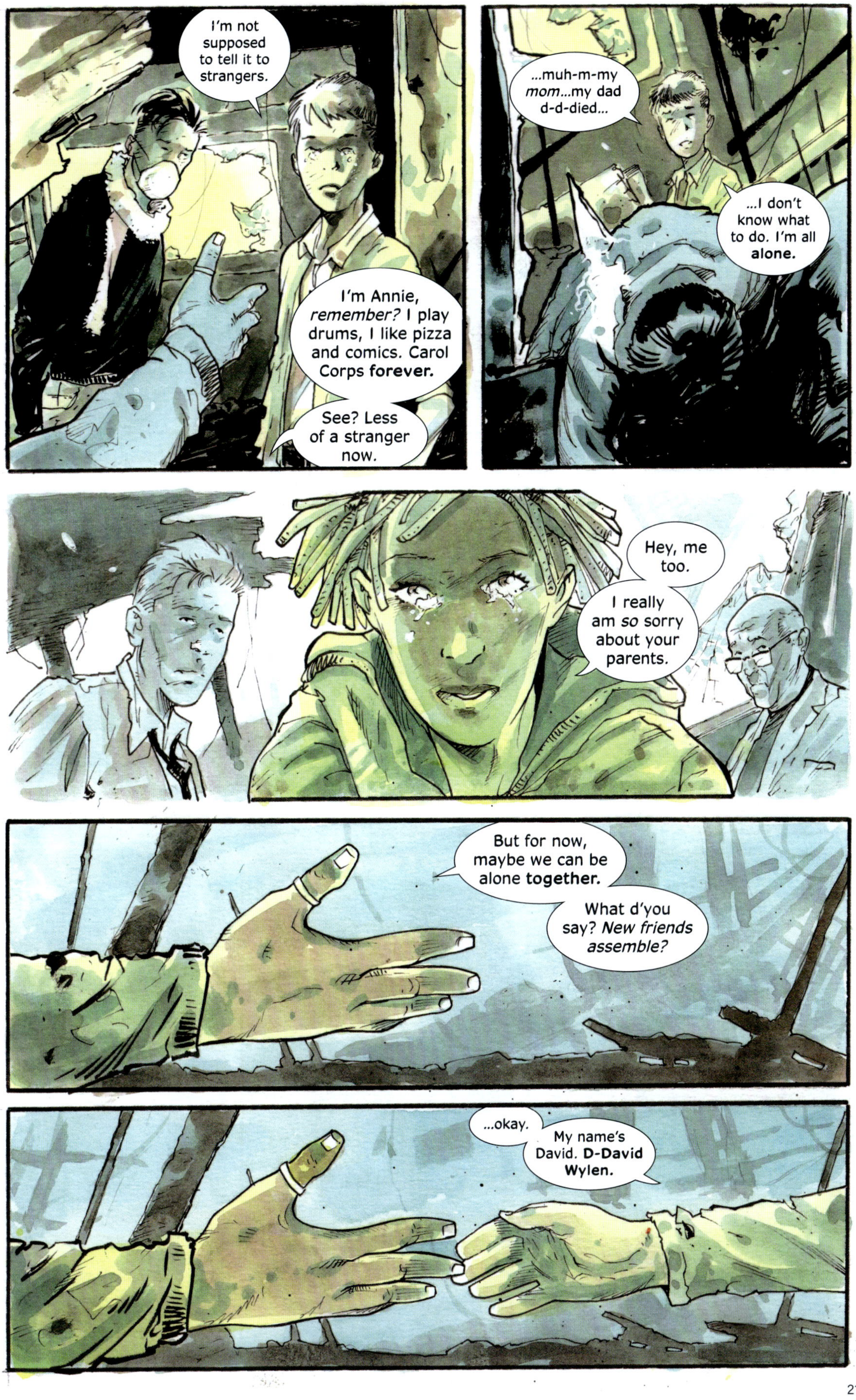
I'm not supposed to tell it to strangers.
I'm Annie, *remember?* I play drums, I like pizza and comics. Carol Corps **forever.**
See? Less of a stranger now.
...muh-m-my *mom*...my dad d-d-died...
...I don't know what to do. I'm all **alone.**
Hey, me too.
I really am *so* sorry about your parents.
But for now, maybe we can be alone **together.**
What d'you say? *New friends assemble?*
...okay.
My name's David. **D-David Wylen.**

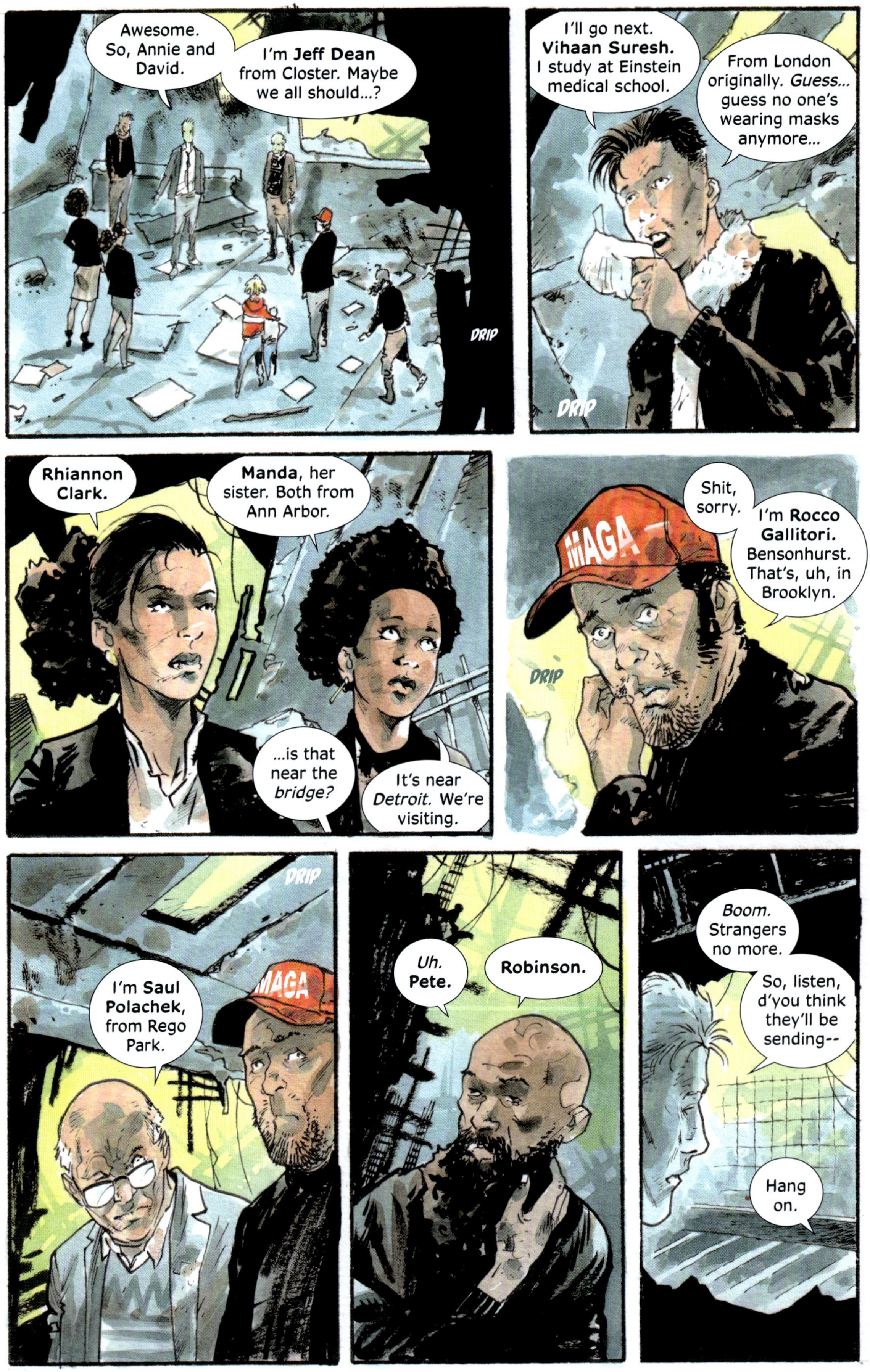
Awesome. So, Annie and David.
I'm **Jeff Dean** from Closter. Maybe we all should...?
DRIP
I'll go next. **Vihaan Suresh.** I study at Einstein medical school.
From London originally. *Guess...* guess no one's wearing masks anymore...
DRIP
Rhiannon Clark.
Manda, her sister. Both from Ann Arbor.
...is that near the *bridge?*
It's near *Detroit.* We're visiting.
MAGA
Shit, sorry.
I'm **Rocco Gallitori.** Bensonhurst. That's, uh, in Brooklyn.
DRIP
DRIP
MAGA
I'm **Saul Polachek,** from Rego Park.
Uh. **Pete.**
Robinson.
Boom. Strangers no more.
So, listen, d'you think they'll be sending--
Hang on.

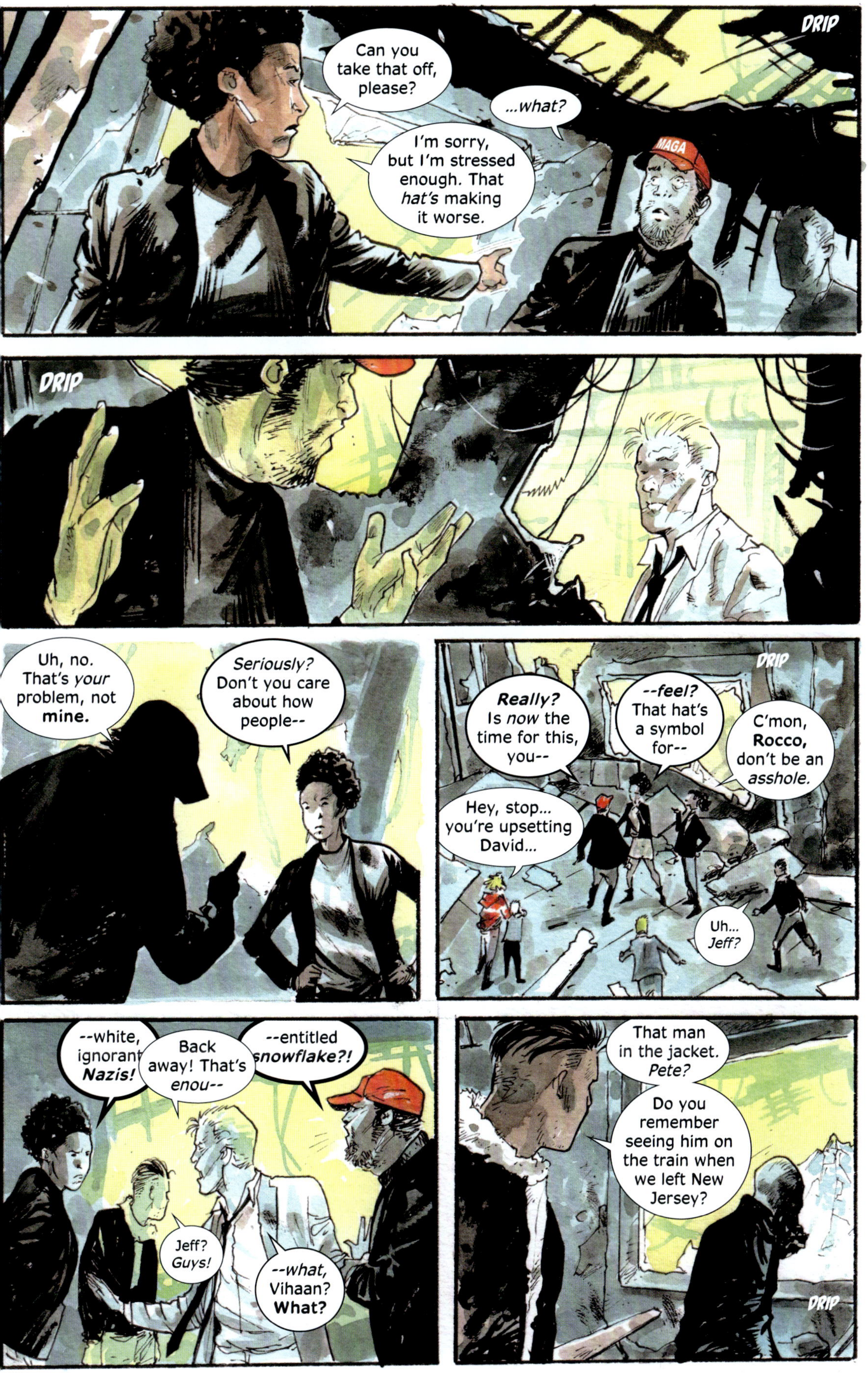
DRIP
Can you take that off, please?
...what?
I'm sorry, but I'm stressed enough. That *hat's* making it worse.
MAGA
DRIP
Uh, no. That's *your* problem, not **mine.**
Seriously? Don't you care about how people--
DRIP
Really? Is *now* the time for this, you--
--feel? That hat's a symbol for--
C'mon, **Rocco,** don't be an *asshole.*
Hey, stop... you're upsetting David...
Uh... *Jeff?*
--white, ignorant ***Nazis!***
Back away! That's *enou--*
--entitled ***snowflake?!***
Jeff? Guys!
--what, Vihaan? **What?**
That man in the jacket. *Pete?*
Do you remember seeing him on the train when we left New Jersey?
DRIP

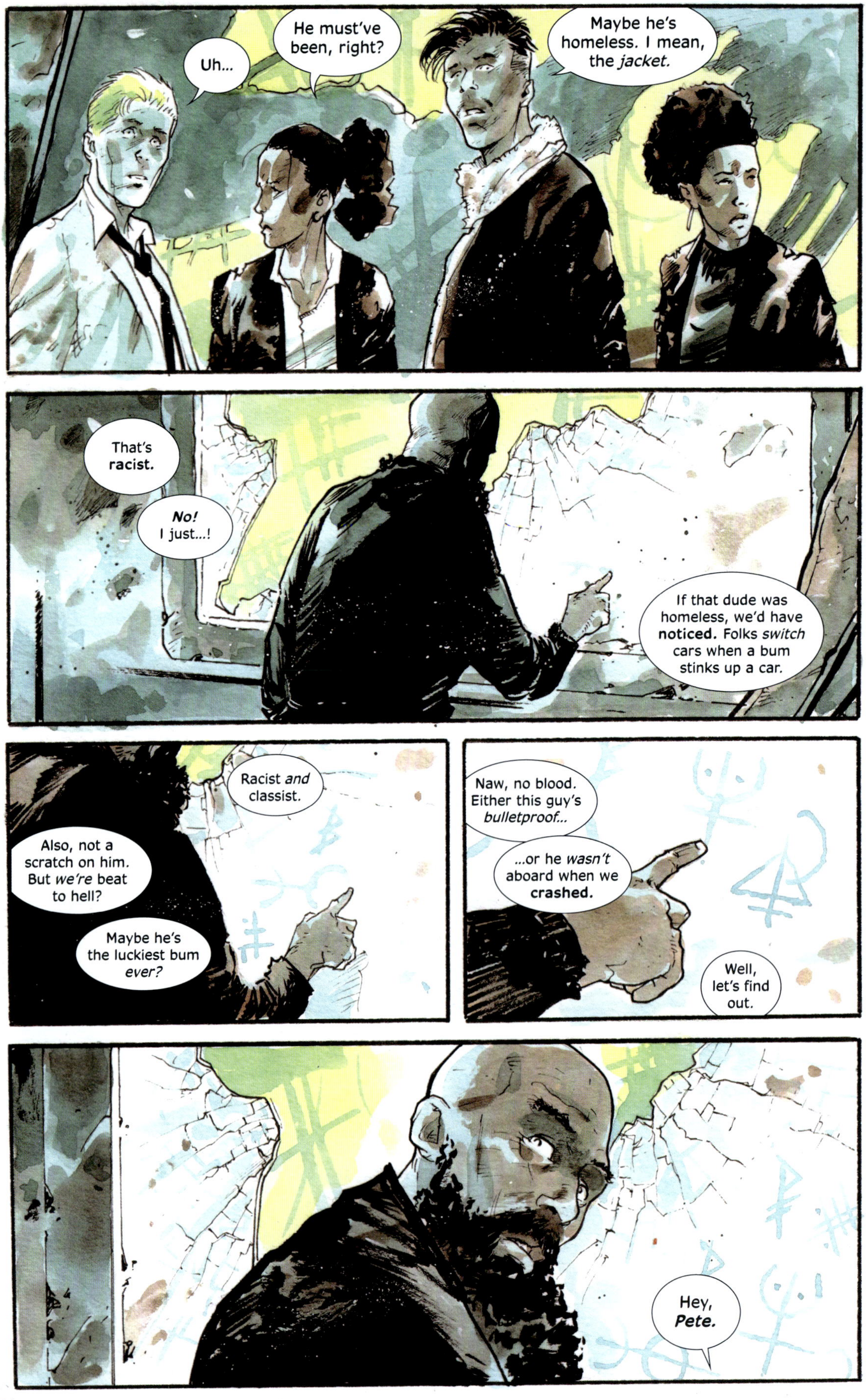
Uh...
He must've been, right?
Maybe he's homeless. I mean, the *jacket.*
That's **racist.**
No! I just...!
If that dude was homeless, we'd have **noticed.** Folks *switch* cars when a bum stinks up a car.
Racist *and* classist.
Also, not a scratch on him. But *we're* beat to hell?
Maybe he's the luckiest bum *ever?*
Naw, no blood. Either this guy's *bulletproof...*
...or he *wasn't* aboard when we **crashed.**
Well, let's find out.
Hey, ***Pete.***

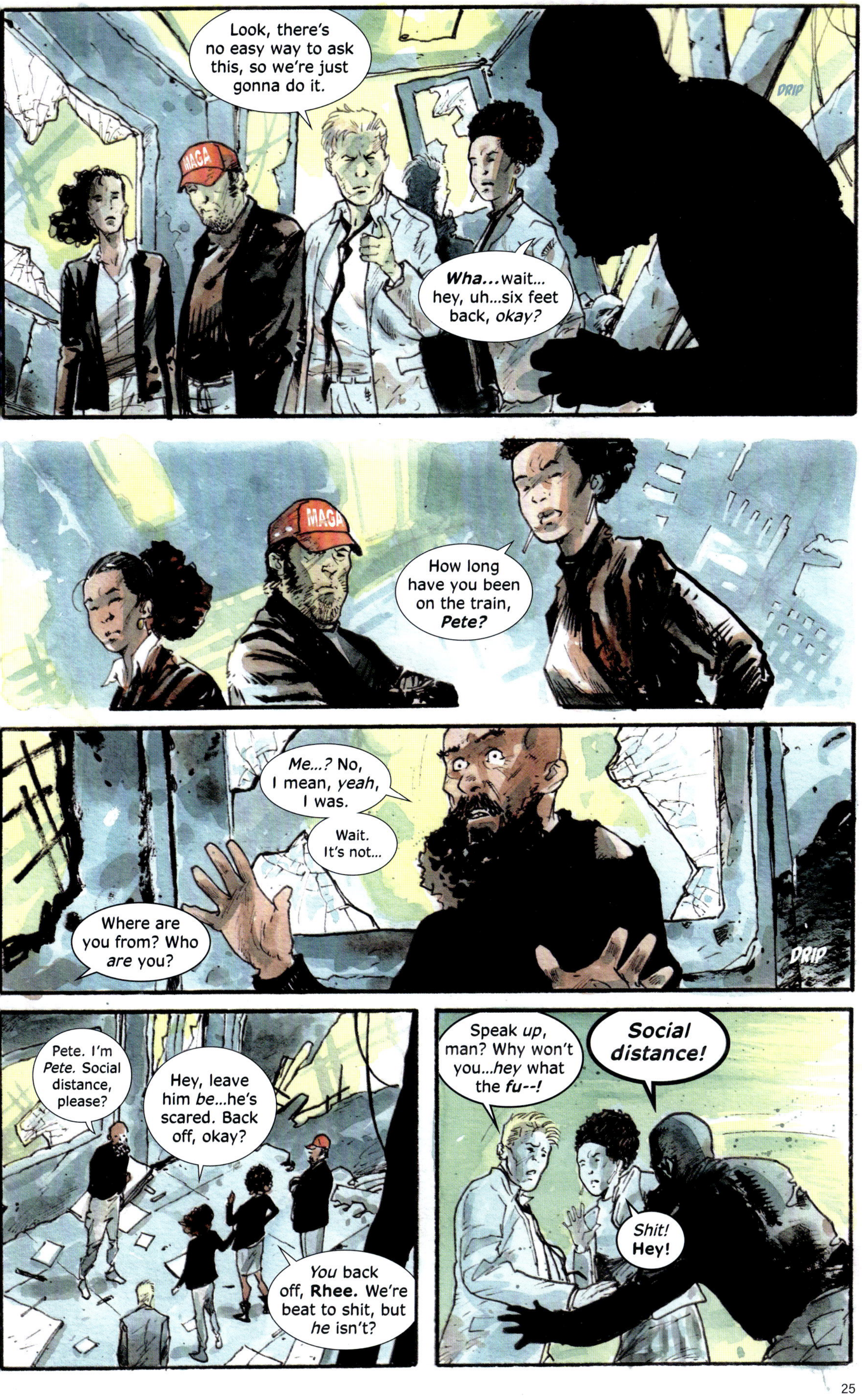

Look, there's no easy way to ask this, so we're just gonna do it.
DRIP
Wha... wait... hey, uh...six feet back, *okay?*
How long have you been on the train, ***Pete?***
Me...? No, I mean, *yeah*, I was.
Wait. It's not...
Where are you from? Who *are* you?
DRIP
Pete. I'm *Pete.* Social distance, please?
Hey, leave him *be*...he's scared. Back off, okay?
You back off, **Rhee.** We're beat to shit, but *he* isn't?
Speak *up*, man? Why won't you...*hey* what the *fu--!*
Social distance!
Shit! **Hey!**

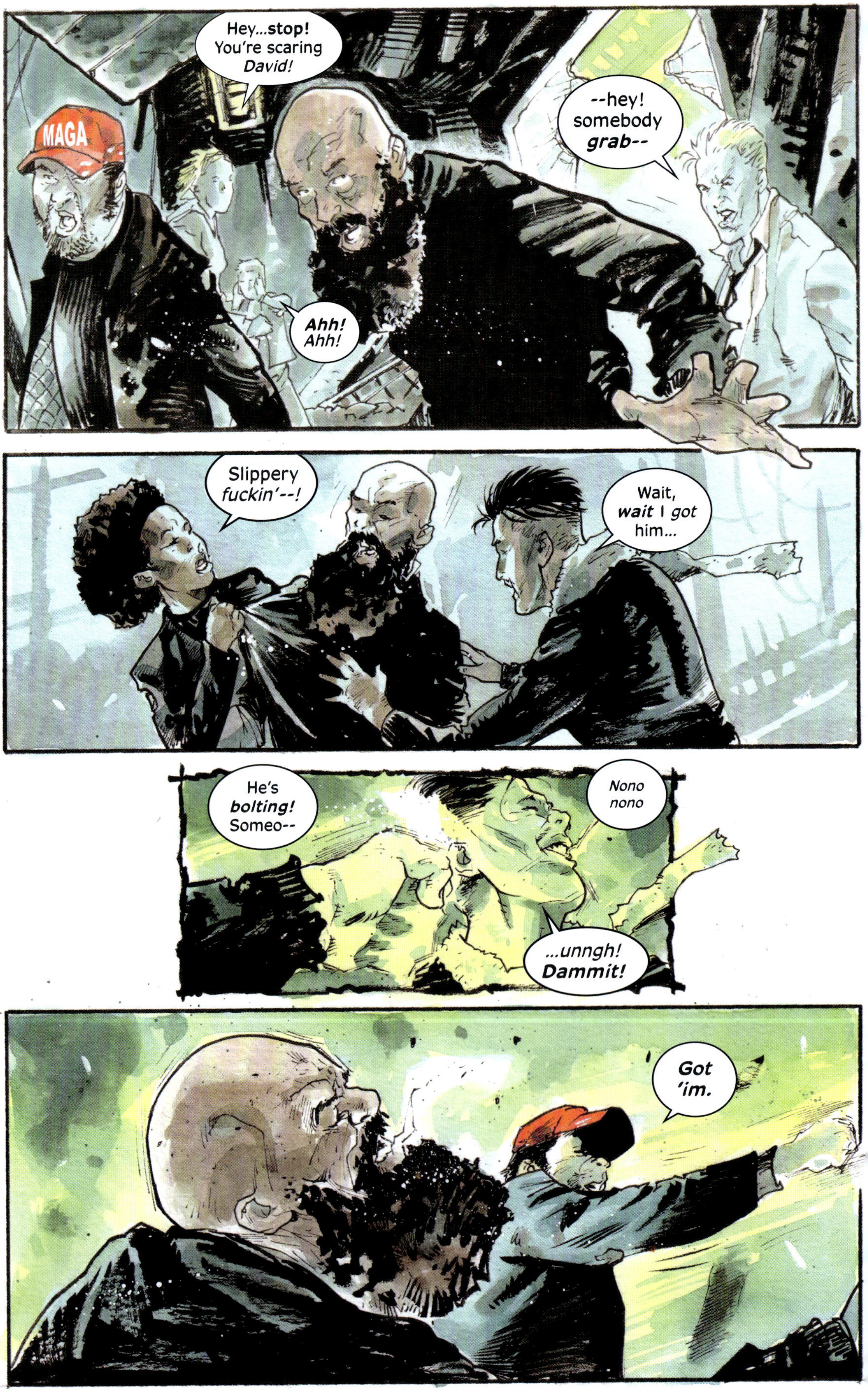
Hey...stop! You're scaring David!
--hey! somebody grab--
Ahh! Ahh!
Slippery fuckin'--!
Wait, wait I got him...
He's bolting! Someo--
Nono nono
...unngh! Dammit!
Got 'im.

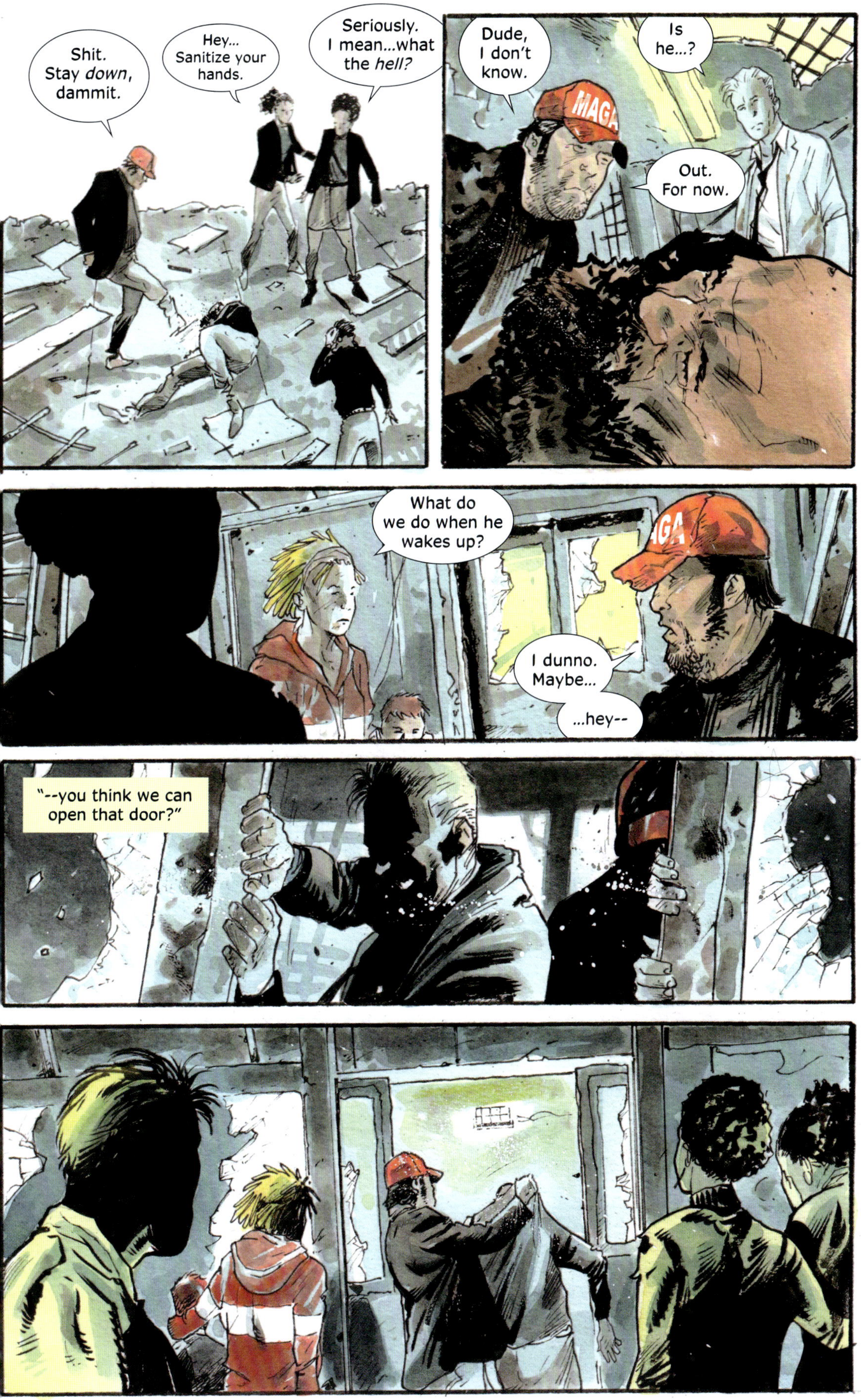
Shit. Stay *down*, dammit.
Hey... Sanitize your hands.
Seriously. I mean...what the *hell?*
Dude, I don't know.
Is he...?
Out. For now.
MAGA
What do we do when he wakes up?
I dunno. Maybe...
...hey--
"--you think we can open that door?"

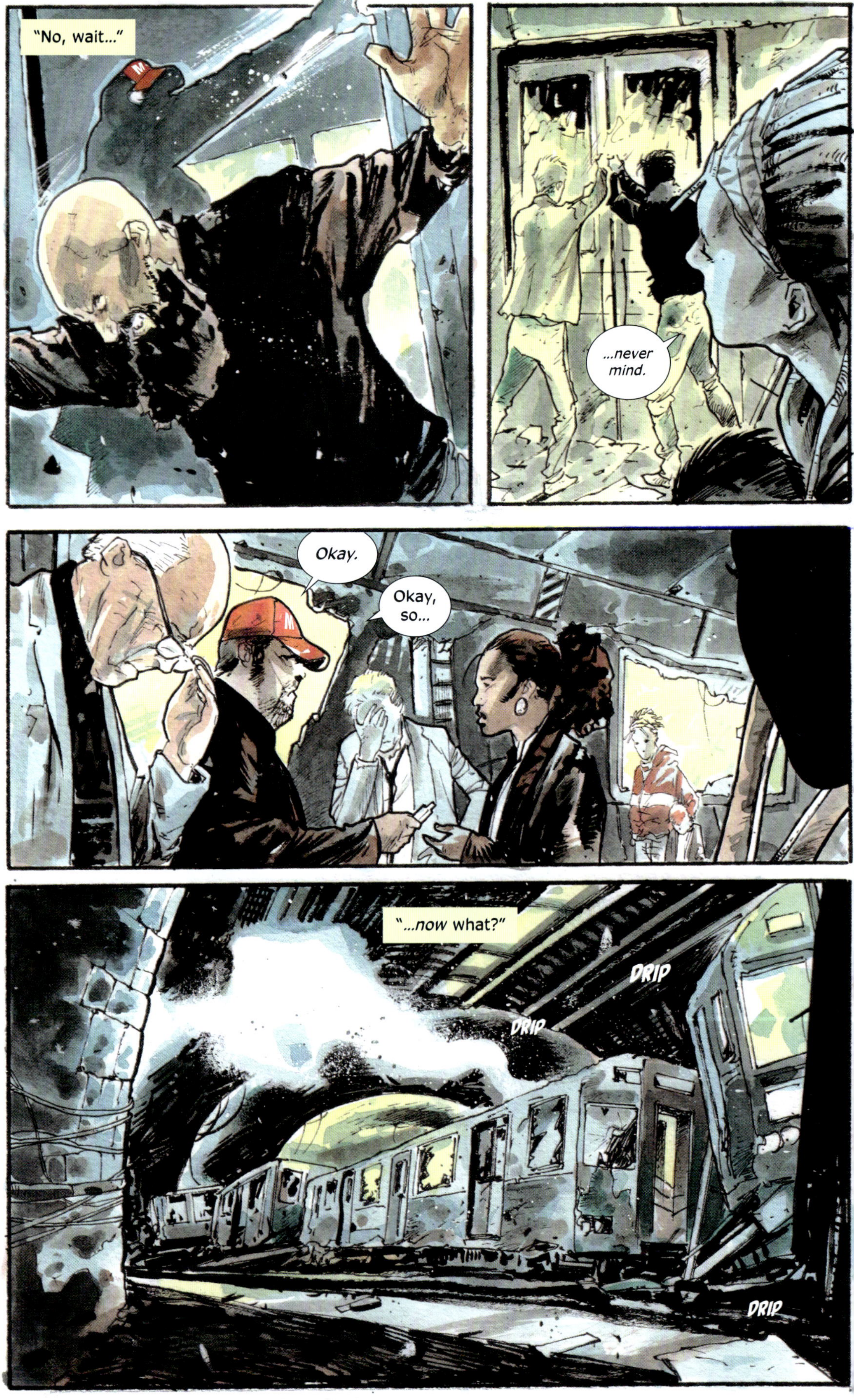
"No, wait..."
...never mind.
Okay.
Okay, so...
"...now what?"
DRIP
DRIP
DRIP

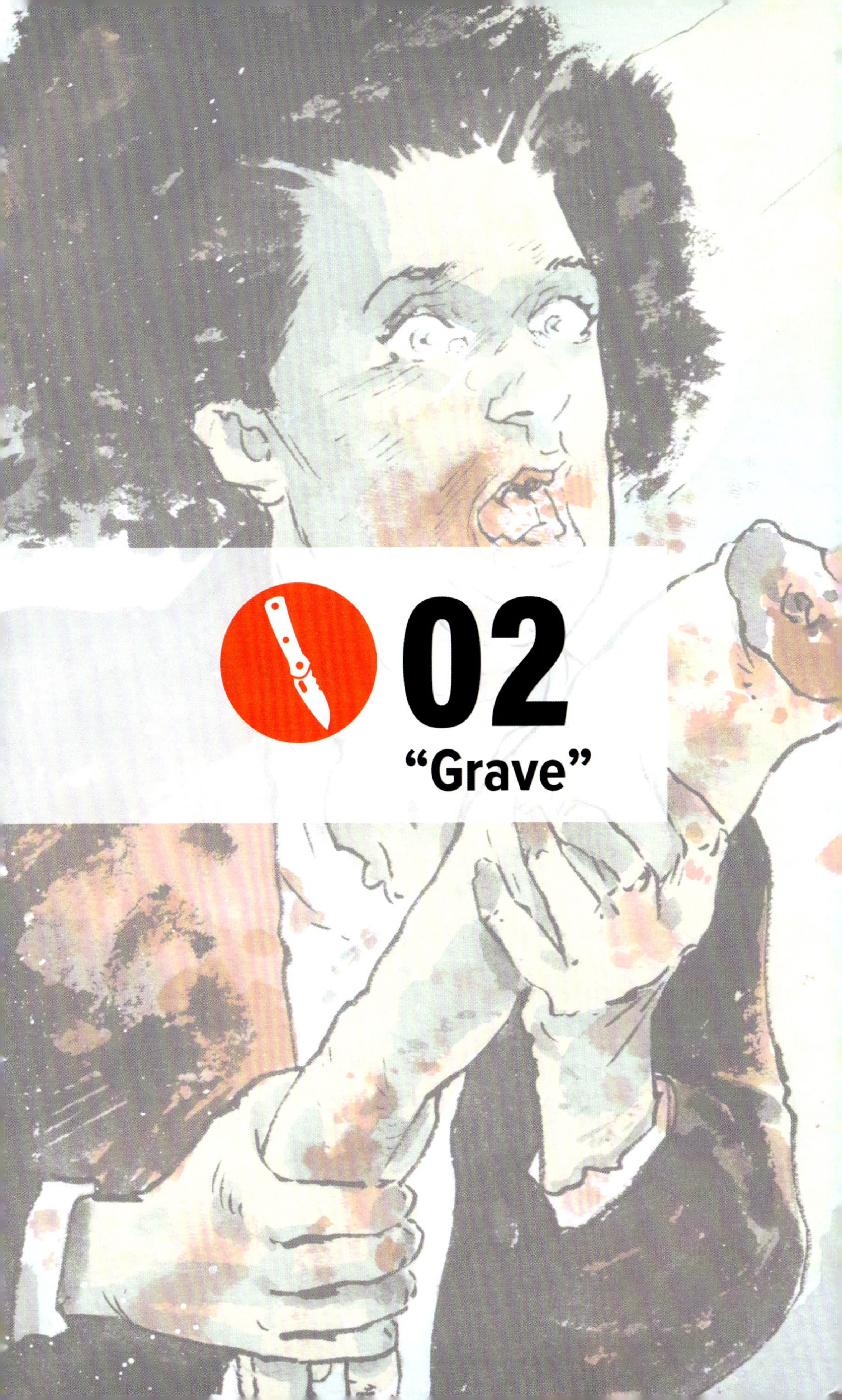
02
“Grave”

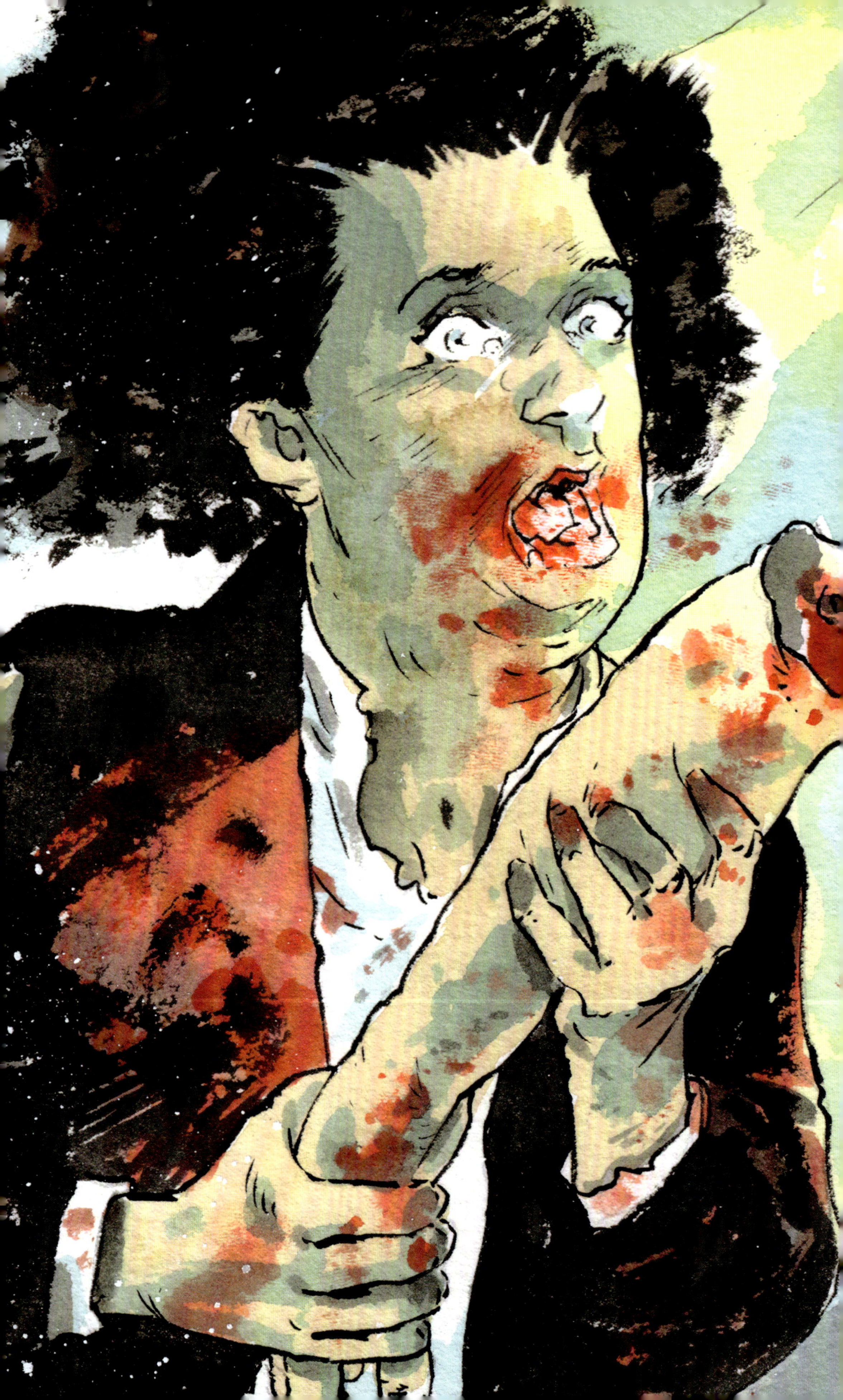

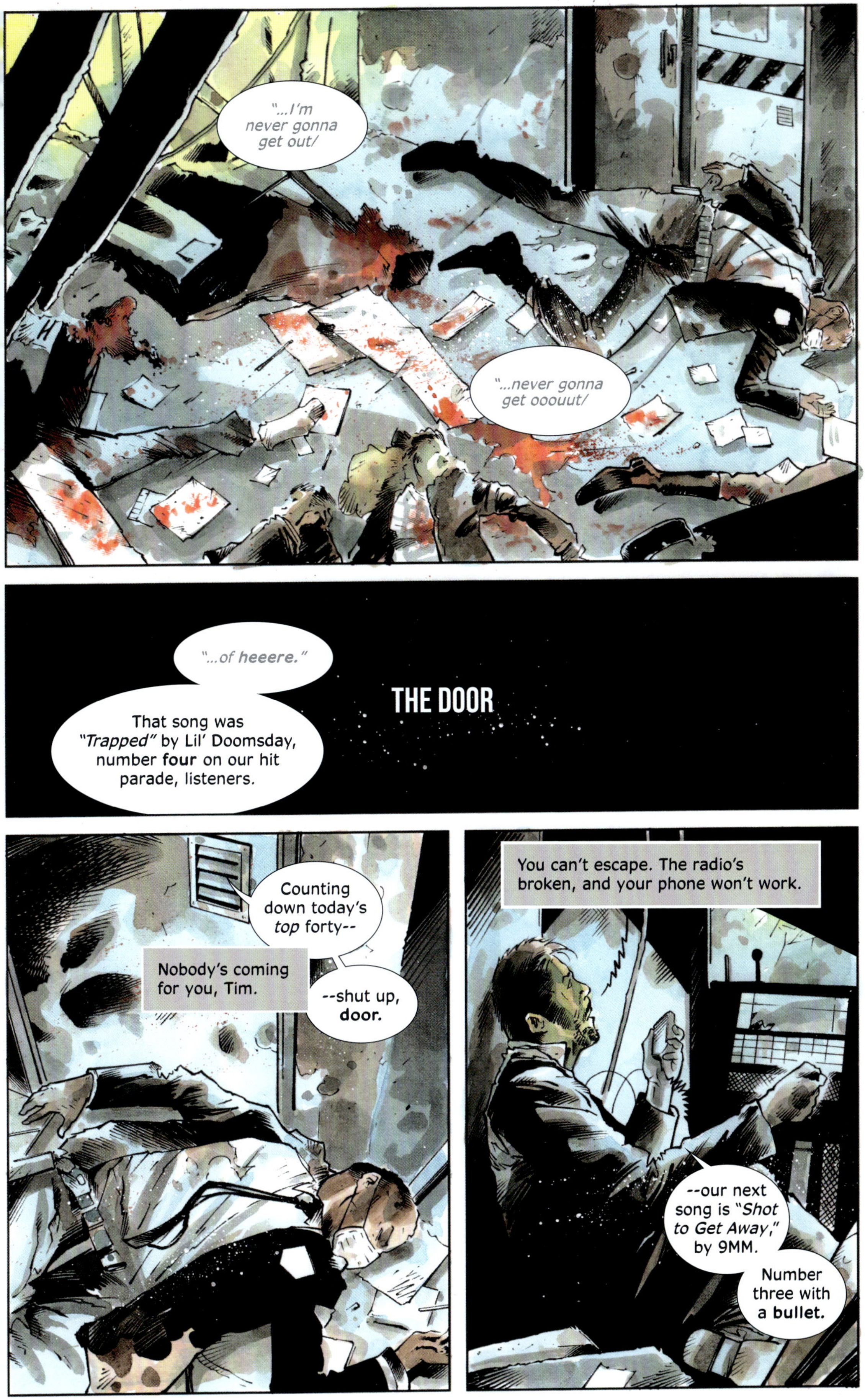
"...I'm never gonna get out/
"...never gonna get ooouut/
"...of *heeere.*"
That song was *"Trapped"* by Lil' Doomsday, number **four** on our hit parade, listeners.
THE DOOR
Counting down today's *top* forty--
Nobody's coming for you, Tim.
--shut up, **door.**
You can't escape. The radio's broken, and your phone won't work.
--our next song is *"Shot to Get Away,"* by 9MM.
Number three with a **bullet.**

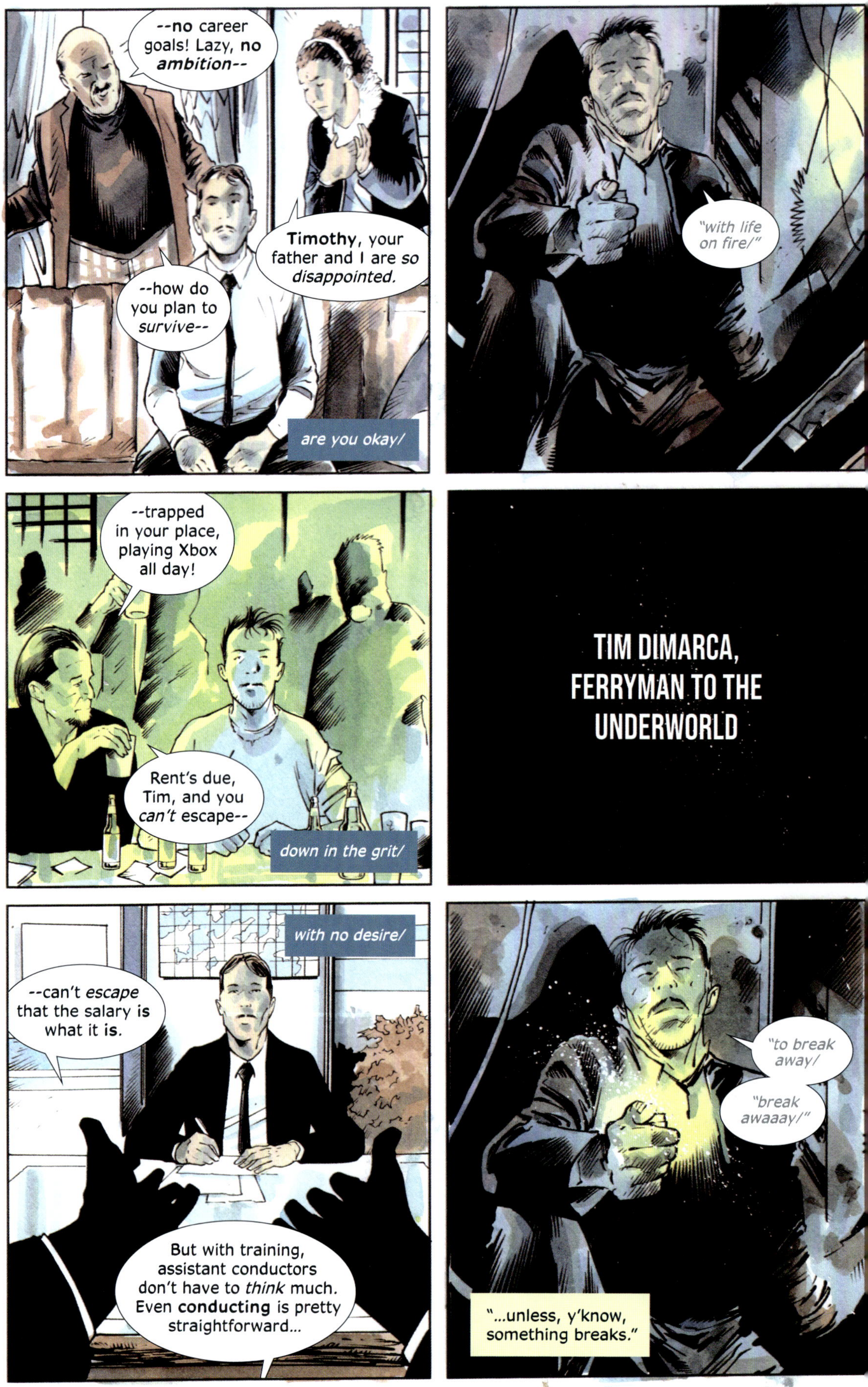
--no career goals! Lazy, no ambition--
Timothy, your father and I are so disappointed.
--how do you plan to survive--
are you okay/
"with life on fire/"
--trapped in your place, playing Xbox all day!
Rent's due, Tim, and you can't escape--
down in the grit/
TIM DIMARCA, FERRYMAN TO THE UNDERWORLD
with no desire/
--can't escape that the salary is what it is.
But with training, assistant conductors don't have to think much. Even conducting is pretty straightforward...
"to break away/
"break awaaay/"
"...unless, y'know, something breaks."

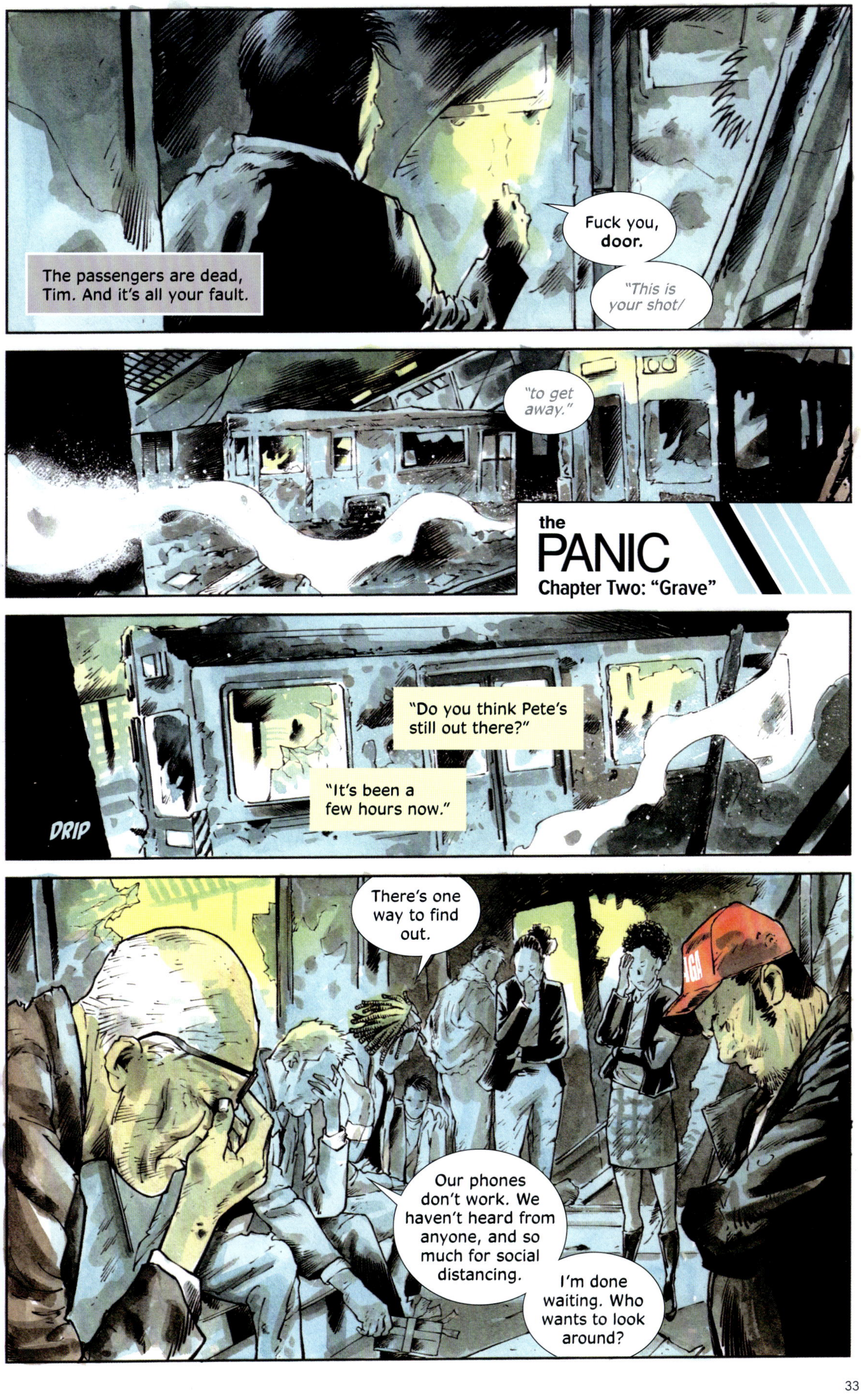
The passengers are dead, Tim. And it's all your fault.
Fuck you, door.
"This is your shot/
"to get away."
the
PANIC
Chapter Two: "Grave"
"Do you think Pete's still out there?"
"It's been a few hours now."
DRIP
There's one way to find out.
Our phones don't work. We haven't heard from anyone, and so much for social distancing.
I'm done waiting. Who wants to look around?

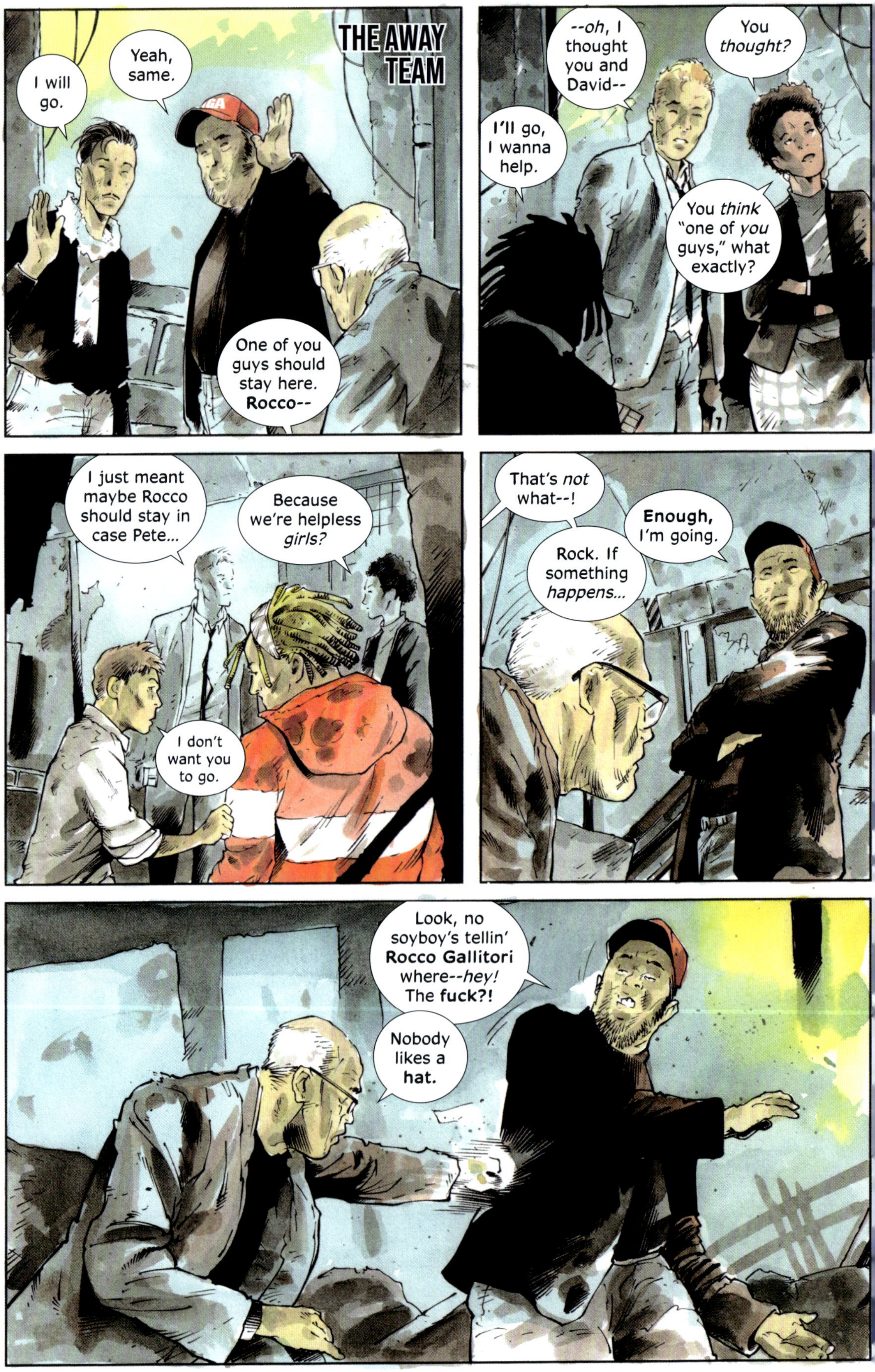
THE AWAY TEAM
I will go.
Yeah, same.
One of you guys should stay here. **Rocco**--
--*oh*, I thought you and David--
You *thought?*
I'll go, I wanna help.
You *think* "one of *you* guys," what exactly?
I just meant maybe Rocco should stay in case Pete...
Because we're helpless *girls?*
I don't want you to go.
That's *not* what--!
Rock. If something *happens*...
Enough, I'm going.
Look, no soyboy's tellin' **Rocco Gallitori** where--*hey!* The **fuck?!**
Nobody likes a **hat.**

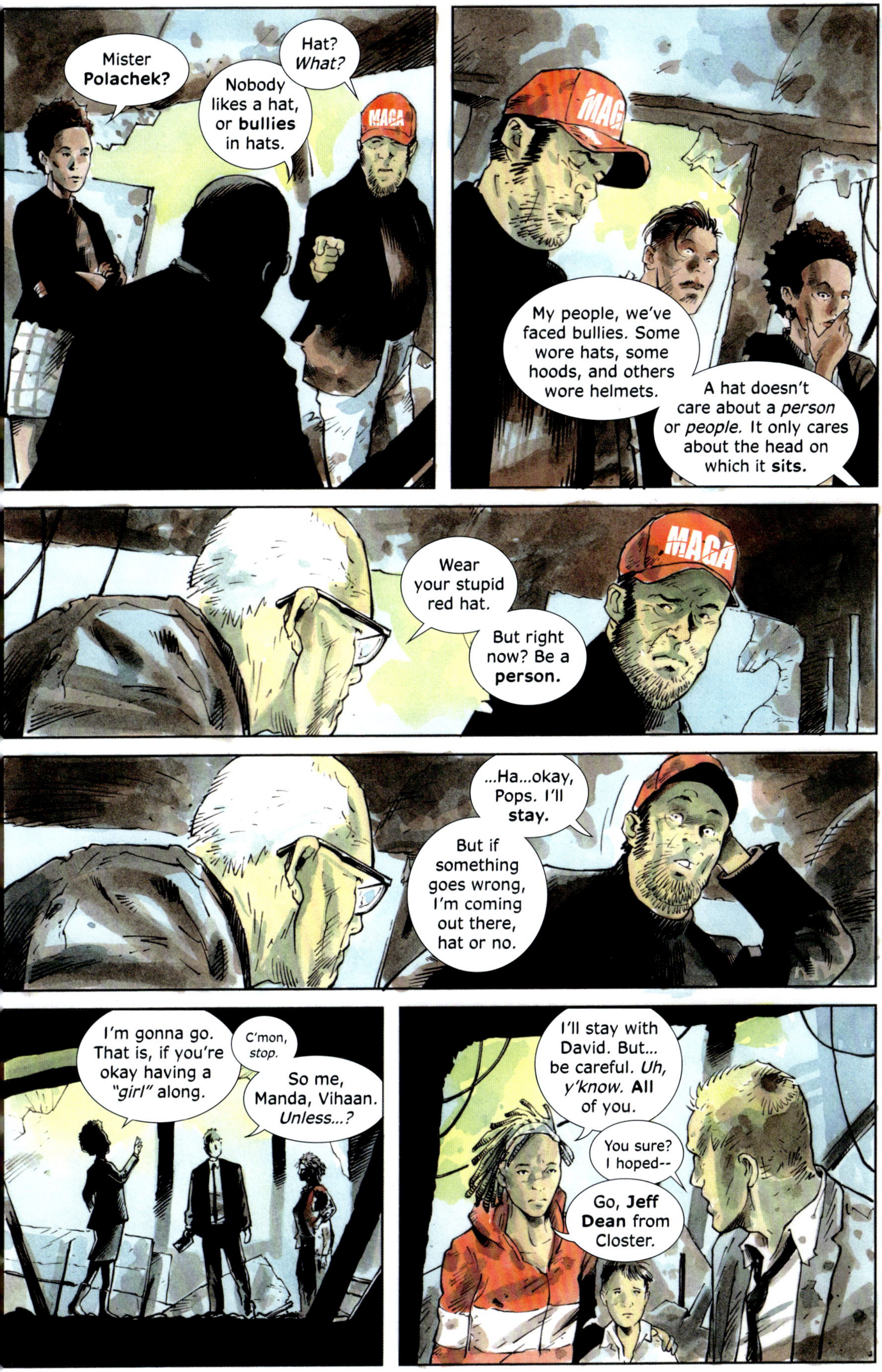
Mister **Polachek?**
Hat? *What?*
Nobody likes a hat, or **bullies** in hats.
My people, we've faced bullies. Some wore hats, some hoods, and others wore helmets.
A hat doesn't care about a *person* or *people.* It only cares about the head on which it **sits.**
Wear your stupid red hat.
But right now? Be a **person.**
...Ha...okay, Pops. I'll **stay.**
But if something goes wrong, I'm coming out there, hat or no.
I'm gonna go. That is, if you're okay having a *"girl"* along.
C'mon, stop.
So me, Manda, Vihaan. *Unless...?*
I'll stay with David. But... be careful. *Uh, y'know.* **All** of you.
You sure? I hoped--
Go, **Jeff Dean** from Closter.

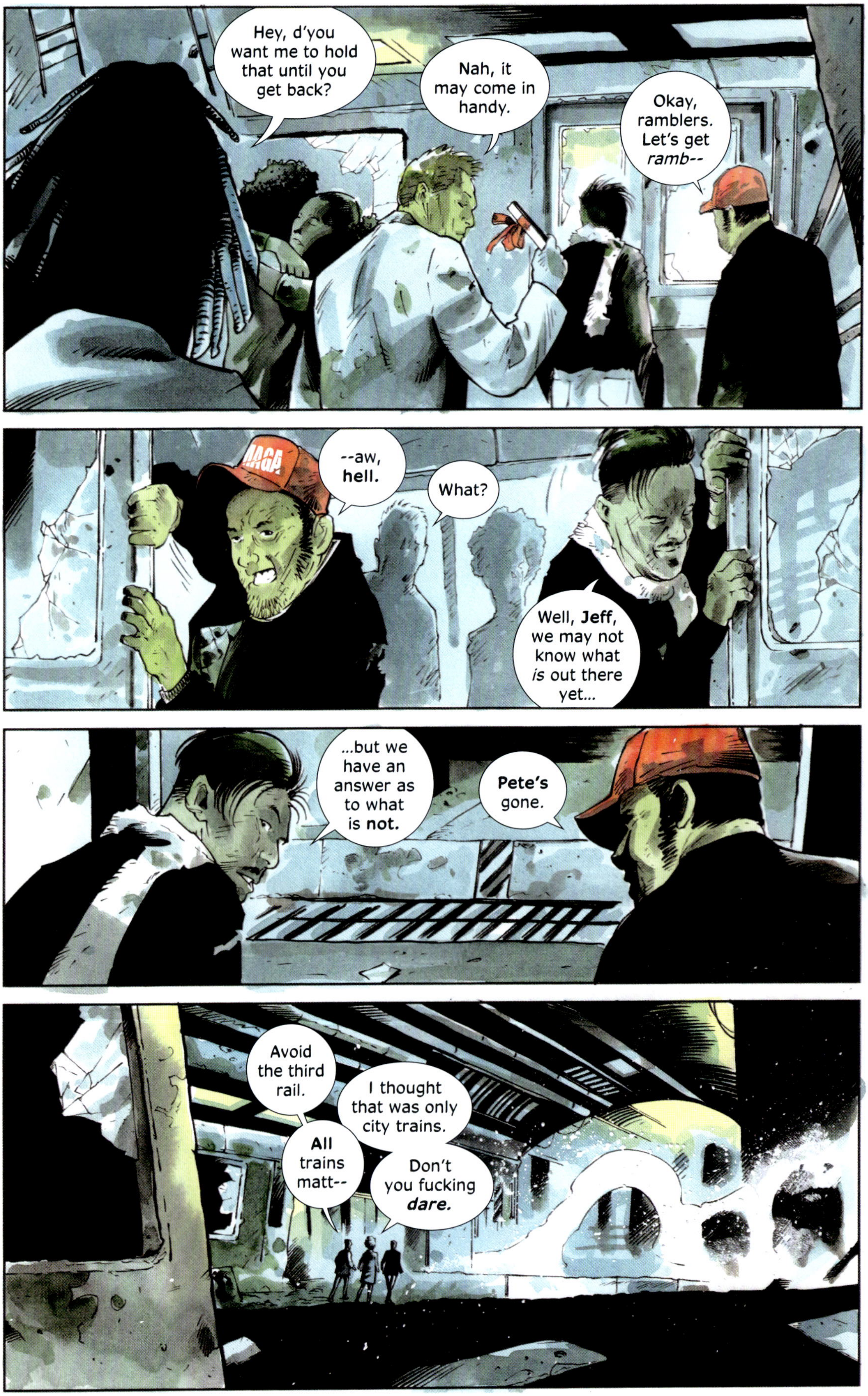
Hey, d'you want me to hold that until you get back?
Nah, it may come in handy.
Okay, ramblers. Let's get *ramb--*
--aw, **hell.**
What?
Well, **Jeff,** we may not know what *is* out there yet...
...but we have an answer as to what is **not.**
Pete's gone.
Avoid the third rail.
I thought that was only city trains.
All trains matt--
Don't you fucking ***dare.***

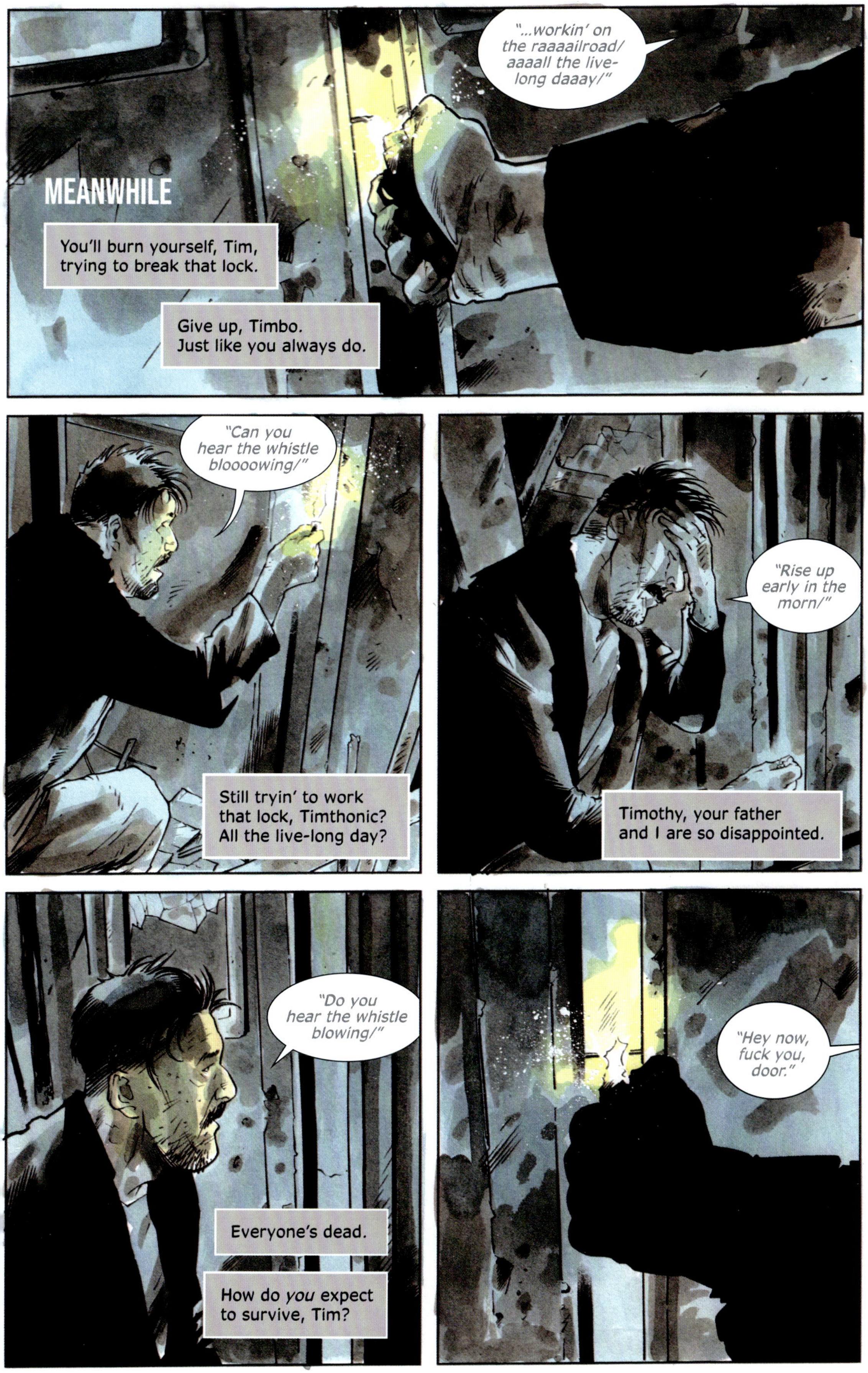
"...workin' on the raaaailroad/ aaaall the live-long daaay/"
MEANWHILE
You'll burn yourself, Tim, trying to break that lock.
Give up, Timbo. Just like you always do.
"Can you hear the whistle bloooowing/"
Still tryin' to work that lock, Timthonic? All the live-long day?
"Rise up early in the morn/"
Timothy, your father and I are so disappointed.
"Do you hear the whistle blowing/"
Everyone's dead.
How do *you* expect to survive, Tim?
"Hey now, fuck you, door."

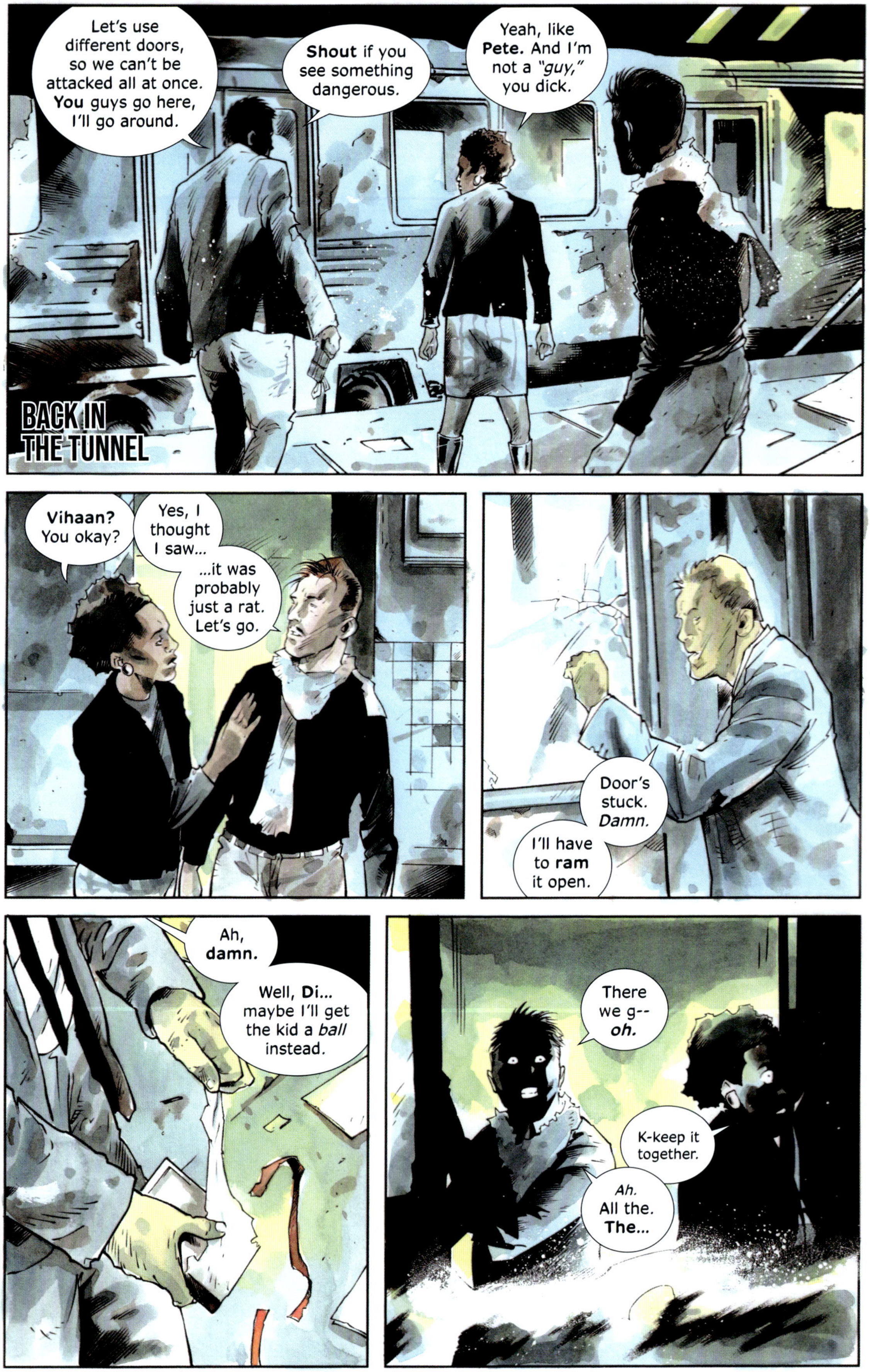
Let's use different doors, so we can't be attacked all at once. **You** guys go here, I'll go around.
Shout if you see something dangerous.
Yeah, like **Pete.** And I'm not a *"guy,"* you dick.
BACK IN THE TUNNEL
Vihaan? You okay?
Yes, I thought I saw...
...it was probably just a rat. Let's go.
Door's stuck. *Damn.*
I'll have to **ram** it open.
Ah, **damn.**
Well, **Di...** maybe I'll get the kid a *ball* instead.
There we g-- ***oh.***
K-keep it together.
Ah. All the. **The...**

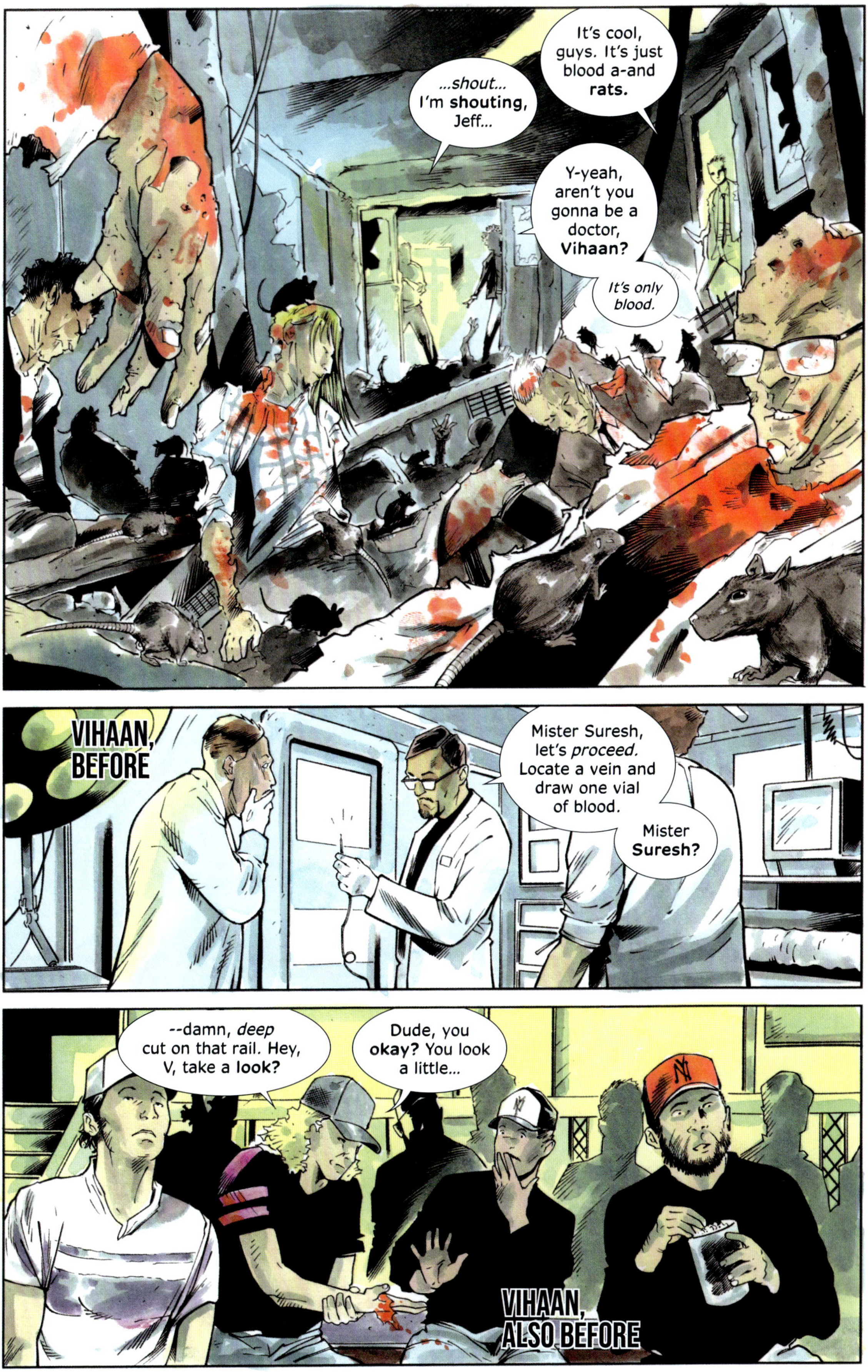
...shout... I'm shouting, Jeff...
It's cool, guys. It's just blood a-and rats.
Y-yeah, aren't you gonna be a doctor, Vihaan?
It's only blood.
VIHAAN, BEFORE
Mister Suresh, let's proceed. Locate a vein and draw one vial of blood.
Mister Suresh?
--damn, deep cut on that rail. Hey, V, take a look?
Dude, you okay? You look a little...
VIHAAN, ALSO BEFORE

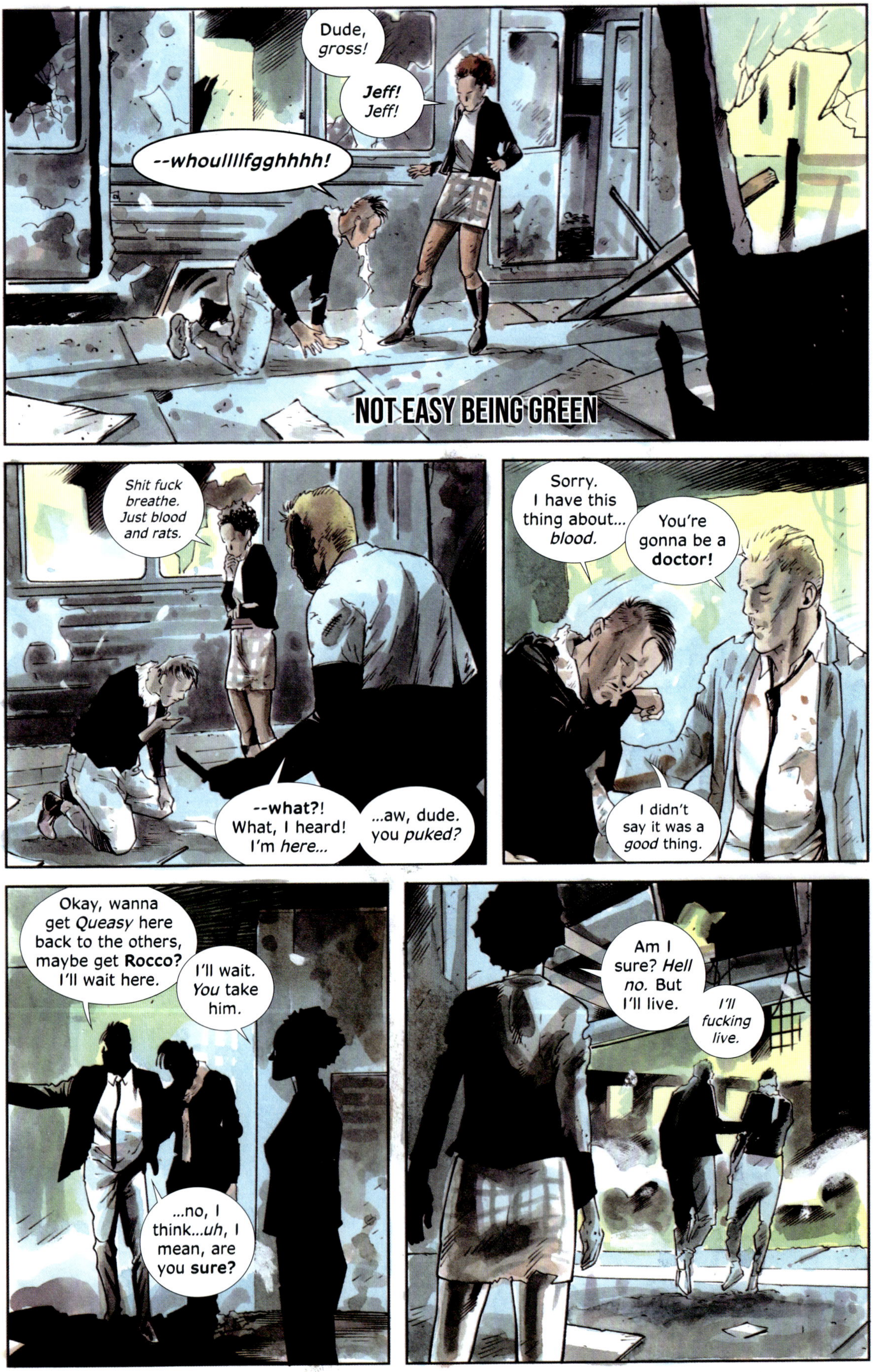

Dude, *gross!*
Jeff! *Jeff!*
--whoulllllfgghhhh!
NOT EASY BEING GREEN
Shit fuck breathe. Just blood and rats.
--what?! What, I heard! I'm *here...*
...aw, dude. you *puked?*
Sorry. I have this thing about... *blood.*
You're gonna be a **doctor!**
I didn't say it was a *good* thing.
Okay, wanna get *Queasy* here back to the others, maybe get **Rocco?** I'll wait here.
I'll wait. *You* take him.
...no, I think...*uh*, I mean, are you **sure?**
Am I sure? *Hell no.* But I'll live.
I'll fucking live.

--who's that? **Jeff...?**
...Pete?
SHUFFLE
Just a rat. *Breathe*, Manda.
You're gonna get *outta* here. You won't be **one more** dead black trans girl.
"You're gonna live."
MEANWHILE
--aw what the **shit?!**
What's *blocking the door?*
WHUMP
You're never getting out, Tim.
No no **no no.** *¡Singa tu madre!*
Fuck you, door!
You're g
to die here.
Fuck... *you...*
You're going
to die
...door!
WHUMP

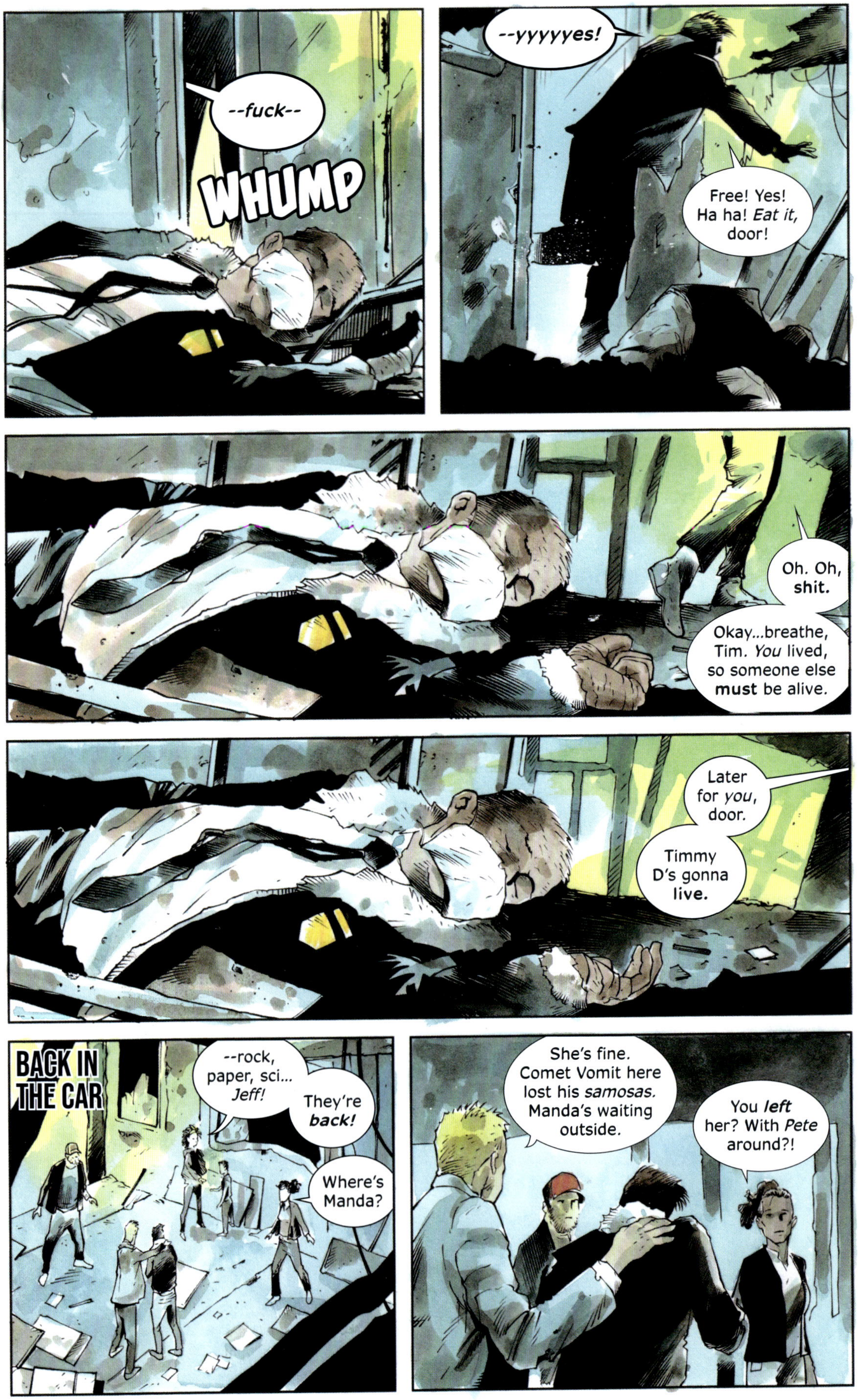
--fuck--
WHUMP
--yyyyyes!
Free! Yes! Ha ha! *Eat it,* door!
Oh. Oh, **shit.**
Okay...breathe, Tim. *You* lived, so someone else **must** be alive.
Later for *you,* door.
Timmy D's gonna **live.**
BACK IN THE CAR
--rock, paper, sci... *Jeff!*
They're *back!*
Where's Manda?
She's fine. Comet Vomit here lost his *samosas.* Manda's waiting outside.
You *left* her? With *Pete* around?!

Asshole! I'm going--
Hang on, *I'll* go--
--you're gonna lose that hand, ***Hat!***
Hey, um, can I go instead?
She's **my** sister...
...who's a badass.
But I can't stare at my dead friend for much longer. I need a break, *please.*
We can both go.
No, I need someone to help David while I go...
I'm not *daycare*. Let Vihaan do it, or **Saul**...
...fuck, fine. Just bring her back. Manda likes Weird Al. You can't be a bad-ass and *also* like Weird Al.
Thanks, **Rhiannon!**
Oh, hey... I don't need *a...aw...*
...oh, hugs are good.
Please don't go, Annie...
Or can I go, too?
It's not safe, David. Rhiannon will talk comics with you for a bit, *okay?*

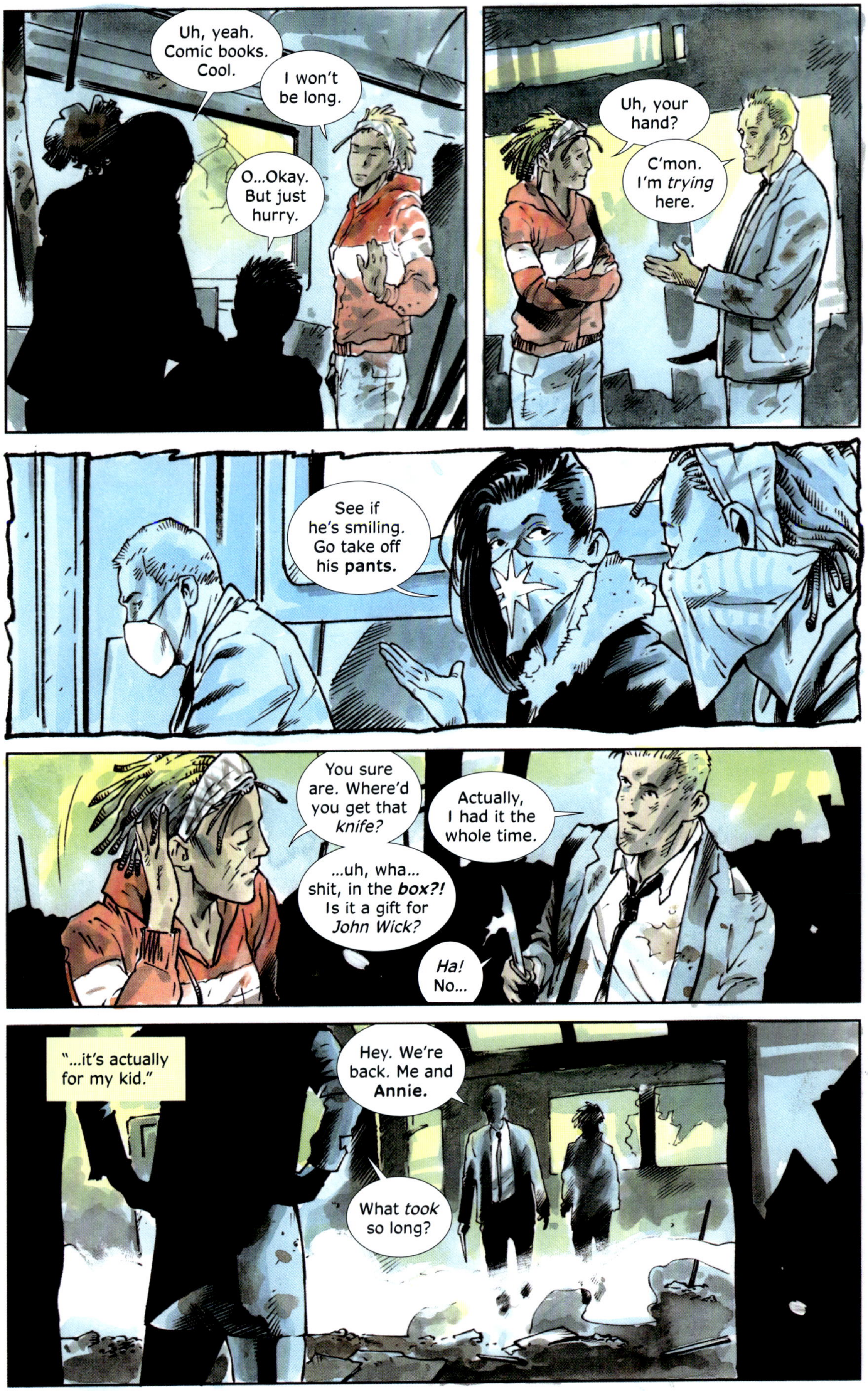
Uh, yeah. Comic books. Cool.
I won't be long.
O...Okay. But just hurry.
Uh, your hand?
C'mon. I'm *trying* here.
See if he's smiling. Go take off his **pants.**
You sure are. Where'd you get that *knife?*
...uh, wha... shit, in the ***box?!*** Is it a gift for *John Wick?*
Actually, I had it the whole time.
Ha! No...
"...it's actually for my kid."
Hey. We're back. Me and **Annie.**
What *took* so long?

Panel 1:
— Sorry. Are you okay?
— Yeah, but I thought that I saw...
— ...forget it. **Vihaan?**
— He's fine. C'mon.

Panel 2:
— Are *you* okay?
— He's got a kid.
— Say again?

Panel 3:
— Never mind.
— Sure, okay.
— Millennials.
— Here we go.

Panel 4:
— Everyone ready?
— No. But it isn't like we have a choice, right?

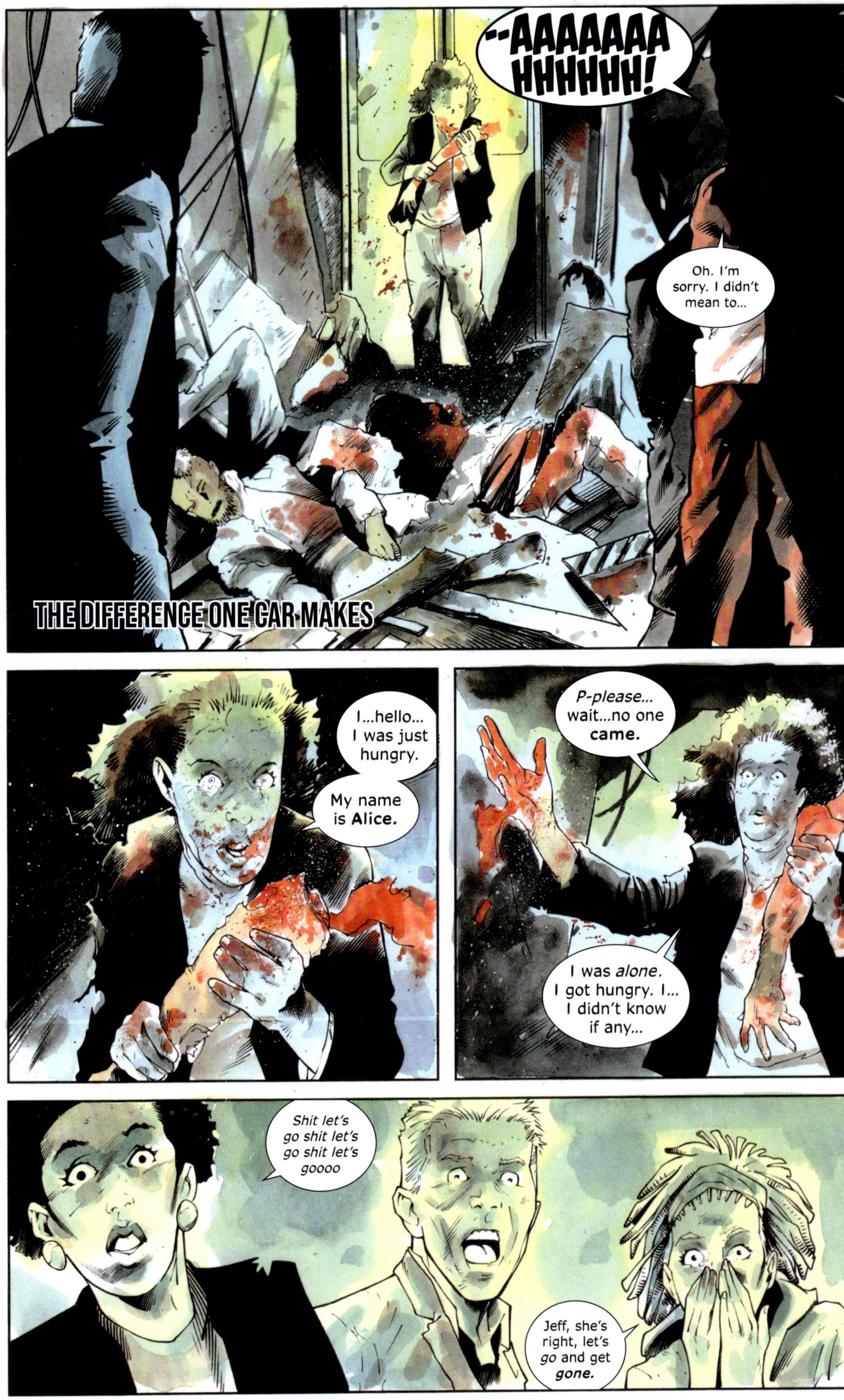
--AAAAAAHHHHHH!
Oh. I'm sorry. I didn't mean to...
THE DIFFERENCE ONE CAR MAKES
I...hello... I was just hungry.
My name is **Alice.**
P-please... wait...no one **came.**
I was *alone.* I got hungry. I... I didn't know if any...
Shit let's go shit let's go shit let's goooo
Jeff, she's right, let's *go* and get **gone.**

Wait, *please.* It's been hours and I was **lonely...** I didn't know if anyone would come...
Will you *stay?* **Join** me?
But, oh...I understand. I must look a **fright.**
You'll take me with you, *right?*
Sorry, but I don't know if that's...
We're g-going to go.
You're going to leave me here? By *myself?*
Oh. Oh **no.**
No no ***no.***
I can't let you do that.

You can't leeeeave me...
Shit! Go-- get to the others!
...Jeff!
...not alone... take me too, please...
Move, move--
Go!
...or stay with me!
--back off, bitc--ahgod-dammit!
No, wait... I just...I'll get Manda. You...
The knife, Jeff! Use the fucking knife!
...hungry... alone...
...ahhh! No! Dad's knife!
shitshit shitshit
Shit.
Don't go.

DON'T GOOOOO!
Aw, hell--
--Annie!
The knife! I'll get the kn--
--ife? Where is it...
...is that Rocco?
Hang on... 'm coming... whozat?
Oh. Oh god.
Get off! Getoff-ame!
Don't go! Don't go! Don't go!
Annieee--
Don't go... don't...
...guh.
--no...oh shiiiiittt

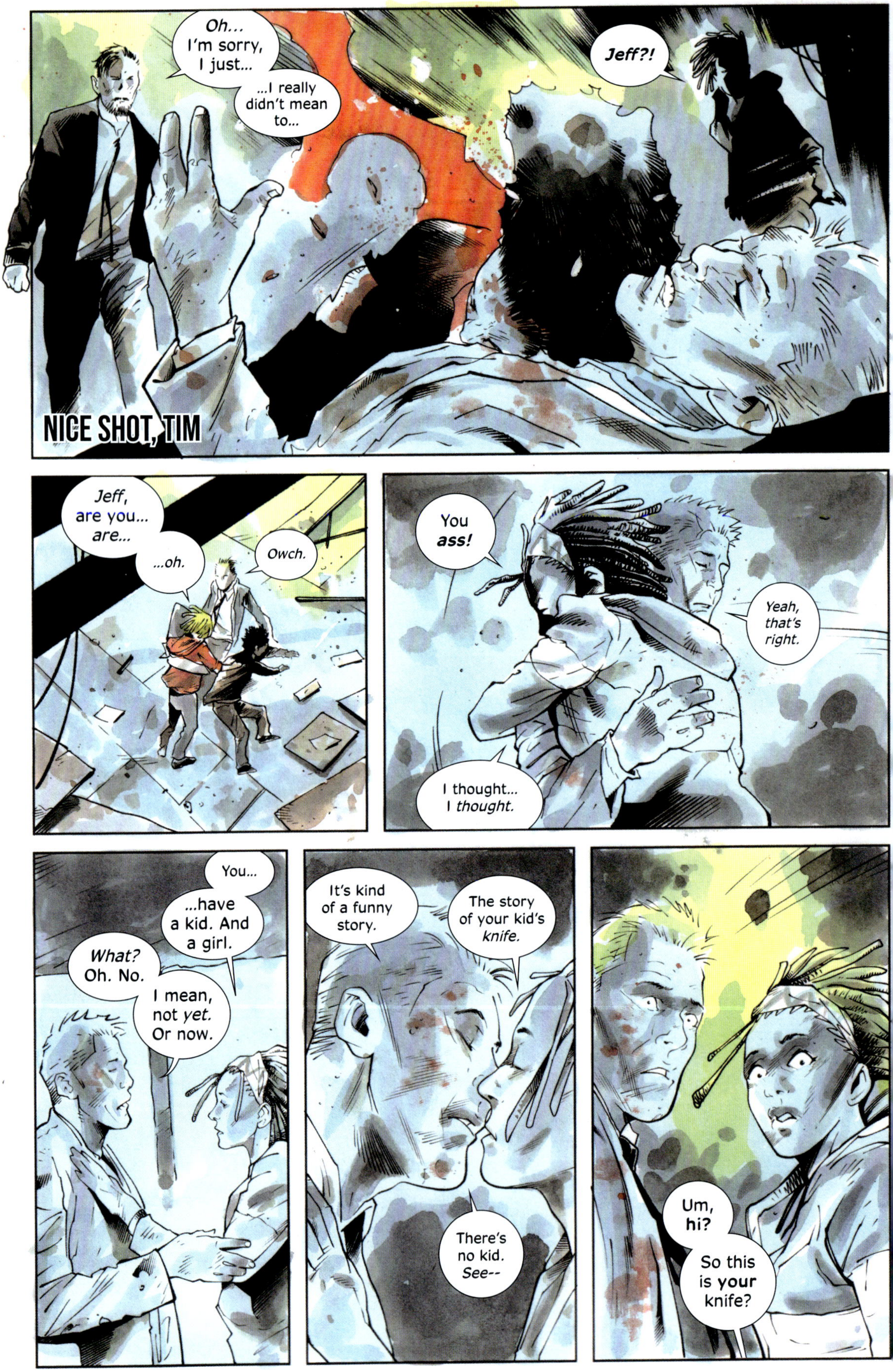
Oh... I'm sorry, I just...
...I really didn't mean to...
Jeff?!
NICE SHOT, TIM
Jeff, are you... are...
...oh.
Owch.
You ass!
Yeah, that's right.
I thought... I thought.
You...
...have a kid. And a girl.
What? Oh. No.
I mean, not yet. Or now.
It's kind of a funny story.
The story of your kid's knife.
There's no kid. See--
Um, hi?
So this is your knife?

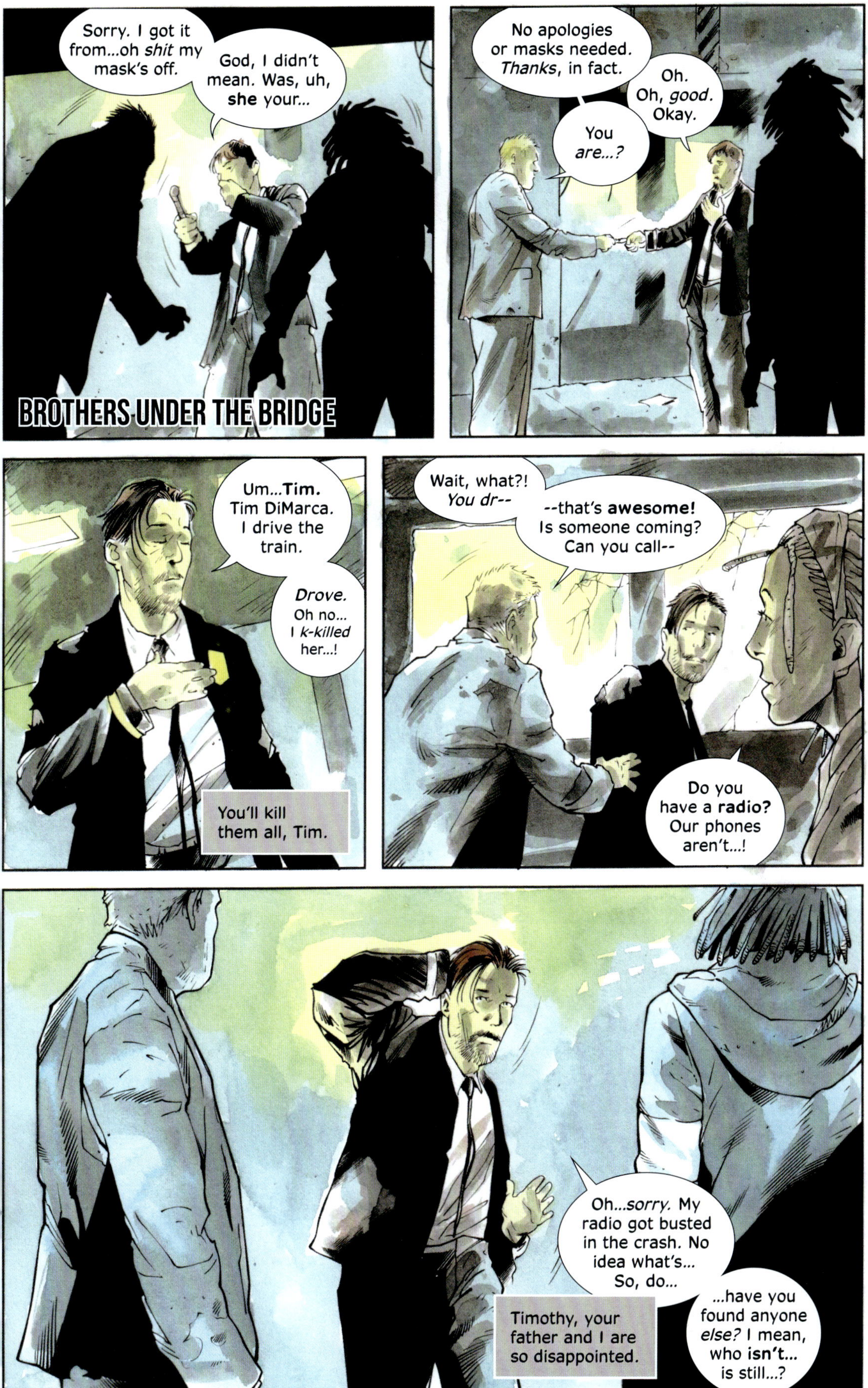

Sorry. I got it from...oh *shit* my mask's off.
God, I didn't mean. Was, uh, **she** your...
BROTHERS UNDER THE BRIDGE
No apologies or masks needed. *Thanks*, in fact.
Oh. Oh, *good*. Okay.
You *are...?*
Um...**Tim.** Tim DiMarca. I drive the train.
Drove. Oh no... I *k-killed* her...!
You'll kill them all, Tim.
Wait, what?! *You dr--*
--that's **awesome!** Is someone coming? Can you call--
Do you have a **radio?** Our phones aren't...!
Oh...*sorry.* My radio got busted in the crash. No idea what's... So, do...
Timothy, your father and I are so disappointed.
...have you found anyone *else?* I mean, who **isn't...** is still...?

Yeah, a few back there. I'm **Annie**, by the way.
Jeff. So, now what?
You're the **Train Guy.** You must know how to get *out*--
No, I don't...
...there are *rats*... and I don't know **why** we crashed. I...I didn't...
Tim, you're the *only* one who can get us out of here...
Don't be too sure of that now.
Now there are **two** of us who can get you out.
Lincoln McNeil, NYPD. Here to help.
You know, in case the *uniform* made you forget.

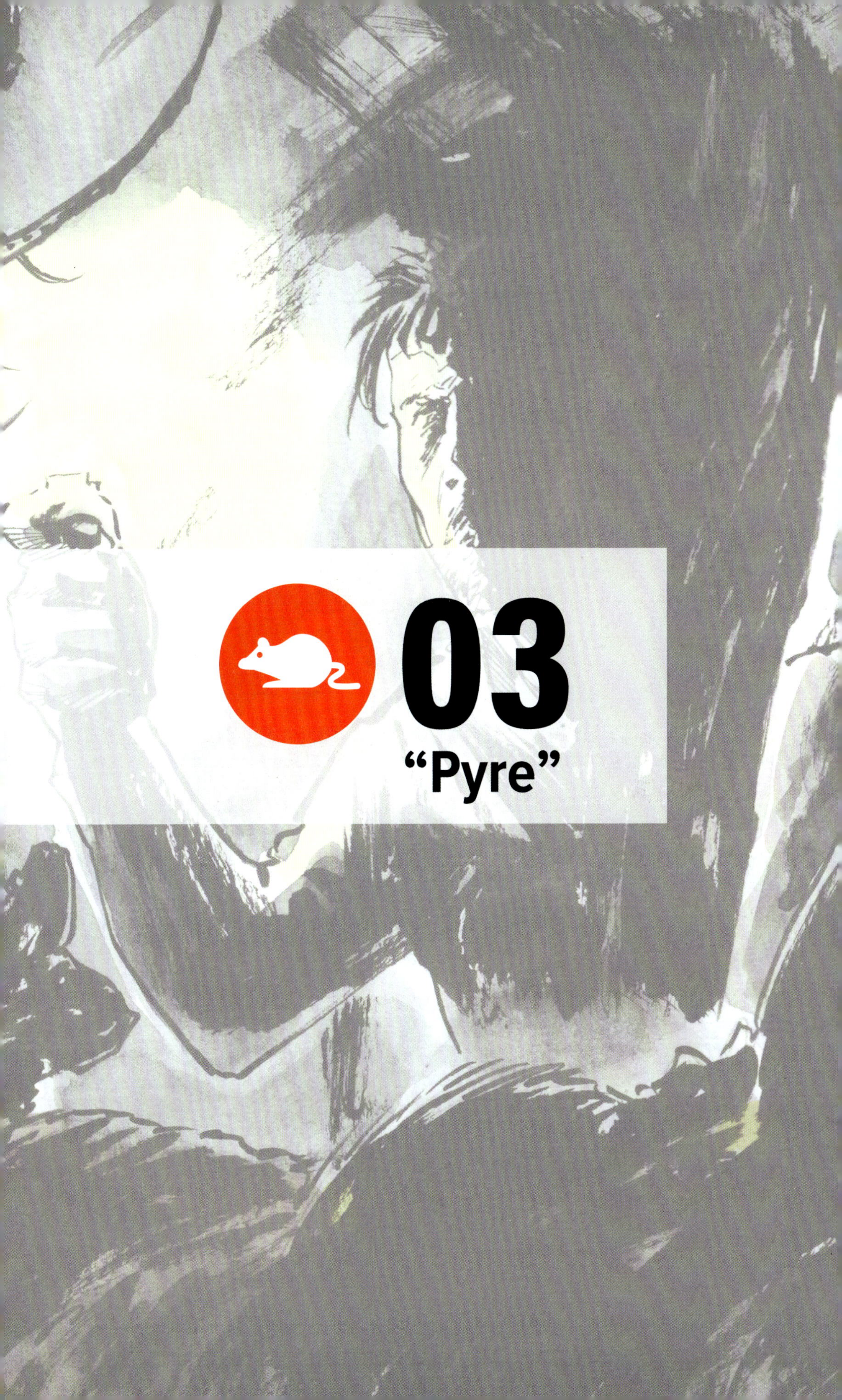

03
“Pyre”

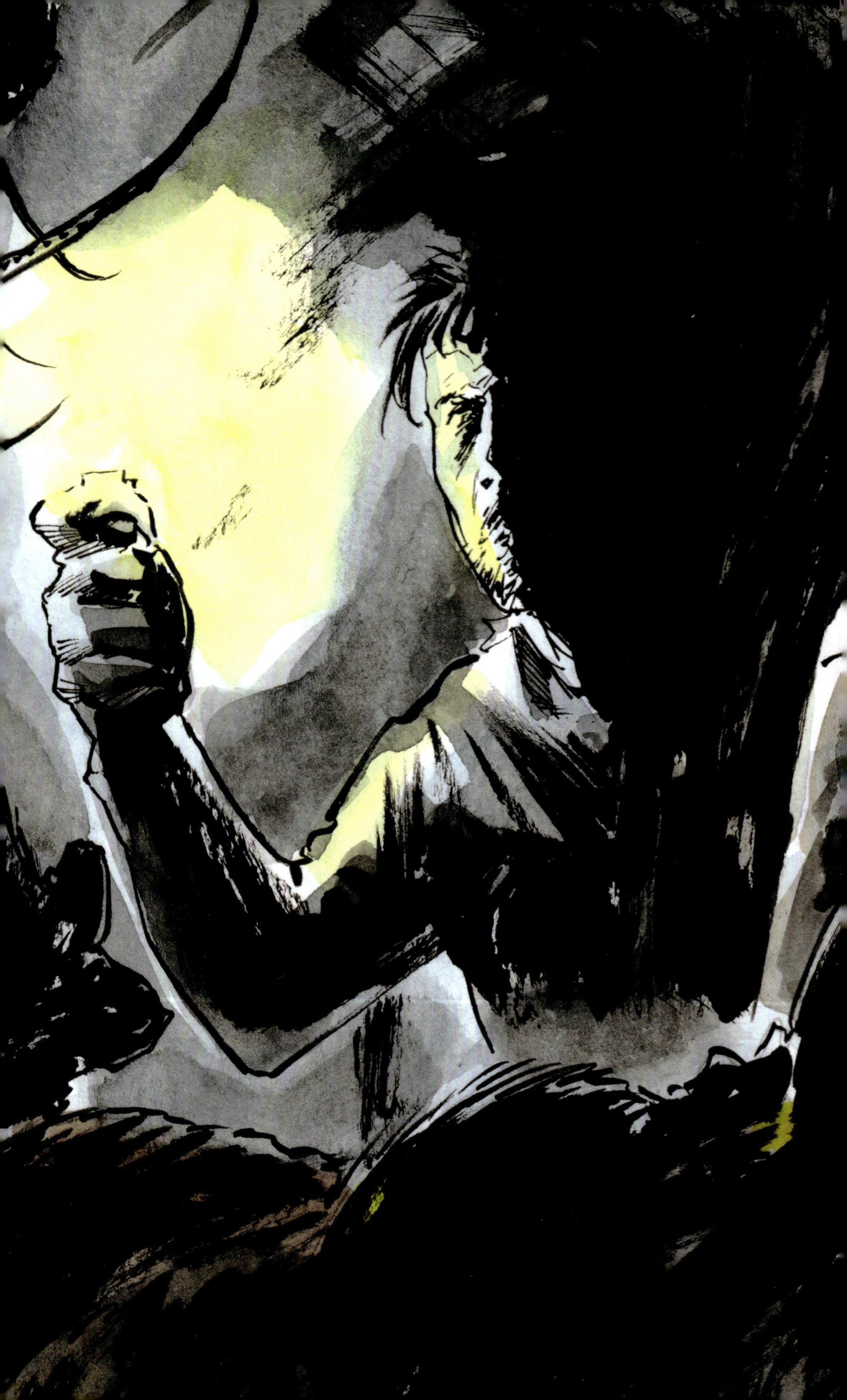

Set me up with your finest iced latte.
I just lost my job.
THE FALL
Sorry to hear that. This one's on **me**, pal.
The name's **Pete.** I'll be fine until I tell my girlfriend.
OCTOBER 2016
That'll be the *worst.*
But it'll get better from there, right?

MARCH 2017
"I'm sorry, Pete, but it's *over*--"
LIQUOR
"--went with another candidate for now--"
"--the position has been **filled**--"
AUGUST 2017
"--owed **months** of rent, Pete--"
"--discontinue your cellular service--"
OCTOBER 2017
"Hey. Hey, **you**."
JANUARY 2018
C'mon, man. There's a place **uptown**.
It isn't much, but it's *warm*.
People up on top are the **worst**.
They treat us like we're *trash*.

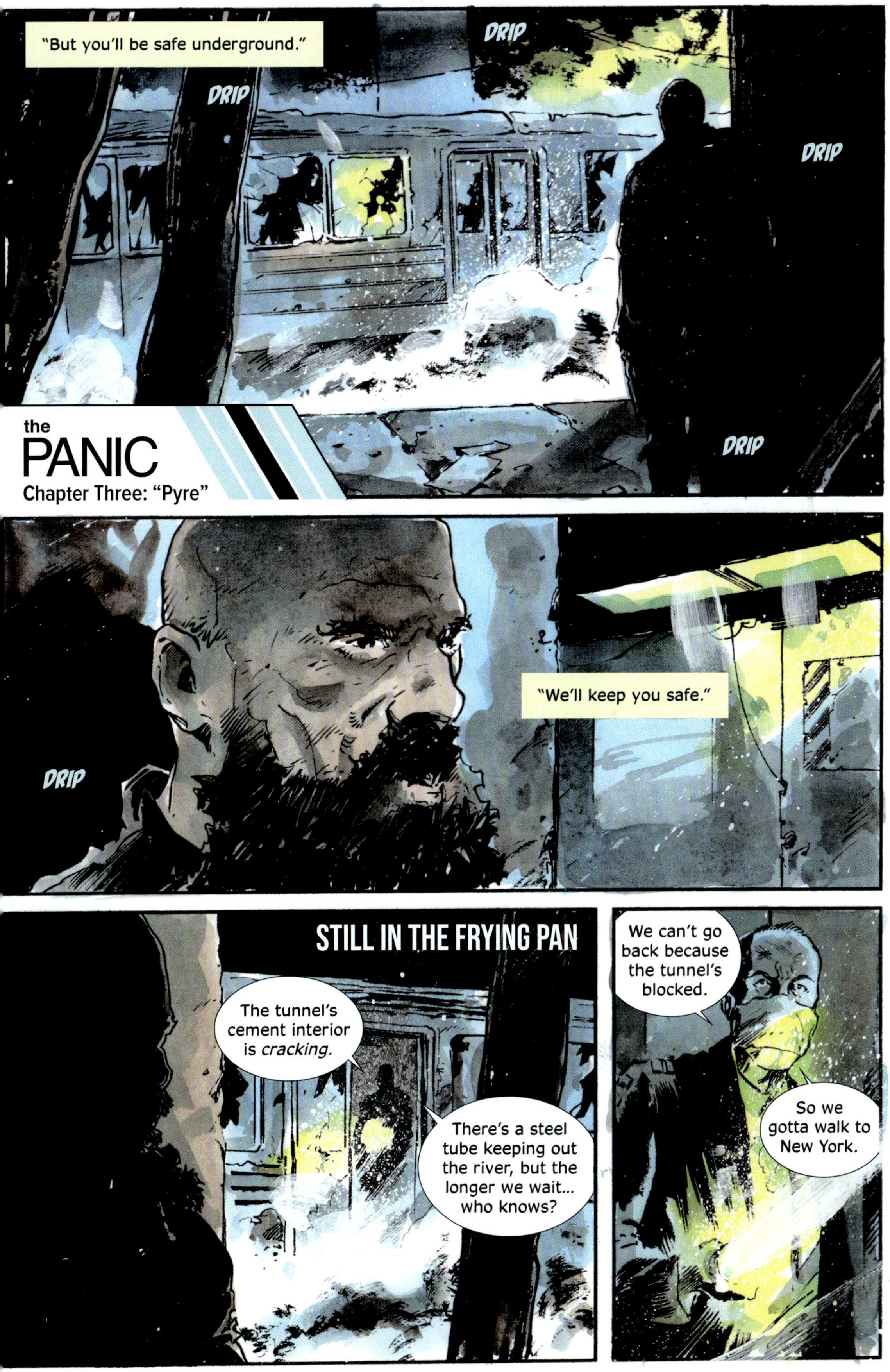
"But you'll be safe underground."
DRIP
DRIP
DRIP
DRIP
the PANIC
Chapter Three: "Pyre"
"We'll keep you safe."
DRIP
STILL IN THE FRYING PAN
The tunnel's cement interior is *cracking.*
There's a steel tube keeping out the river, but the longer we wait... who knows?
We can't go back because the tunnel's blocked.
So we gotta walk to New York.

And why should we listen to **you?**
Because you'll *die* if you stay. For starters.
Still. Badge and gun don't just put you in charge.
Hey, **Manda**, ease *off.*
Look, my brother, we just went through something here, okay?
Tim, the driver? He *killed* a lady. And this *dude*, Pete...I mean, look...
...none of us *knows* you.
Okay, fine. Hey, what up? **Lincoln McNeil**. Friends call me *Mick*. I'm a cop, I'm a gamer.
Got two kids in Astoria I'd like to see. We *cool?*
Yeah, *cool.* So, I'm **Jeff**...
What? No. Not *"cool."*
What's the *problem?* He's a **cop!** He's got a light, a radio, and a gun.

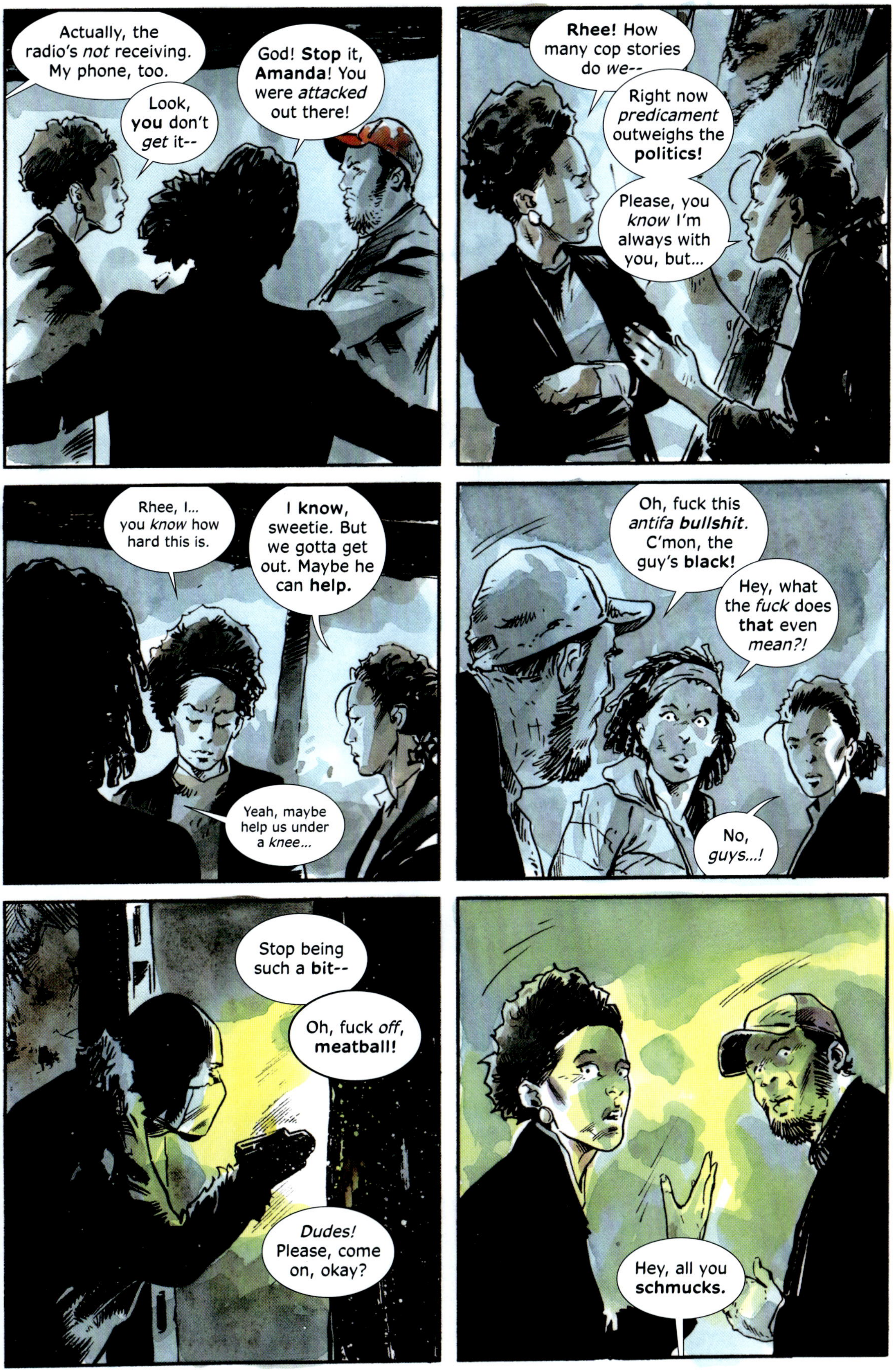
Actually, the radio's *not* receiving. My phone, too.
Look, **you** don't *get* it--
God! **Stop** it, **Amanda**! You were *attacked* out there!
Rhee! How many cop stories do *we*--
Right now *predicament* outweighs the **politics!**
Please, you *know* I'm always with you, but...
Rhee, I... you *know* how hard this is.
I know, sweetie. But we gotta get out. Maybe he can **help.**
Yeah, maybe help us under a *knee*...
Oh, fuck this *antifa* **bullshit**. C'mon, the guy's **black!**
Hey, what the *fuck* does **that** even *mean?!*
No, *guys...!*
Stop being such a **bit--**
Oh, fuck *off*, **meatball!**
Dudes! Please, come on, okay?
Hey, all you **schmucks.**

All the tantrums finished?
You, the liberals? And Mister the Hat? Done? Okay, **good.**
Listen: love or hate each other...all of that is *bupkis* right now.
This here? This is **danger.** You...we...are in *danger.*
Red, black, blue, rainbow-I-don't-know-what...
Hang up your hats and get *over* it.
Because if you *don't*, this **tunnel** will be the last hat you ever wear.
The cop's got a flashlight. *This* guy knows the tunnel.
So, *nu* what are we waiting for? *Mashiach?*

Yeah, I don't know what *"mashiak"* is, but hard agree.
...what, David?
Annie... *Annie*, we *can't.*
We *don't...* I mean, I can't...
...what about my *mom and dad?*
Oh. Oh, man. *Why* did I *volun...?*
Sweetie, I know this sucks, but we can't **stay.**
Your mom, my *friend...*
...I *dunno*, maybe some-one can come back here to **get** them?
But it isn't safe here.
But, my **mom...!**
Oh...oh, *c'mon*...I'm no good at *this--*
Hey. Let *me* try.

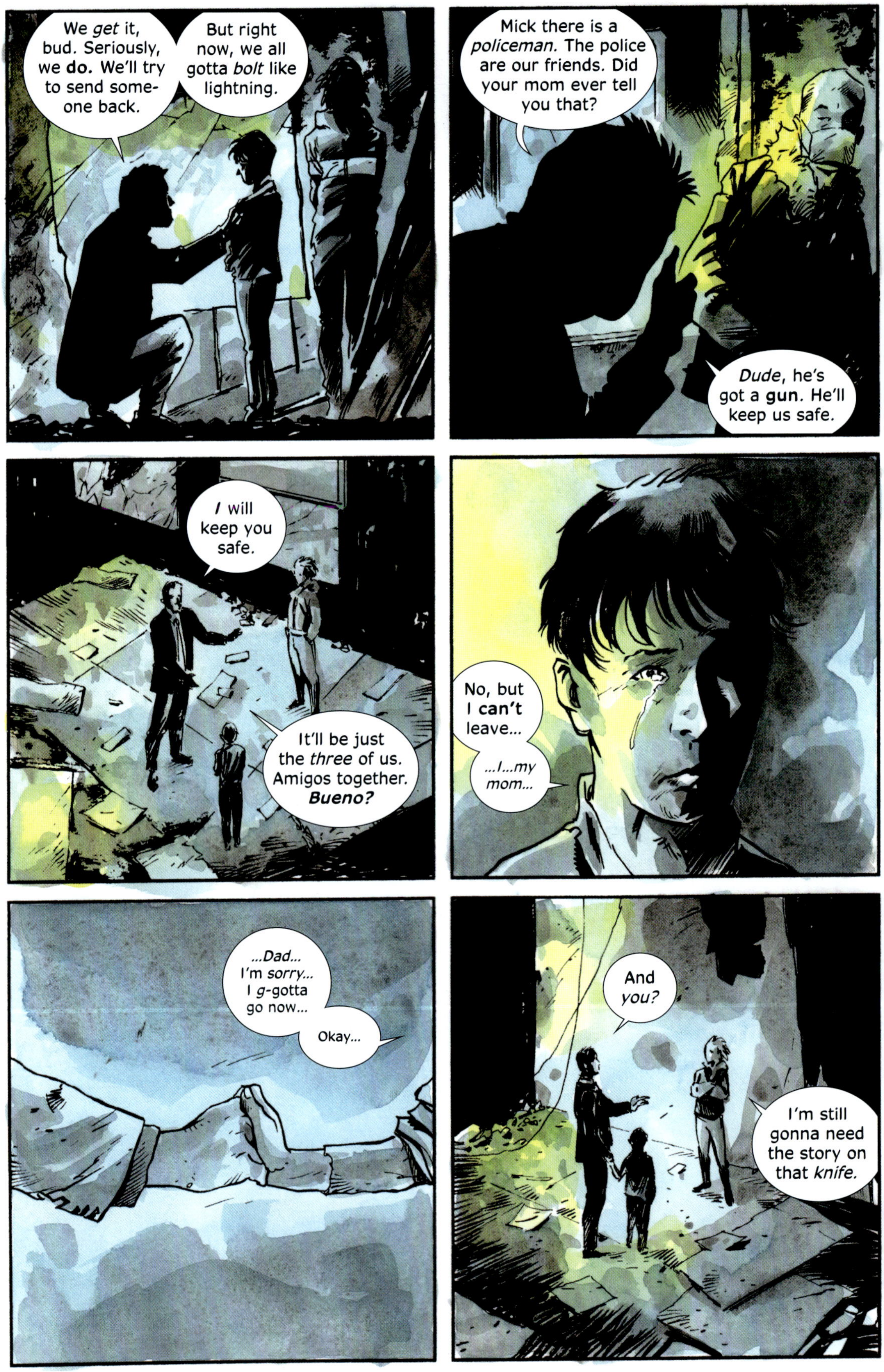
We *get* it, bud. Seriously, we **do.** We'll try to send someone back.
But right now, we all gotta *bolt* like lightning.
Mick there is a *policeman.* The police are our friends. Did your mom ever tell you that?
Dude, he's got a **gun.** He'll keep us safe.
I will keep you safe.
It'll be just the *three* of us. Amigos together. ***Bueno?***
No, but I **can't** leave...
...I...my mom...
...Dad... I'm *sorry...* I *g*-gotta go now...
Okay...
And *you?*
I'm still gonna need the story on that *knife.*

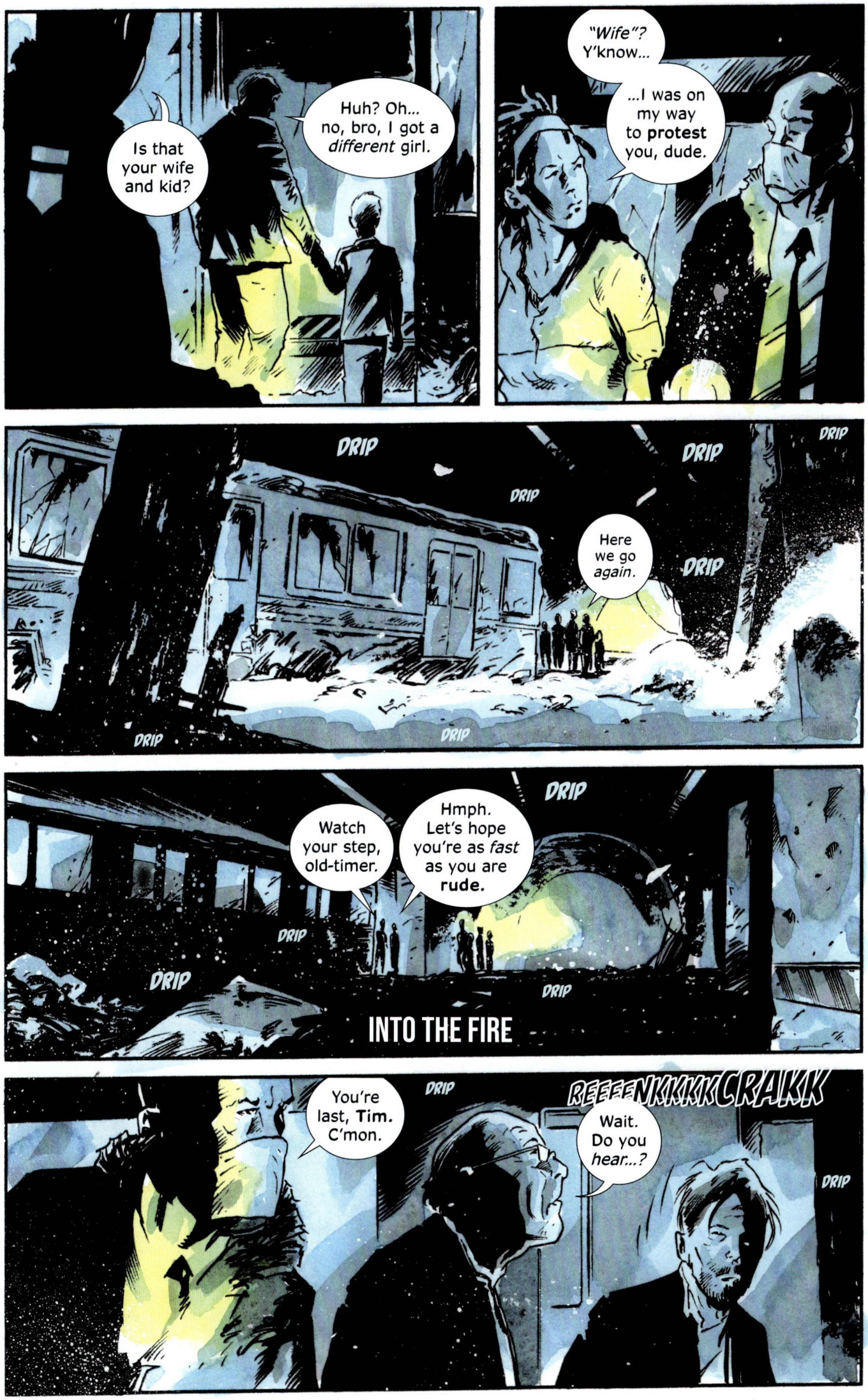
Is that your wife and kid?
Huh? Oh... no, bro, I got a *different* girl.
"*Wife*"? Y'know...
...I was on my way to **protest** you, dude.
DRIP
DRIP
DRIP
DRIP
Here we go *again*.
DRIP
DRIP
DRIP
DRIP
Watch your step, old-timer.
Hmph. Let's hope you're as *fast* as you are **rude.**
DRIP
DRIP
DRIP
DRIP
INTO THE FIRE
DRIP
REEEENKKKKCRAKK
You're last, **Tim.** C'mon.
Wait. Do you *hear...?*
DRIP

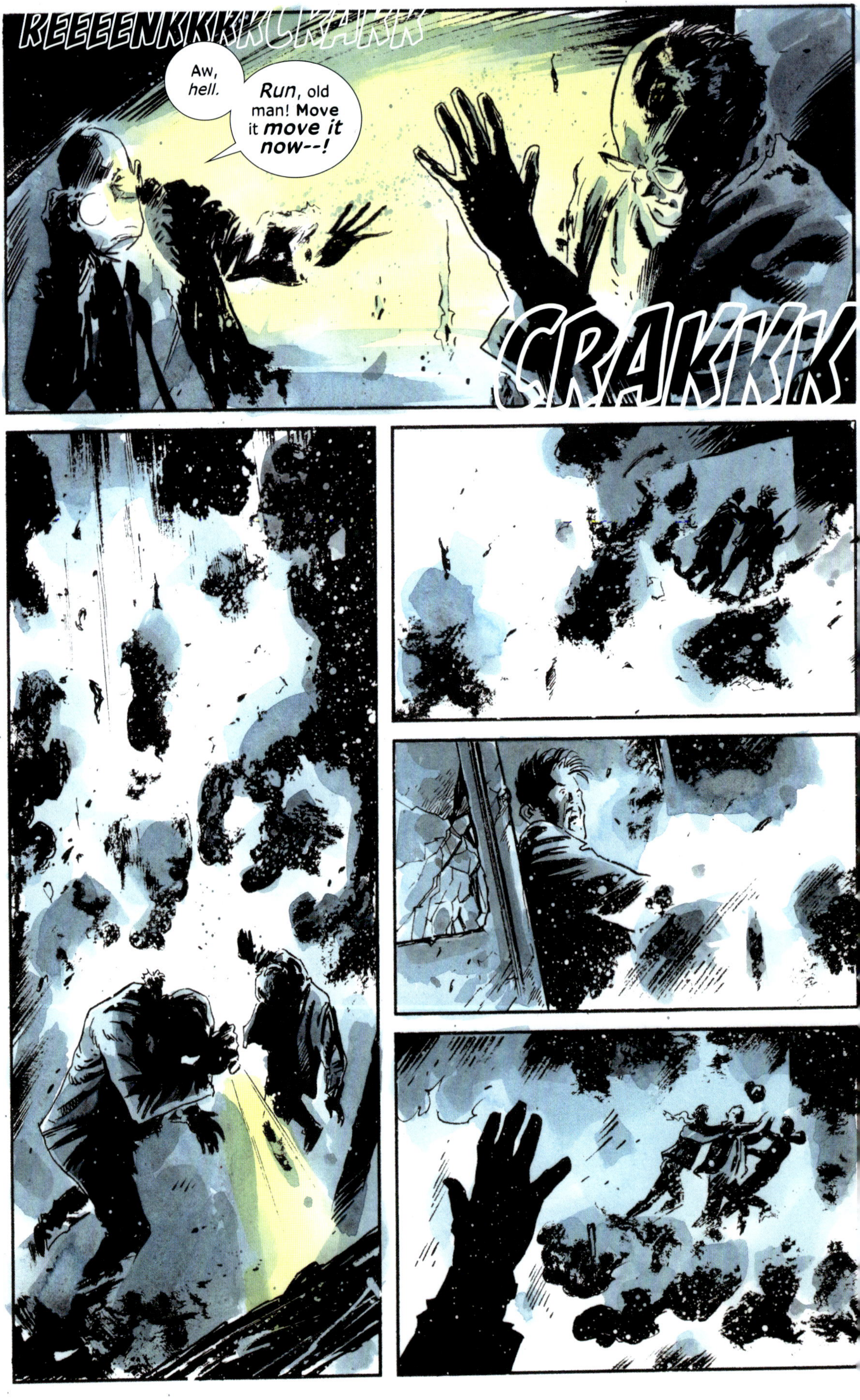
REEEENKKKKCRAKK
Aw, hell.
Run, old man! Move it move it now--!
CRAKKK

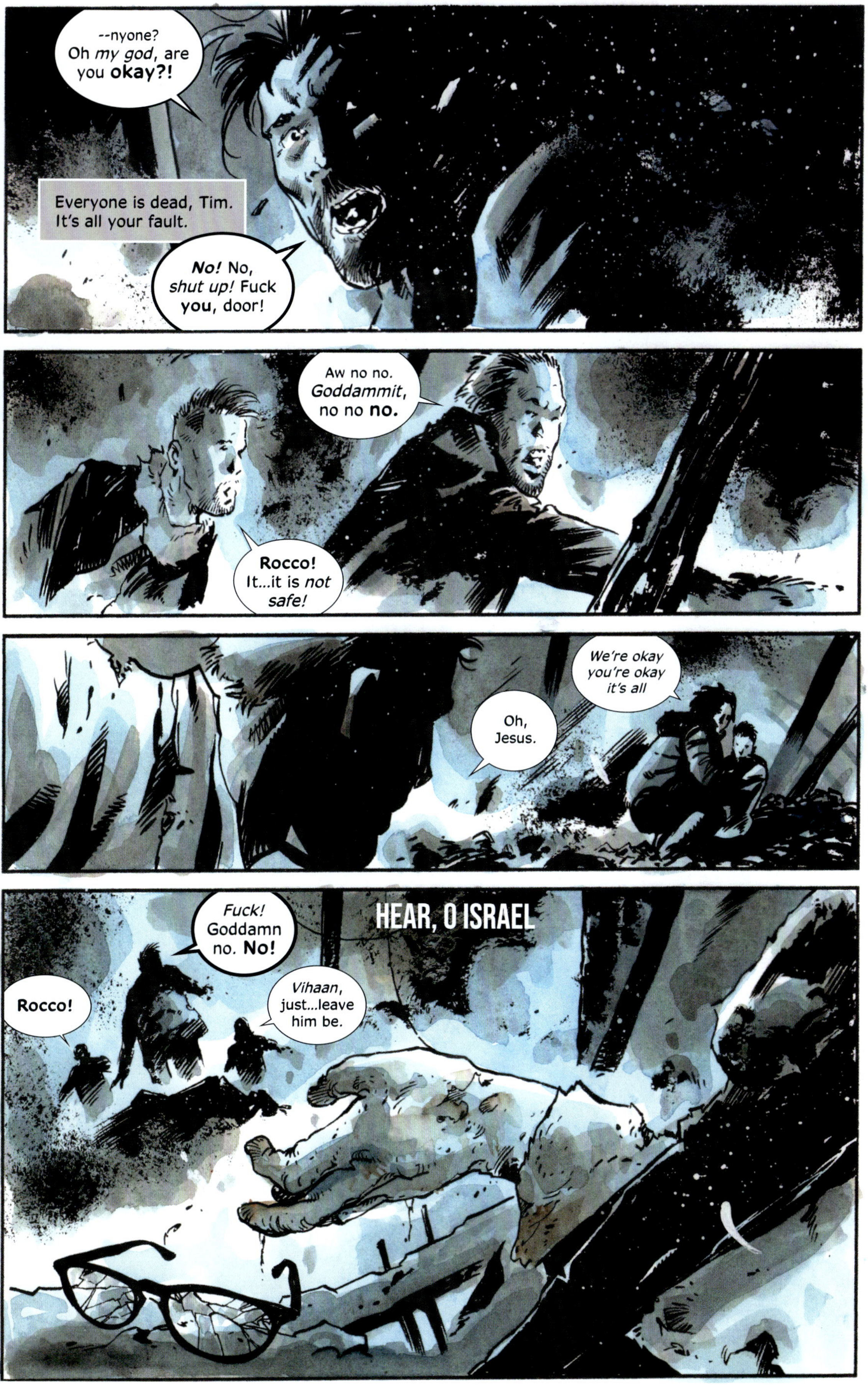
--nyone? Oh *my god*, are you **okay?!**
Everyone is dead, Tim. It's all your fault.
No! No, *shut up!* Fuck **you**, door!
Aw no no. *Goddammit*, no no **no.**
Rocco! It...it is *not safe!*
We're okay you're okay it's all
Oh, Jesus.
Fuck! Goddamn no. **No!**
HEAR, O ISRAEL
Rocco!
Vihaan, just...leave him be.

Oh...oh, poor Mister Polachek.
He was just. I mean, I didn't want him to...
Hey! Hey, you **guys!** Over...
It's McNeil. I think that he's...
...ah. Oh. His leg...
Aaaahhh... Tim? Hey, *d-did...* you're...**did** I...
...the old guy?
Dead, sorry. Your flashlight, too, I think.
Aw, shit. Ow. My leg...you'll have to carry or leave me.
Or I could babysit the crash 'til you get back, but the tunnel may cave in again, or...
Or Pete.
Okay, I will carry McNeil.
Yeah, **Guru Puke**? With the *blood* and all?
Solid good point...

I'll do it.
But we take Polachek, *too*, got it?
Rocco, we can't carry them both.
He's *right*. It's a tricky walk and my light just broke.
Uh... I've got a lighter.
There might be *gas* in the tunnel.
I just thought maybe...
Maybe farther from the crash. For *now*, the light on my **phone** works.
Listen. Polachek. The guy hated me, but...
But then we gotta take David's parents. And my friend, and...
...yeah, yeah. I get it.
MAGA
I just wanna *do* something. A **prayer,** maybe...
Yeah? Do you know any prayers?
Shit.
None that'll do him any good.

I got a prayer: *"Hey, Timbo? Let there be light."*
Huh?! *What* did you call...? Oh...
Right. *Sorry.*
C'mon, lead us out. Walk carefully. But, y'know, also fast.
A-are we sure I should be the one in *front?*
Timothy, your father and I are so disappointed.
I *crashed* us, so...
...I mean, I'm n...no leader. I, like, I killed that lady, and...
Hey, **Tim.**
You got this. *Remember?* You're **Train Guy.**
Slow and steady. But, y'know, also fast.
...Train Guy?
Right. T-train Guy.
Fast but steady. I guess.

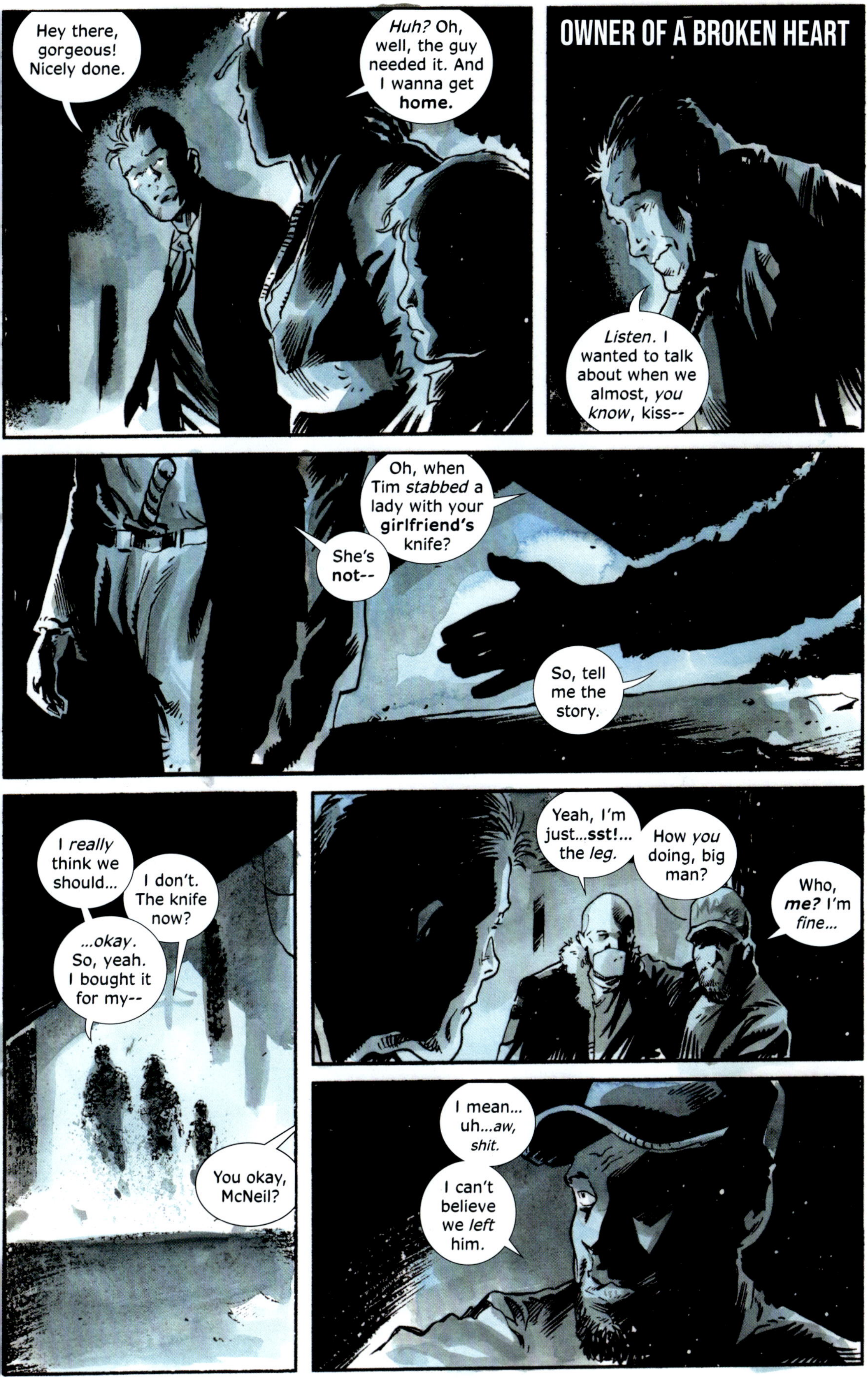
Hey there, gorgeous! Nicely done.
Huh? Oh, well, the guy needed it. And I wanna get **home.**
OWNER OF A BROKEN HEART
Listen. I wanted to talk about when we almost, *you know*, kiss--
Oh, when Tim *stabbed* a lady with your **girlfriend's** knife?
She's **not--**
So, tell me the story.
I *really* think we should...
I don't. The knife now?
...*okay*. So, yeah. I bought it for my--
You okay, McNeil?
Yeah, I'm just...**sst!**... the *leg.*
How *you* doing, big man?
Who, ***me?*** I'm *fine...*
I mean... uh...*aw, shit.*
I can't believe we *left* him.

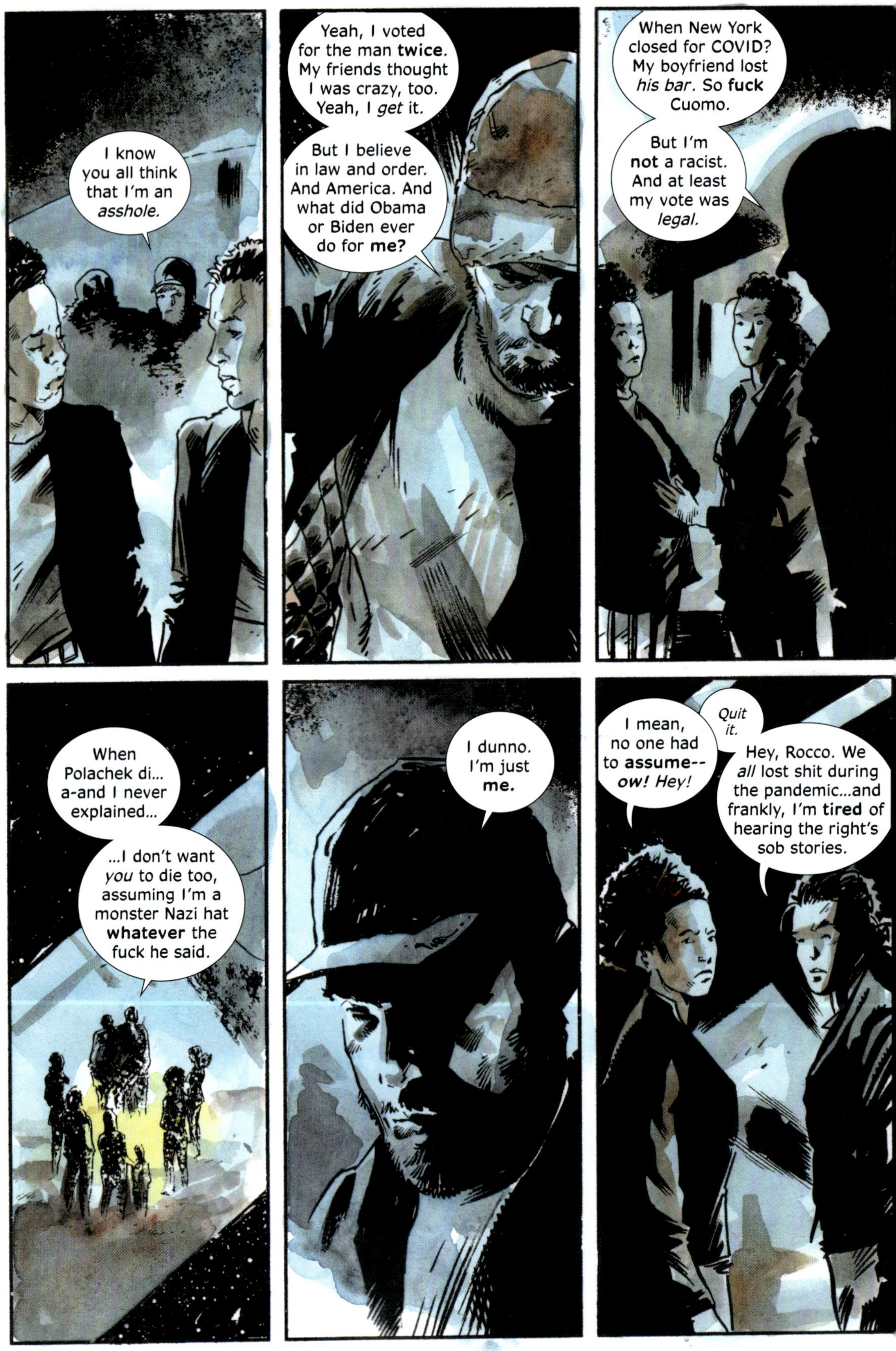
I know you all think that I'm an *asshole.*
Yeah, I voted for the man **twice.** My friends thought I was crazy, too. Yeah, I *get* it.
But I believe in law and order. And America. And what did Obama or Biden ever do for **me?**
When New York closed for COVID? My boyfriend lost *his bar.* So **fuck** Cuomo.
But I'm **not** a racist. And at least my vote was *legal.*
When Polachek di... a-and I never explained...
...I don't want *you* to die too, assuming I'm a monster Nazi hat **whatever** the fuck he said.
I dunno. I'm just **me.**
I mean, no one had to **assume--** ***ow! Hey!***
Quit it.
Hey, Rocco. We *all* lost shit during the pandemic...and frankly, I'm **tired** of hearing the right's sob stories.

Manda and I lost a furniture store. It fucking *sucked*, man.
But we didn't go and kidnap governors. Or attack other people. We tried to **help.**
Yes, this is why I came here. New Yorkers stand up for other New Yorkers.
Fuckin' *naive.* But you're new, Vihaan. you'll **learn.**
This is true. I have never even eaten from a street cart.
See? Learning already. And "Rhee," the left *did* attack other people.
Look, I protest, but it's for tolerance and inclusion...not for *hate.*
Am I an antifa badass? Maybe so. But with COVID, and with men? I'm also constantly scared out there.
So why can't I protect myself?
Someone's coming...
You're justifying lots of shitty things. You want to *honor* Polachek? Show us you're **not** one of those things.
How is **rioting** you protecti--
Hey, *fuck* you too.
Can you stop? 'Cause my leg's not getting any better.
Oh. *Sorry.* Hey, switch with me, **Tim.**
So, *uh,* Annie...about my *knife--*
Hang on. **David**, what'd you say?
I heard... something coming.

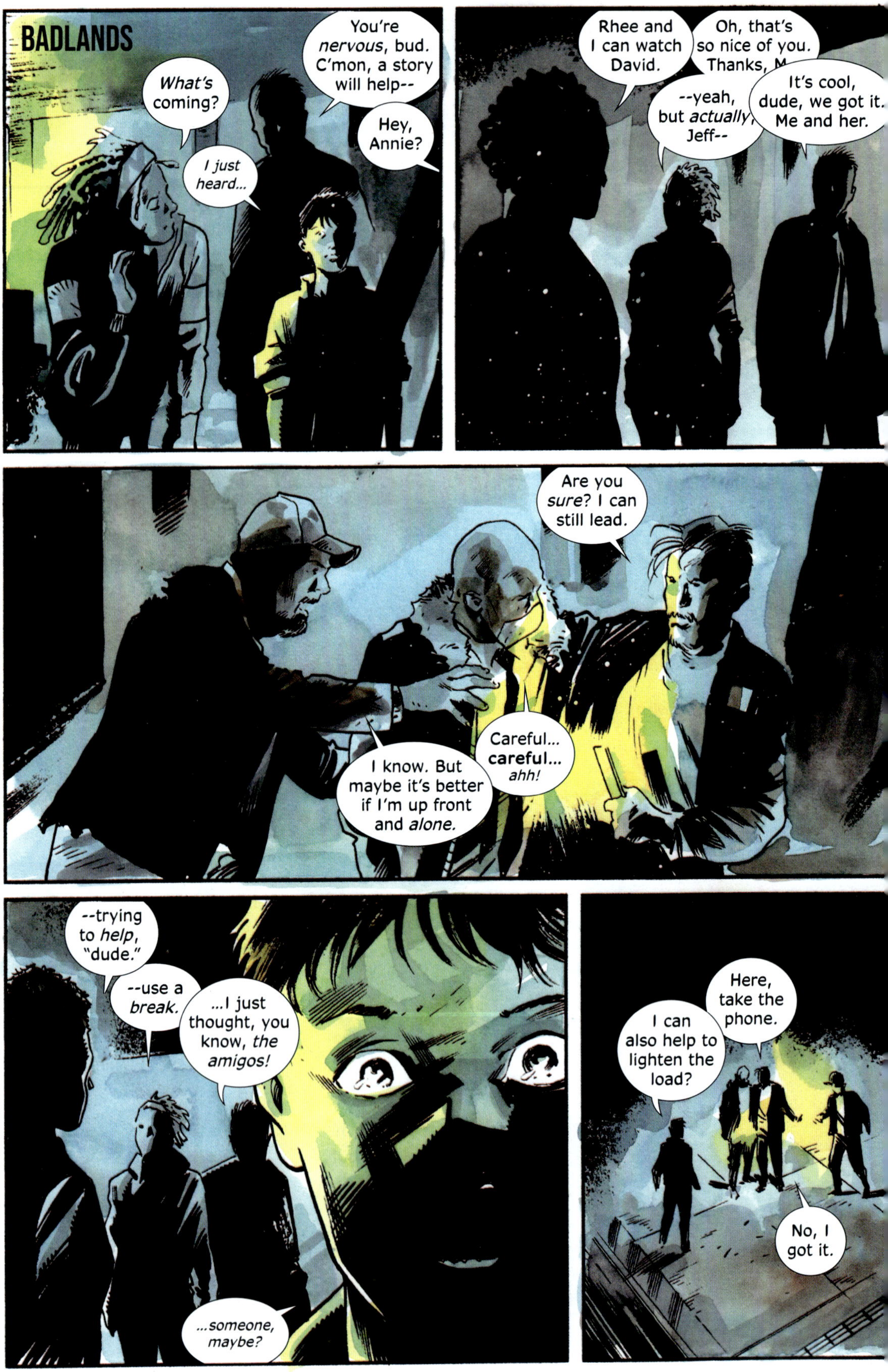
BADLANDS
What's coming?
I just heard...
You're nervous, bud. C'mon, a story will help--
Hey, Annie?
Rhee and I can watch David.
Oh, that's so nice of you. Thanks, M--
--yeah, but actually, Jeff--
It's cool, dude, we got it. Me and her.
Are you sure? I can still lead.
Careful... careful... ahh!
I know. But maybe it's better if I'm up front and alone.
--trying to help, "dude."
--use a break.
...I just thought, you know, the amigos!
...someone, maybe?
I can also help to lighten the load?
Here, take the phone.
No, I got it.

--fine on my *own*, **Jeff!** I'm a grown-ass woman.
I just thought...
I said *no!* We *just* met and you're **smotheri--**
Hey, uh, we cool over here...?
Yeah, **Fredo**, we're *cool.* Annie, let--
Very cool. Just give me my space.
Sure you're fine?
...he just keeps *pushing* me...
Lots of someones maybe...
C'mon, we gotta move!
Fuck your Fredo! *You're* acting like a creep.
Not your *business*, bro!
You guys...?
--I mean, he has a *girlfriend--*
Maybe *back off* Annie just a *litt--*
Why don't *you* back off, Rocco?!
Hey!
Not the *phone...!*

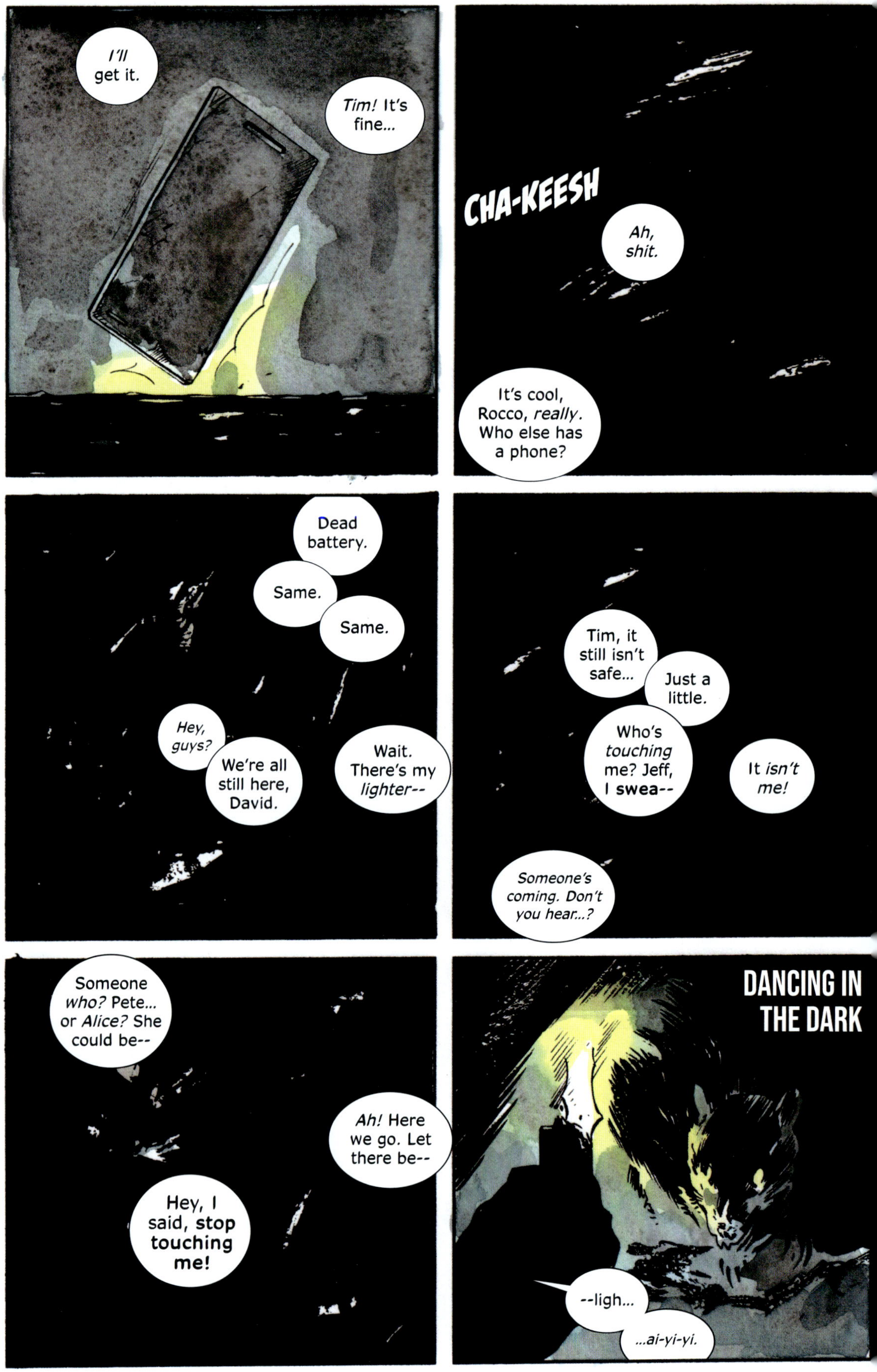
I'll get it.
Tim! It's fine...
CHA-KEESH
Ah, shit.
It's cool, Rocco, really. Who else has a phone?
Dead battery.
Same.
Same.
Hey, guys?
We're all still here, David.
Wait. There's my lighter--
Tim, it still isn't safe...
Just a little.
Who's touching me? Jeff, I swea--
It isn't me!
Someone's coming. Don't you hear...?
Someone who? Pete... or Alice? She could be--
Ah! Here we go. Let there be--
Hey, I said, stop touching me!
DANCING IN THE DARK
--ligh...
...ai-yi-yi.

Tim? What is i*aaaaahh!* ***Ahhh!***
Shit *shit* **Getitoff** *get* **off**
Ahh...
...just, ahh... just rats...just a coupla...
David...!
I *tried* to tell you...
What do we...*should we...?*
Pick 'im up, *V!* C'mon, we gotta... ***...Tim!***
Tim, we gotta go *now!*
Tim!

Shit what do we *do* shit what do we ***do...?!***
What do we *do?*
We run like **hell.**

04
“Tomb”

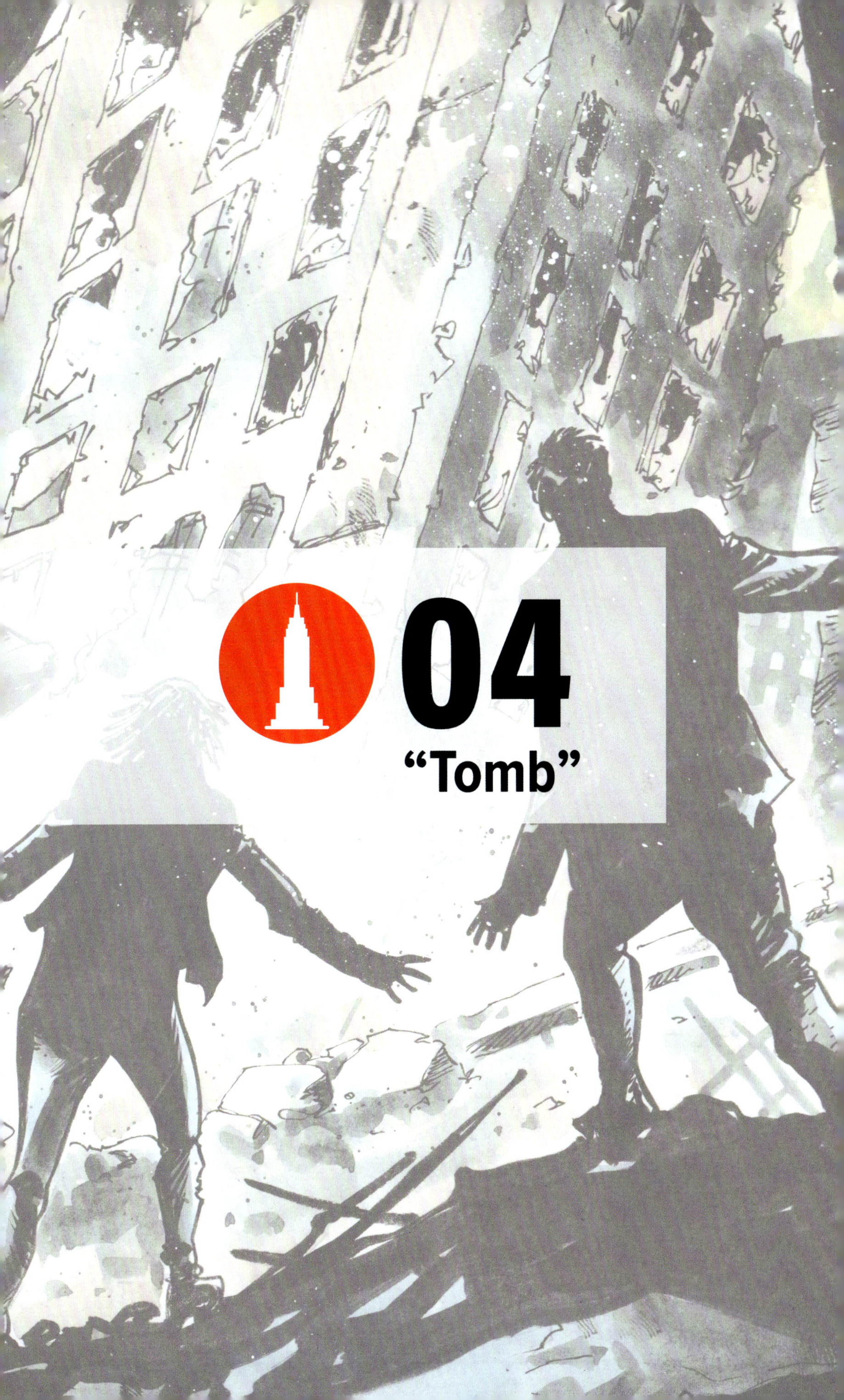

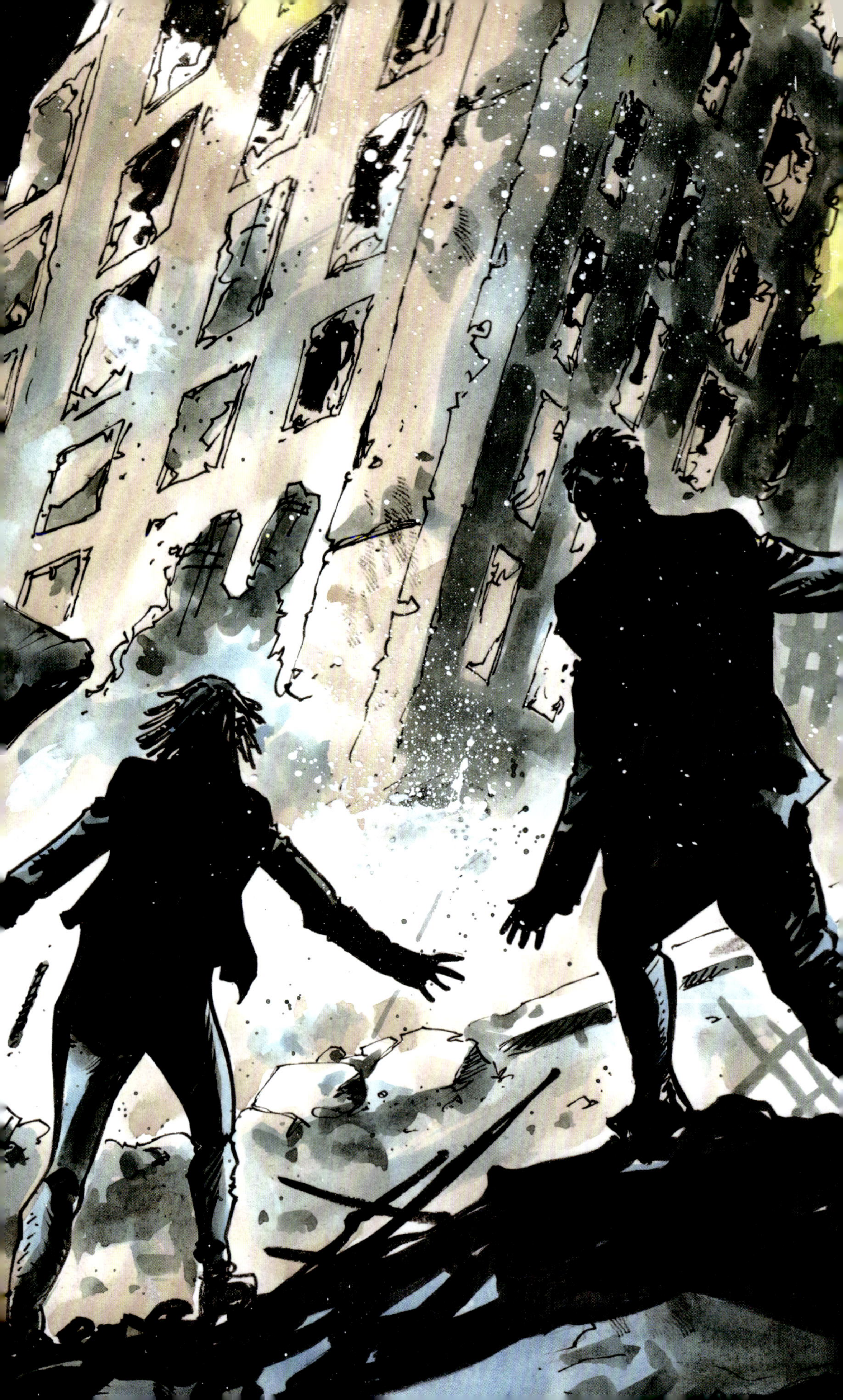

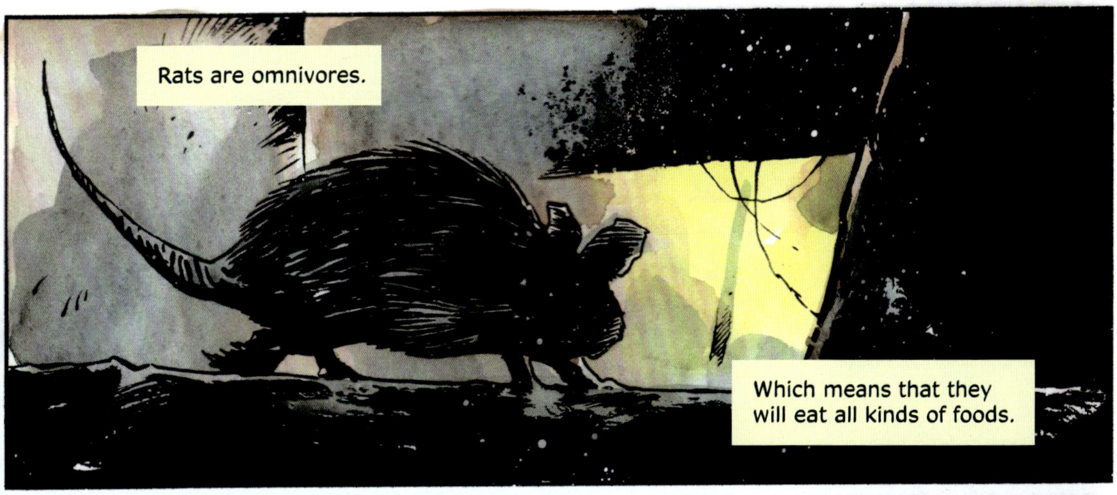
Rats are omnivores.
Which means that they will eat all kinds of foods.

ALL GOD'S RATS ARE HUNGRY

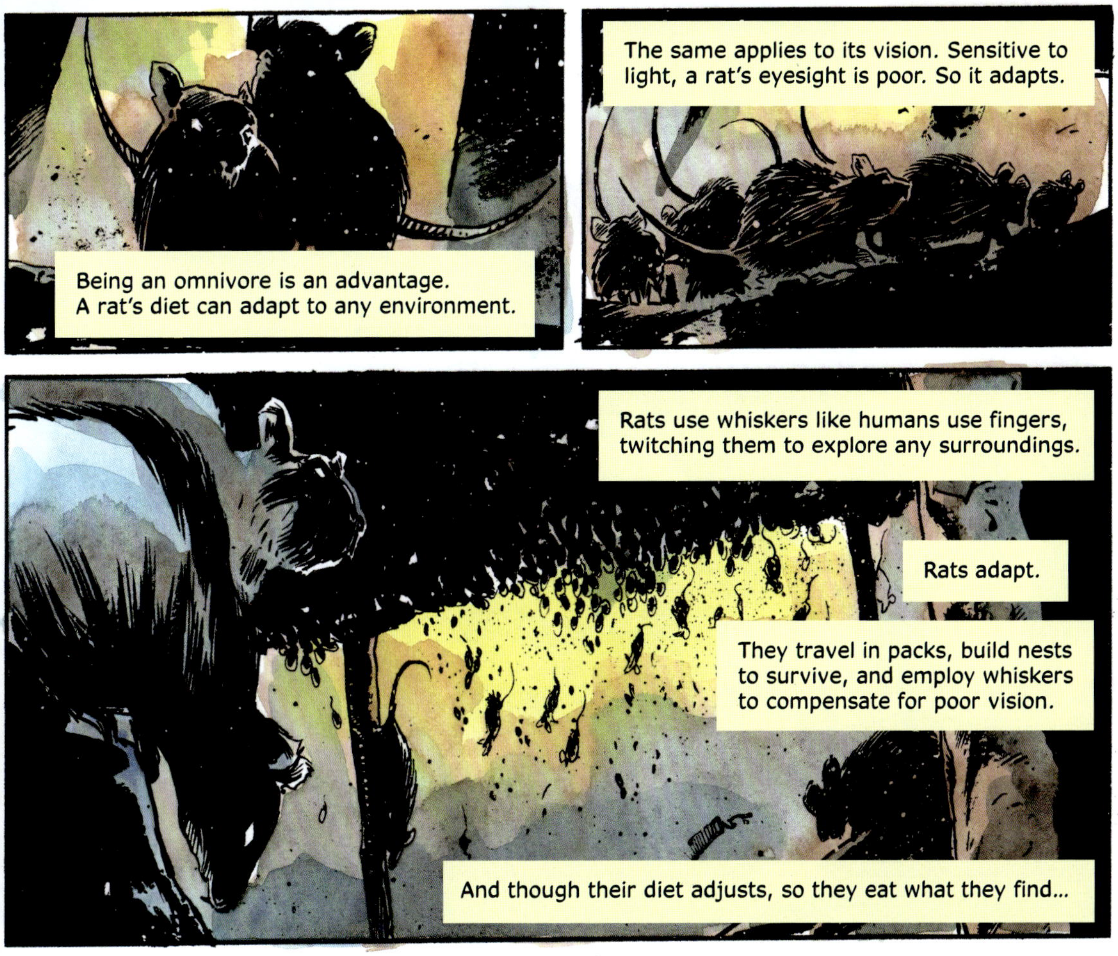
Being an omnivore is an advantage. A rat's diet can adapt to any environment.
The same applies to its vision. Sensitive to light, a rat's eyesight is poor. So it adapts.
Rats use whiskers like humans use fingers, twitching them to explore any surroundings.
Rats adapt.
They travel in packs, build nests to survive, and employ whiskers to compensate for poor vision.
And though their diet adjusts, so they eat what they find...

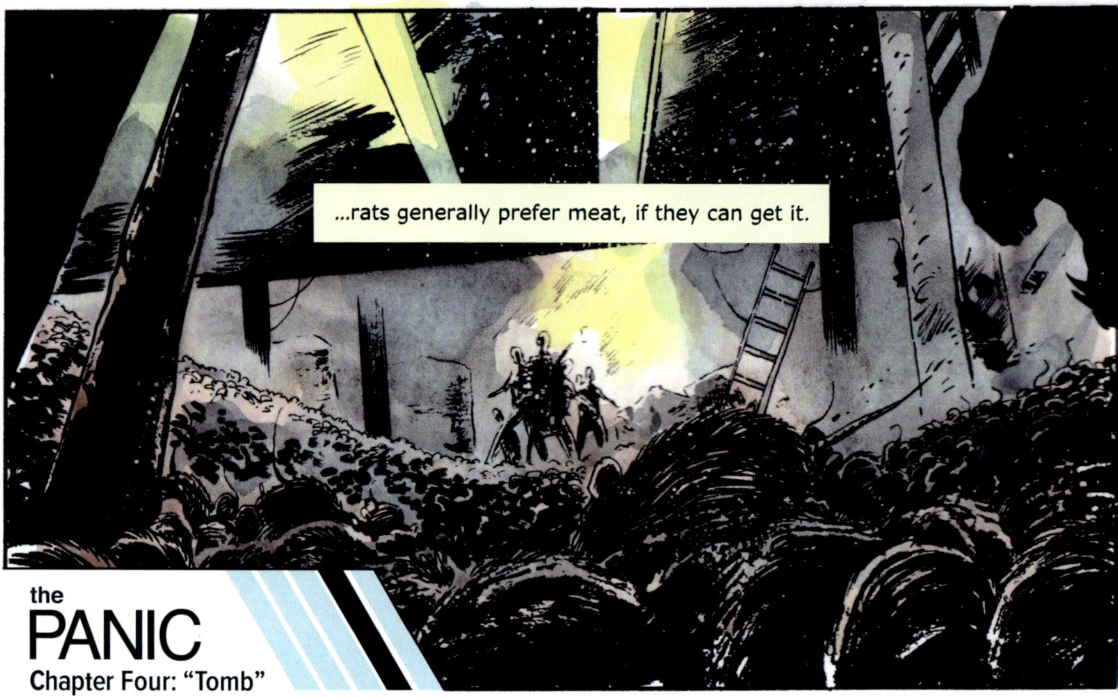
...rats generally prefer meat, if they can get it.

the
PANIC
Chapter Four: "Tomb"

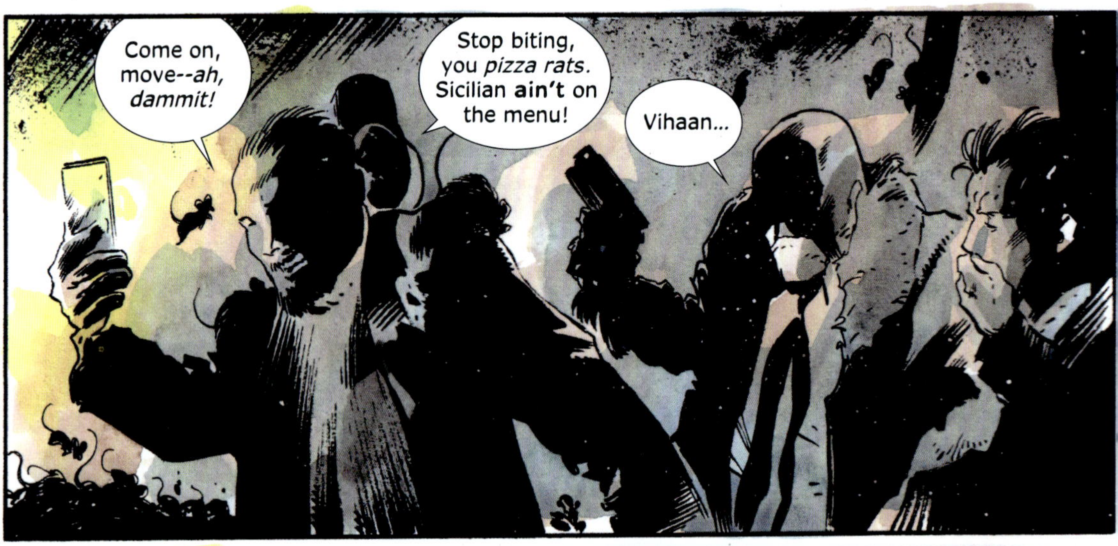
Come on, move--*ah, dammit!*
Stop biting, you *pizza rats.* Sicilian **ain't** on the menu!
Vihaan...

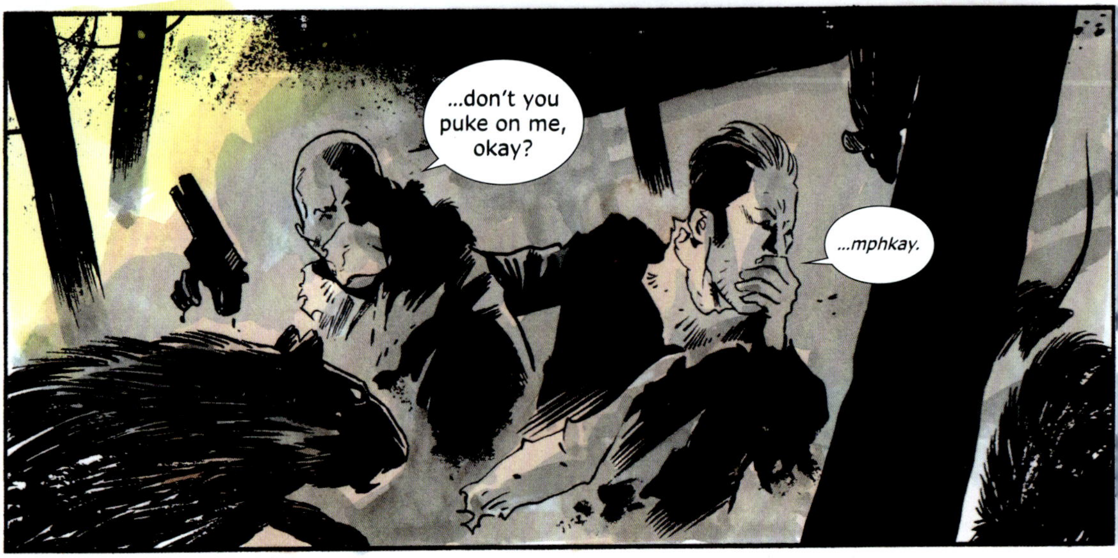
...don't you puke on me, okay?
...mphkay.

We all gotta! *Keep!* ***Moving!***
BLAM!
Rocco. Pick me up, make a hole, and run for your *fucking life.*
And run for **mine,** too.

Ah, shit!
I have lost
my foot...
FWHAM!
...nyaah
howw!
Ow...
W-what...did
I just run into...
aaaahhhh...

...is that... a building? Hey...
...friends! Something is blocking our way! We--
Don't care. Keep moving.
Up and through.
Here, Annie, let me help--
I've got it, Jeff, okay?!
Some-one is still coming...
Rats are coming, David!
Move, Tim--anywhere's better than here!
Aaahhhh

Wait, I *don't*...what *happe--*
Oh. Oh, **Rhee**, don't turn--
--ned to the *rats?*
Oh. They're eating people. Oh, *god...*
...the rats are *leaving*, eating...
...but where the *fuck* did all these bodies come from?
Thanks, **Manda.**
I'm not from New York, but there shouldn't be a *building* here in the middle of...*right?*
Right. No, there really *shouldn't.*
Who are all of these people...?
Hey, *guys.* What...

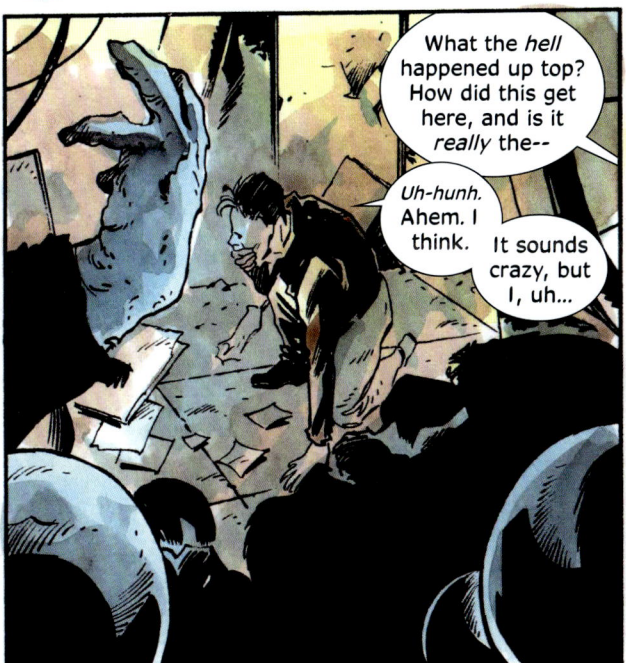

LANDMARK

...what is this place?

Monster movie-*Godzilla*-level shit.

I think it's--

hurrrrrrk

What the *hell* happened up top? How did this get here, and is it *really* the--

Uh-hunh. Ahem. I think.

It sounds crazy, but I, uh...

Holy *shit*.

Is this the motherfucking *Empire State Building*?

Can't be. That's on 34th and 5th. We're west, under the **Hudson.**
She's right. This is part of an observatory. Those are tourists. Put me *there.*
Guys, the rats stopped to eat--
--hey, I've been here before.
Yeah, we all have, genius.
Not all. Not *real* New Yorkers. It's a tourist trap.
Yeah? *--whoof!--*well, now it's just a **trap.**
Officer McNeil, might I check your wounds? Any bites ...your leg?
Sure, just don't *puke.* Hey, listen. Those rats will want **more** than just an appetizer.
We gotta **go.**

We need a minute. Tim. You *okay?*
Don't *have* a minute, babe. Get that cute butt in gear.
Annie?
Jeff's right. Building water pressure from the river may crack through and flood that shaft.
And I already lost one of you that way.
That's not helping.
Uh. *Jinx?*
Forget it. You lost the hat, But that doesn't change what's *under* it.
No, I...aw, whatever. So no Coke?
Oh, god. I'd *love* a Coke.

Same. The fat guy's hungry, who knew?
A Coke and fries *does* sound great.
Hey, Annie?
I'm also hungry...and I *still* hear someone.
Oh, David. You're hearing *rats.* Once we get out I'll buy you something.
Why wait?
Snack bar's *over there.*
It's not farm to table, and you may have to fight off Remy and his ratty cousins.
But it's **packaged.** Who wants a pop?
Hey, Annie. What can I get for you and our man David?
What? Oh, no, that's okay, Jeff. We have hands.
Shut up, Rocco.
I'll take a licorice, if you're asking.
Dude, you *gotta* know you're making it **worse** with her.

If you like Annie, maybe back off her a little?
You back off, paisan! Mind your biznatch.
Right now, my *"biznatch"* is **Twizzlers.**
"But as long as we're depending on one another, it's also anything that makes our lives harder."
Tim, hold up a sec.
Oh...did you want a soda?
Soon. But first I have something for *you.*
TIMMY'S GOT A GUN
Quick, take it.
Take... *what?!* No, I'm **not**--
Shhh. Listen.
We're the only ones here in any *official* capacity.
Which means I know you had fuck all to do with the train crash, or *whatever* this is.
And I can trust you to use this to get the others out while I stay behind.

...*what?!* No, Mick! No **way!**
There's *no way* we're leaving you here.
Shhh... *quiet.*
I'm slowing us down, Tim.
This way you move fast, and then send back help.
Lead them out. It isn't far to go.
The *others* won't--
Let *me* worry about the others.
It isn't far, but it's **dangerous.** Rats...
...and who *knows* what's waiting for us up top.
The group dynamic is... *tense*, Tim. You see it, right?
Honestly, I *doubt* you'll need it. But if you *do*, I trust you to use the gun responsibly.
You'll kill them all, Tim.
Take it. Better safe than sorry.
It'll be your fault.

Oh, fuck. Fuck it fuck, okay, give it here.
Better safe than sorry.
But, you staying here's a *bad* idea--
--ahhh, no, I didn't mean...
Who's staying here?
Me. That is to say, *I'm* staying.
Like I told Tim, it's best for the group. I've been slowing us down.
Like hell. C'mon.
Jeff, you're all tired.
So? That doesn't mean you're--
You are. We're nearly out. So I won't be waiting all that long.
Right! That's why--
We're not gonna leave you with the rats, and...
...if, if that ceiling gives? Then you'll *drown!*

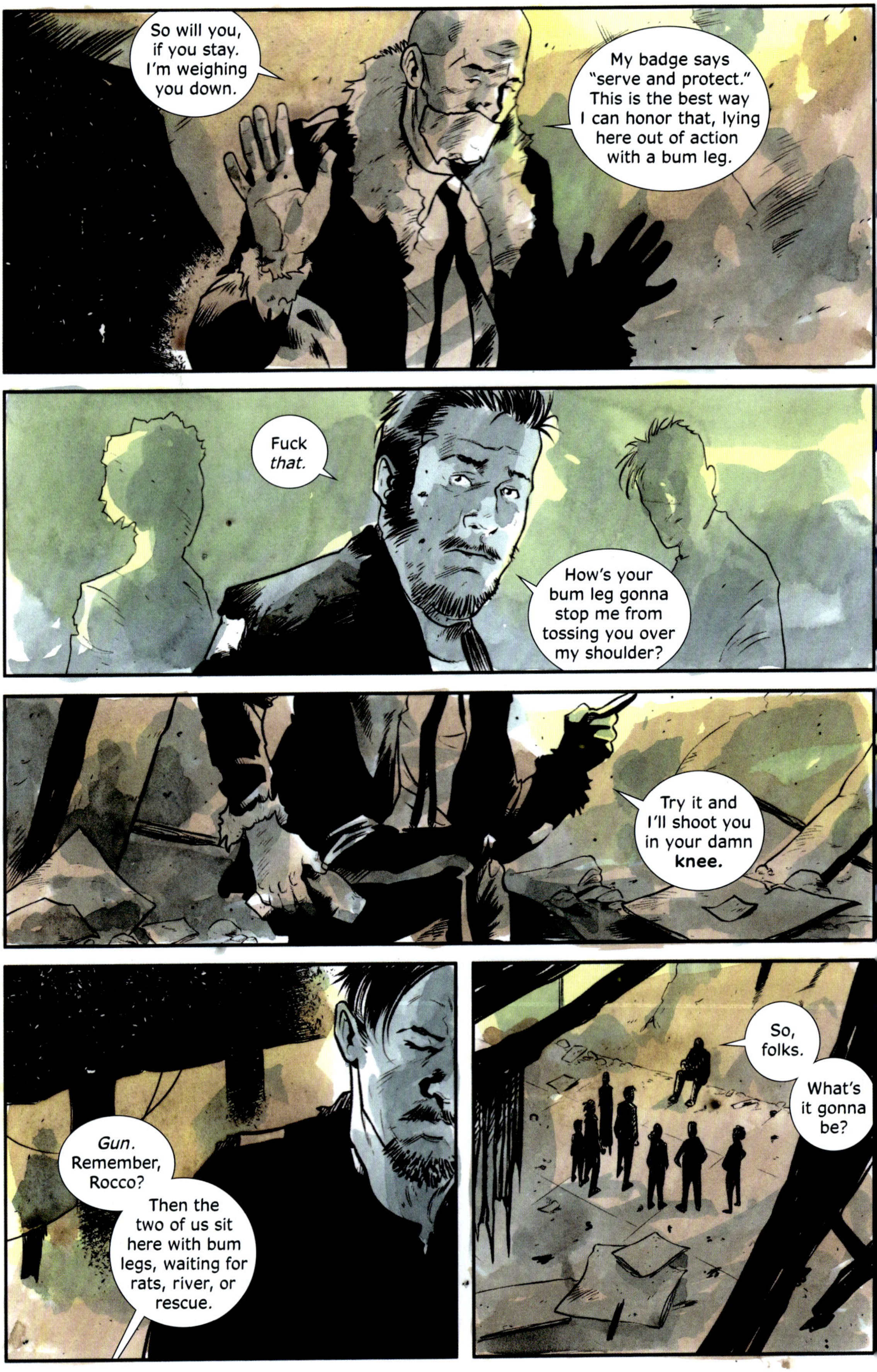
So will you, if you stay. I'm weighing you down.
My badge says "serve and protect." This is the best way I can honor that, lying here out of action with a bum leg.
Fuck *that.*
How's your bum leg gonna stop me from tossing you over my shoulder?
Try it and I'll shoot you in your damn **knee.**
Gun. Remember, Rocco?
Then the two of us sit here with bum legs, waiting for rats, river, or rescue.
So, folks.
What's it gonna be?

Shall we vote?
Well. I, uh. I vote we *leave him.*
Mick makes sense, if you think about it clearly--
What d'you--
Yeah, big *shocker.*
You *wanted* this, dude. You *hate* not being in charge.
No! That ’t--
Plus, you're *white.*
Whoa! That has *nothing* to d--
Yes, that is *true.*
You are a *very* large racist.
And a *creep.*
Oh! Oh, yes. A creep for *certain.*
Oh, *fuck* you **both!** Fine--*you* decide!

I say *take* him. He won't shoot me.
I'd take that bet.
Manda...
We're *not* leaving him...
Weren't you anti-cop earlier, Annie?
This isn't a *protest*, asshole. He's a human with *kids.*
"Asshole"? Even after we almost kissed?
...what?! Are you *mental?*
Hey, *Annie?*
...Empire State is in the Hudson! Rats are *eating* **tourists!** And *you* want to leave a man *behind!*
How do we say, *"Yes, sacrifice yourself for us"*? Does Mick get to *make* that choice?
Do *you,* Tim? *Me?*
Annie...
What? ***What?!***
I think the decision has been *made.*
Here, Mick... I'll help you get comfortable.

David, *no...* didn't you hear someone coming? We *can't* ju--
Maybe it was *rats.* Mick's right, Annie. We gotta move *faster.*
Annie, I'll be *fine.*
You don't *know* that!
David, this is ...it's hard, but leaving Mick...
Mick's got a gun. He'll be safe.
And *we* can't stay here.
We'll send someone back. For him *and* my parents.
You, me, and Jeff.
Amigos. But *we* gotta go. Mick has to *stay.*
Annie...it could be worse. I could have a case of "*blue flu,*" am I right?
I'll be *fine*, kid. You will, too.
Ha...no. No, Officer Token.
I really don't think I will.

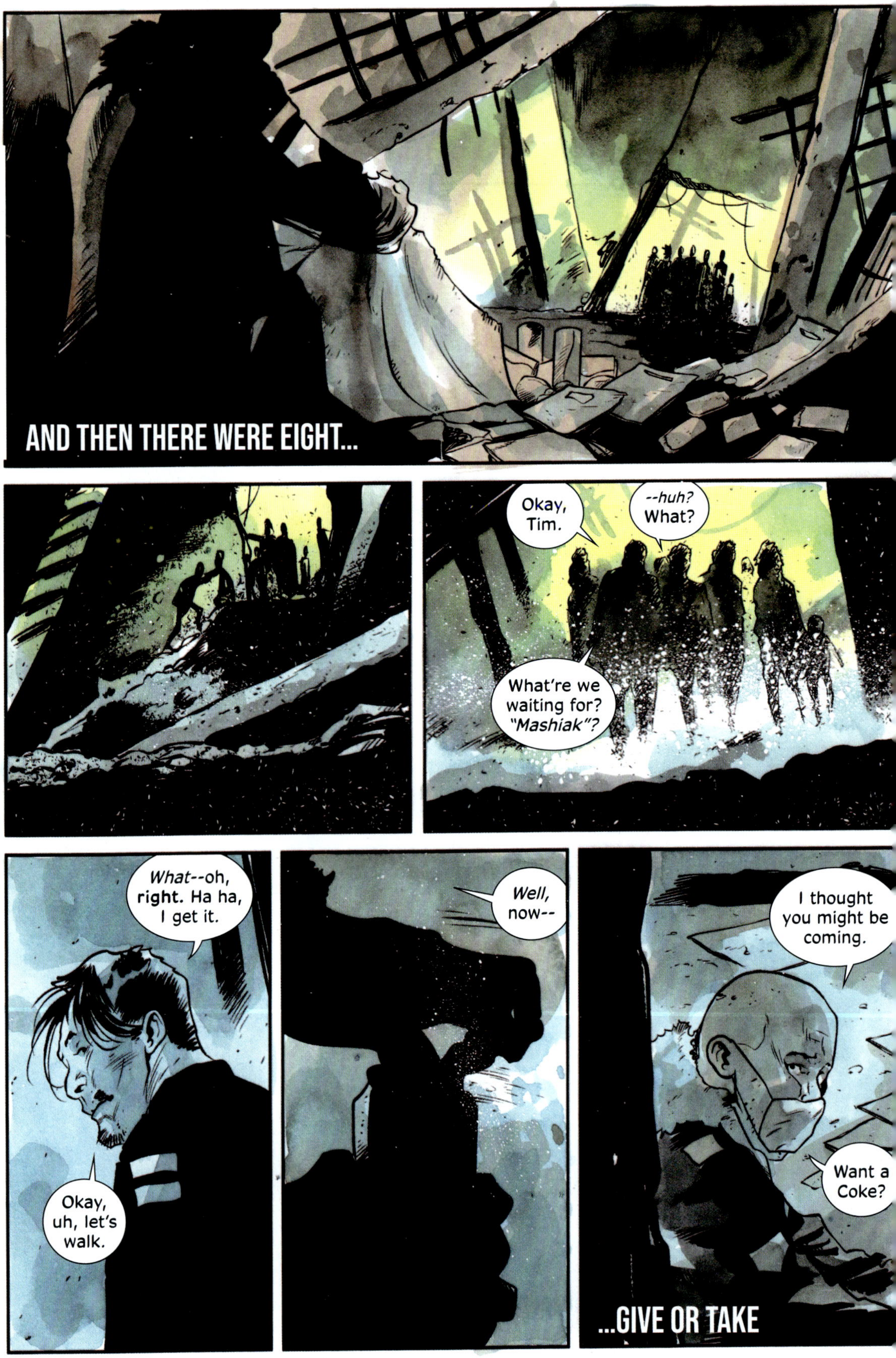
AND THEN THERE WERE EIGHT...
Okay, Tim.
--huh? What?
What're we waiting for? "Mashiak"?
What--oh, right. Ha ha, I get it.
Okay, uh, let's walk.
Well, now--
I thought you might be coming.
Want a Coke?
...GIVE OR TAKE

I am not a creep.
Oh, *Jesus,* here we go...
Hey, *shut...* listen, Annie, I just thought we had a...
Yes, I *have* a girlfriend. But she isn't...
...I was gonna tell you about this *knife,* right?
I *promise.* Once you hear the story, you'll *see--*
Oh my *god,* just fucking ***stop it!!***
Now? *Really?* Is *now* the time?

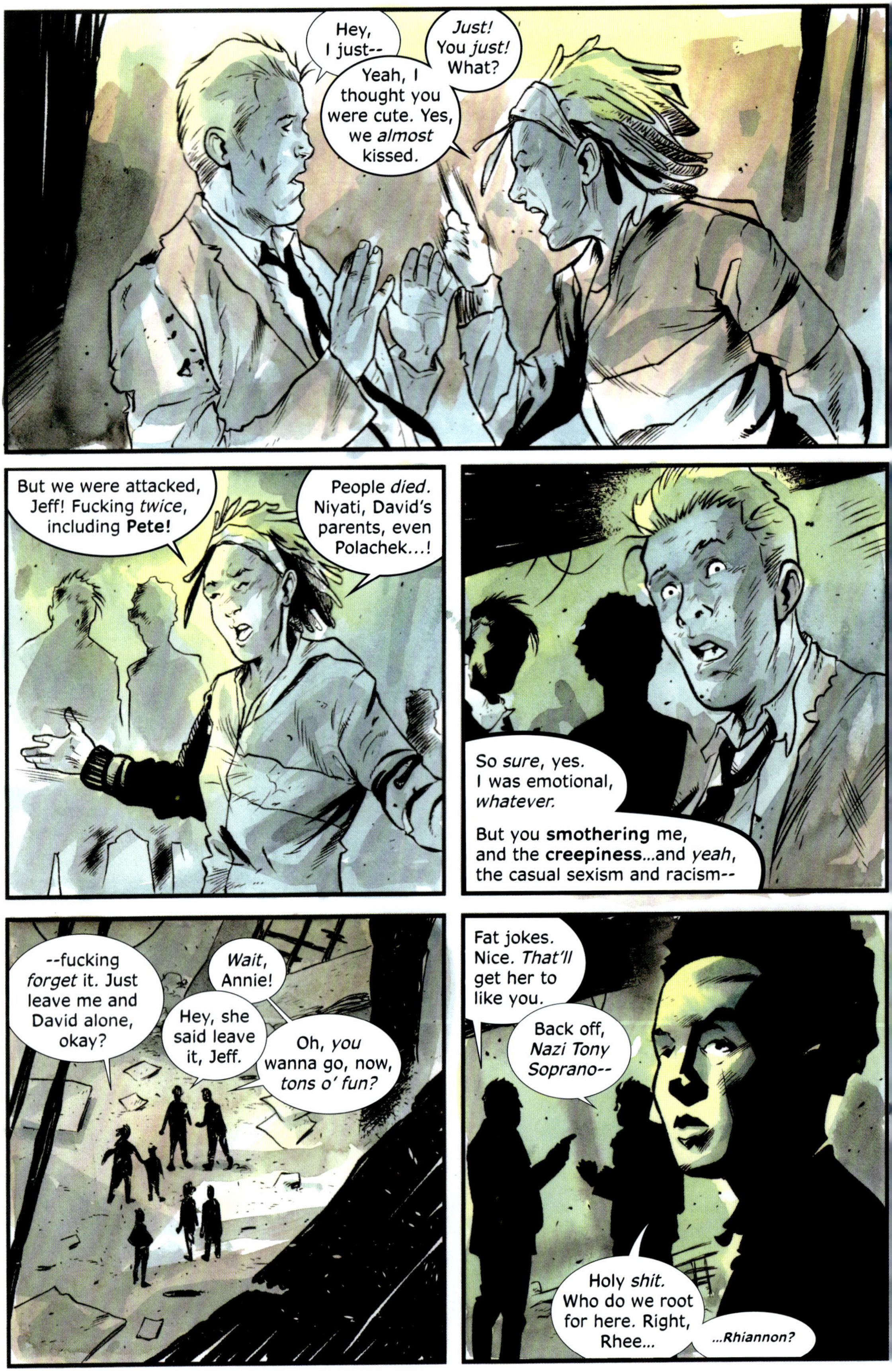
Hey, I just--
Just! You just! What?
Yeah, I thought you were cute. Yes, we almost kissed.
But we were attacked, Jeff! Fucking twice, including Pete!
People died. Niyati, David's parents, even Polachek...!
So sure, yes. I was emotional, whatever.
But you smothering me, and the creepiness...and yeah, the casual sexism and racism--
--fucking forget it. Just leave me and David alone, okay?
Wait, Annie!
Hey, she said leave it, Jeff.
Oh, you wanna go, now, tons o' fun?
Fat jokes. Nice. That'll get her to like you.
Back off, Nazi Tony Soprano--
Holy shit. Who do we root for here. Right, Rhee...
...Rhiannon?

Rhee! Where *are* you?
Has anyone... *Rhee!*
Manda?
...what fucking now?
She's not... d-did she go back? We left... we gotta--
Manda, we will find her. *Rhiannon!* Are you *there?*
She can't be *far...*
...she's always doing *stupid shit!*
Hey, she's gonna be fine, *okay?*
Yeah, we can retrace her...
Rhiannon! ***Rhee!***
Girl, when I *find* you, if you *ain't* dead, I'm gonna--
--kill you.
Omi-god.

Oh, you son of a *bitch.*
Hey, guys.
It's **Pete,** *remember?* I've been following you.
And, well...
...I brought *my* friends, see?
And now, I really think we should *talk.*

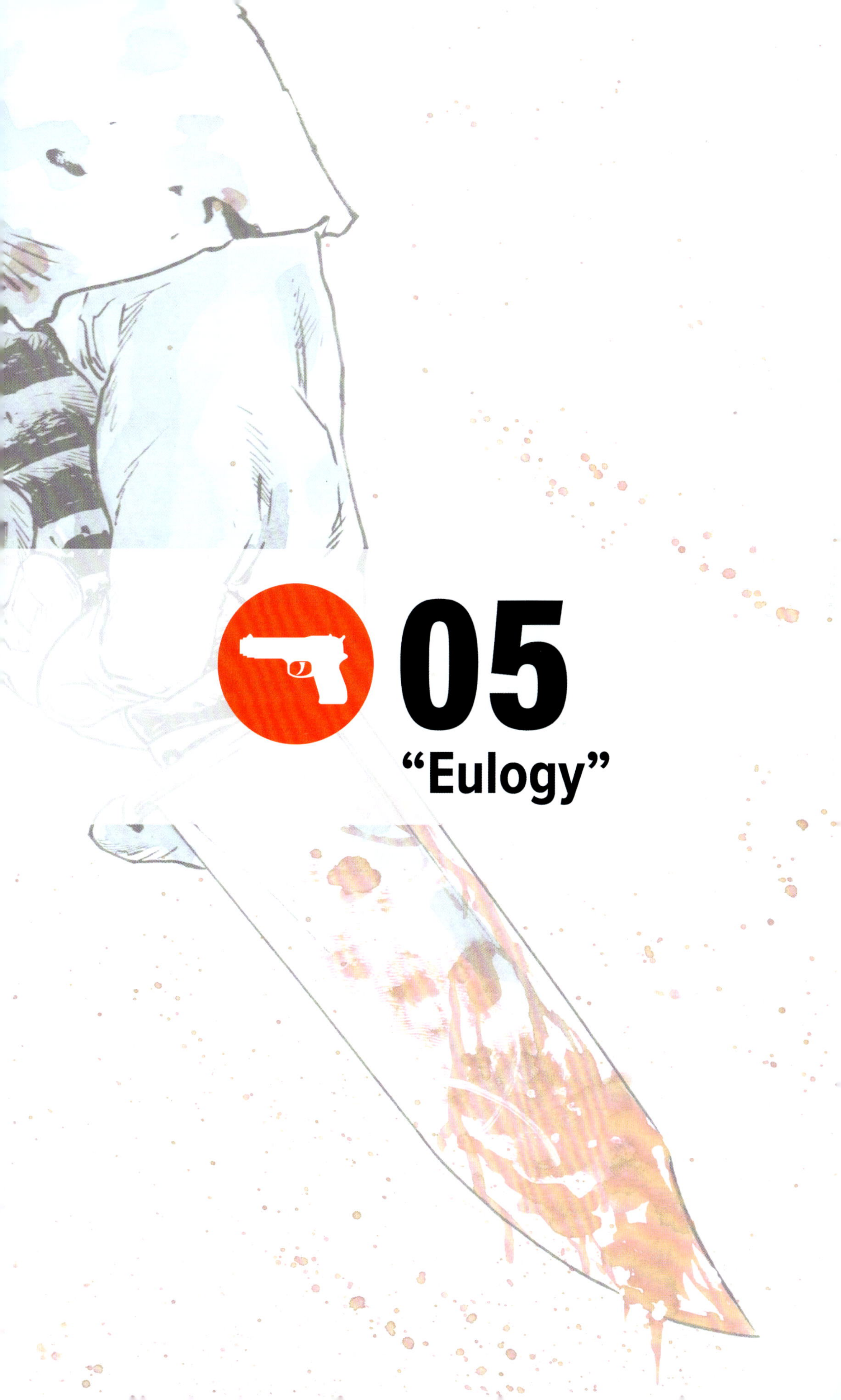

05
“Eulogy”

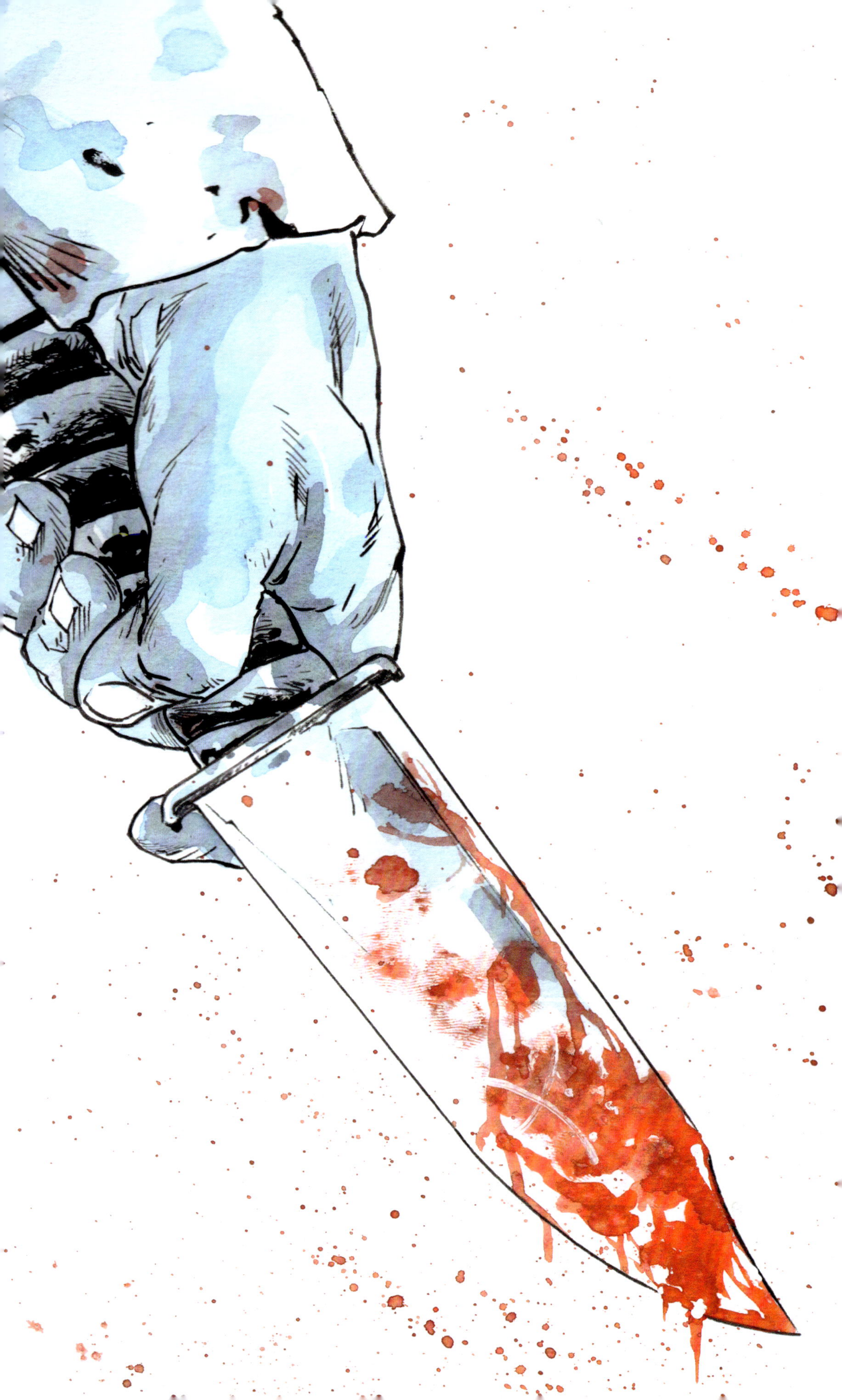

"So, the **knife.**
"It was my dad's.
"It belonged to my grandpa before that. He carried that knife everywhere he went.
"Even during summers at the lake, remember?"
Uncle Frank once used it to slice a soda can *in half.*
The can was **full**, but *whatever.*
"Look, we loved that knife, us kids.
"And one night, Dad was sleeping off a Jets loss, so I took it.

"He never said anything.
"Maybe he wanted me to have it? Like, I dunno, me taking it was him passively bequeathing the knife?"
It's like...my **legacy**, Diana. See?
I mean, I *guess* I remember. So, what...you want to buy a knife?
No...that's not...legacy. *Legacy* is what I mean, Di.
You. Me. **Ours.**
"Ours"?
What are you rambling about, **Jeff?**
THE KNIFE
"...yes, ours. And I'm not talking about a *knife*...
"...I'm talking about **a life."**

We've been dating off and on since high school, Di.
Okay...?
We have history. It isn't "legacy," but it *could* be.
Jeff, what...
Stories. Memories. That knife. I want to hand it down.
I want to build a *legacy.*
I want to build it with **you.**
Wait... *Jeff...*
Yes, **Diana.**
I want us to have a *baby.*
You know.
Like... together.

Wait, hear me out--
Are you out of your mind?
Look, this is fun, and we have history, but I'm seeing other guys.
--sure, but I'd hoped...
"Jeff, I don't even know if I want a kid. Like, ever.
"And, seriously? A knife?! A baseball, sure. But a knife?"
That knife carries history for us, Diana. Memories--
What? Your drunk uncle cutting Fanta cans?
--and one day I'll gift it to you.
"It's gonna start our legacy.
"Then you'll see how I use that knife to connect to and protect the ones I love.

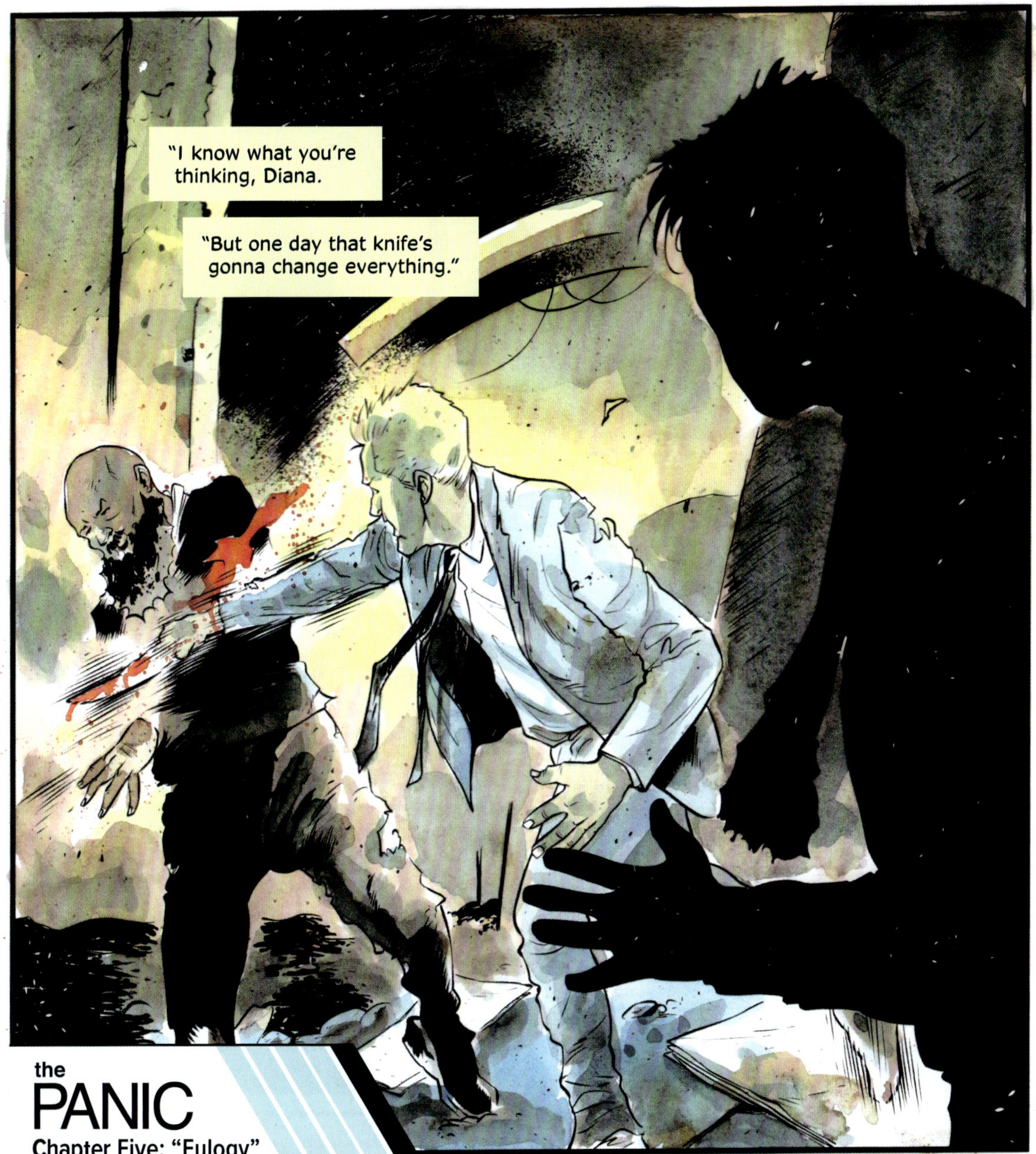
"I know what you're thinking, Diana.
"But one day that knife's gonna change everything."

the PANIC
Chapter Five: "Eulogy"

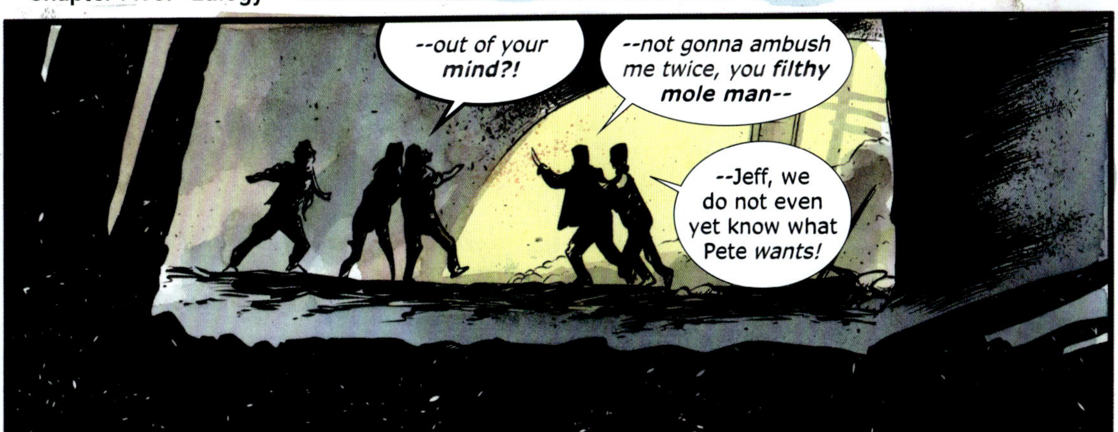
--out of your mind?!
--not gonna ambush me twice, you filthy mole man--
--Jeff, we do not even yet know what Pete wants!

Rhee! Rhiannon?! Are you...hey, getoffme!
Wait, listen to us--
Yo! Back away from the girl, stinky!
We just wanted to help! Pete...are you okay?
Is it deep?
...hunh... I'll live...
Let go! Pete attacked us and you hold me back?!
Jeff. Give me the knife...
Jeff--
Breathe, Pete.
You people came at me first, and now look...
...aw, fuck this.
Fuck this? Fuck you, bro!
Jeff, wai--ah! Dammit, Jeff!

...ah, shit.
They're gonna die, Tim.
are you okay/
Your father and I are so disappointed, Timothy.
with life on fire/
down in the grit/
with no desire/
"to break away/"
I can trust you to use this.
They're gonna die, Tim.
...they won't...
Timothy--

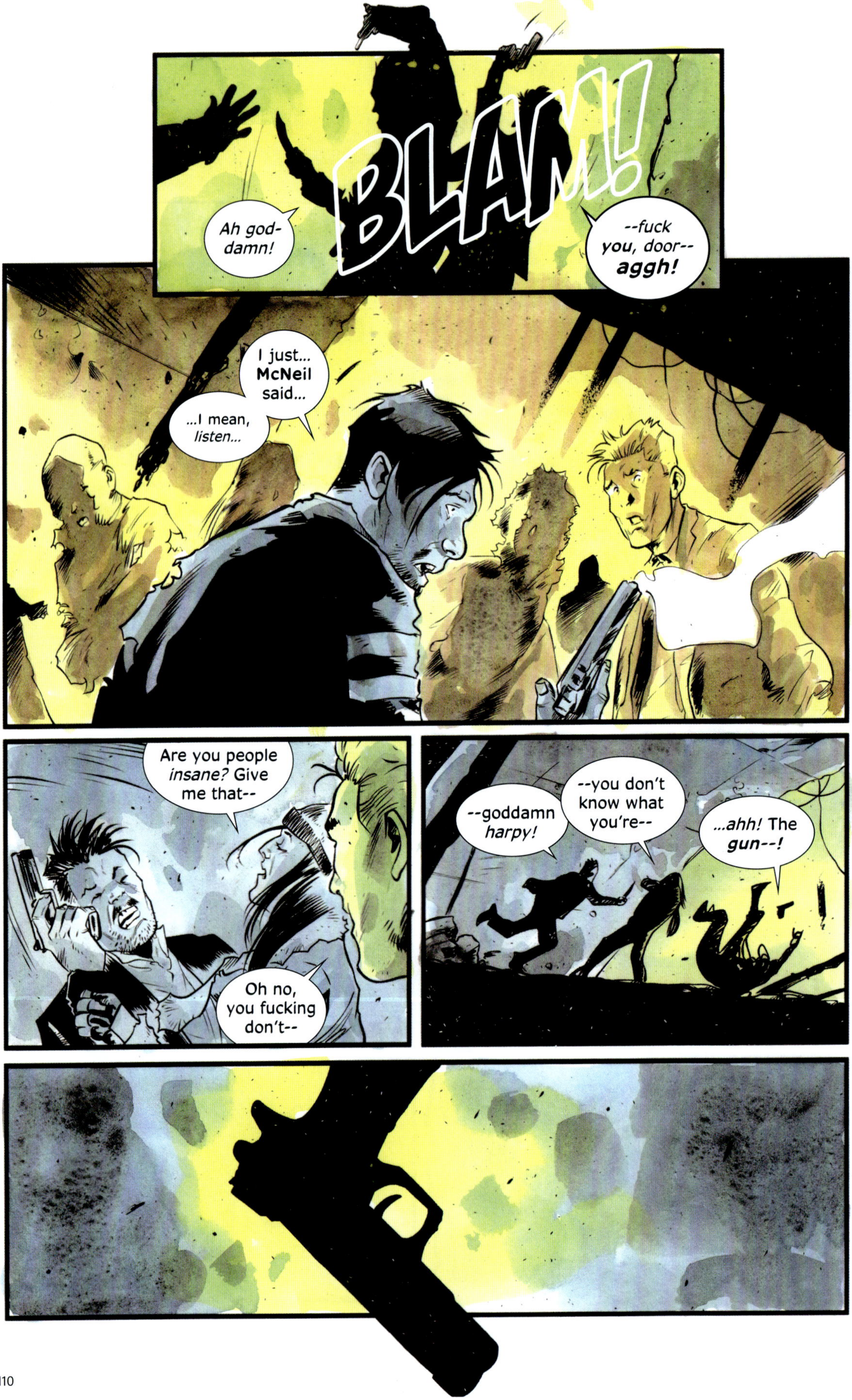
BLAM!
Ah god-damn!
--fuck you, door--aggh!
I just... McNeil said...
...I mean, listen...
Are you people insane? Give me that--
Oh no, you fucking don't--
--goddamn harpy!
--you don't know what you're--
...ahh! The gun--!

Almost **got** it--!
Oh no, **don't--**
--even **think** about it, you greasy bitch...!
Where... where'd it go? The *gun...*
Jeff!
Jeff, *wait...!*
...where is...did she...
...where'd Annie...***Oh.*** No no...
Jeff!
...No, no...

...no! *Annie!* Wait a sec!
Keep *away* from us, **Jeff!**
Annie. Should we...?
Keep going. *Look,* David--
--we're almost **out.**
Wait! We need to ***talk!***
Get away, you *creepy*--
Annie, I just wanna *talk* to you *before*--
Hey, *Jeff...* **wait...**
--we leave...what **--who...**
Hey! I said **wait!**

Aaaa aahhh!
...fuckin' distance, asshole!
...aw hell not again...
What, scum fuck? Leave us alone, Pete!
...was only trying to help...
Can't you see we're a family?!
Can't you fuckin' see--
Jeff. T...turn around.
G-get away from him.

I mean it, Jeff. *Walk away.*
You're out of control.
Annie?
You have the...
...this *nobody* attacked our **family.** Back when we crashed.
Shut up, *Pete!*
...not... no...
I'm...we're not your "family," okay? You're *crazy.*
You're... you need to **stop.**
Can't stop, babe.
We **are** family. We shared this... *connection.* You, me...David.
Amigos *together,* right??
...amigos.
David...?
Know it, *bud.* I love you **both.**

Love us? *Dude*, you don't even *know* us.
Family? You're out of your mind.
Are you out of your *mind?*
...d-don't say that. Please, not *that.*
Dave, c'mere. She's *not* gonna shoot me.
We almost *kissed*, Annie. Remember?
Stop it! Can't you see how **scary** you're...
...David? *Wait--*
--Annie?
--Tim? He...!
Get *over* here, bud!
Annie...?

BLAM!
...no, he was so... and I just...he grabbed...
...and Tim...
...no.
...Annie?
We almost...
...almost k-kissed...
...thought you I-I... liked...
...Oh. Dian... Di...

...j-just...wanted ...legacy...
...with you...
Jeff?! Jeff! No--
H-holy shit...is he--
I killed him.
THOK
Oh...I... killed...
Annie? Wait...
Annie!
NEW YORK CHANGED THAT NIGHT.

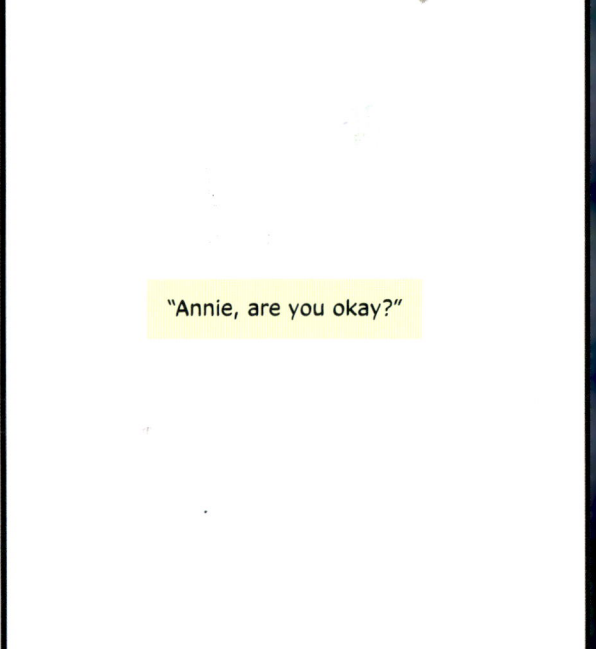

AND THERE WERE MORE IMPORTANT THINGS AT STAKE THAN THE FATE OF A RUNAWAY TRAIN.

...I just wanted...

...didn't mean to kill...

BUT TELL THAT TO THE SURVIVORS.

...so sorry...

"Annie!

"Annie, we need you!

"Annie, are you okay?"

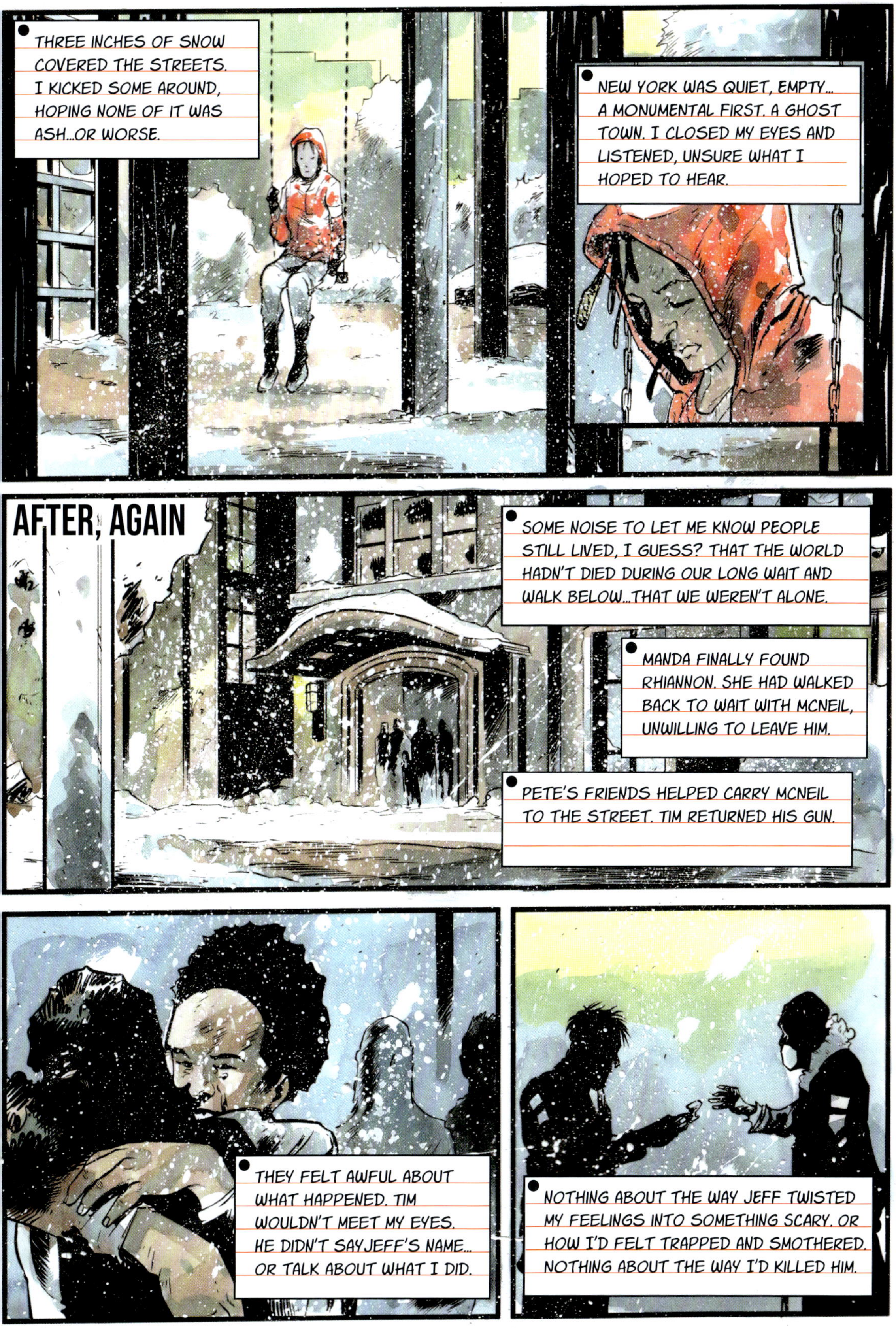
THREE INCHES OF SNOW COVERED THE STREETS. I KICKED SOME AROUND, HOPING NONE OF IT WAS ASH...OR WORSE.
NEW YORK WAS QUIET, EMPTY... A MONUMENTAL FIRST. A GHOST TOWN. I CLOSED MY EYES AND LISTENED, UNSURE WHAT I HOPED TO HEAR.
AFTER, AGAIN
SOME NOISE TO LET ME KNOW PEOPLE STILL LIVED, I GUESS? THAT THE WORLD HADN'T DIED DURING OUR LONG WAIT AND WALK BELOW...THAT WE WEREN'T ALONE.
MANDA FINALLY FOUND RHIANNON. SHE HAD WALKED BACK TO WAIT WITH MCNEIL, UNWILLING TO LEAVE HIM.
PETE'S FRIENDS HELPED CARRY MCNEIL TO THE STREET. TIM RETURNED HIS GUN.
THEY FELT AWFUL ABOUT WHAT HAPPENED. TIM WOULDN'T MEET MY EYES. HE DIDN'T SAY JEFF'S NAME... OR TALK ABOUT WHAT I DID.
NOTHING ABOUT THE WAY JEFF TWISTED MY FEELINGS INTO SOMETHING SCARY. OR HOW I'D FELT TRAPPED AND SMOTHERED. NOTHING ABOUT THE WAY I'D KILLED HIM.

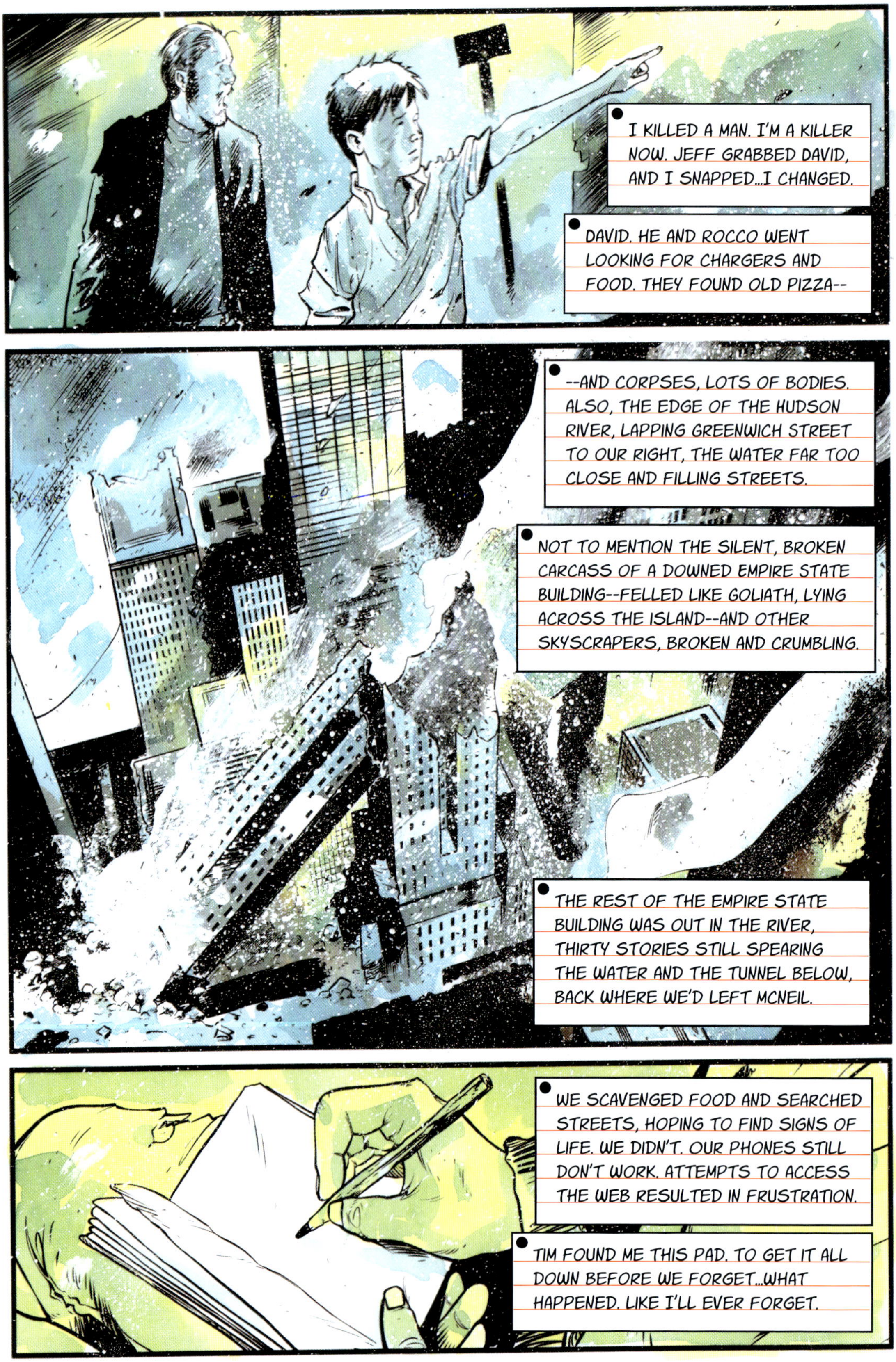
I KILLED A MAN. I'M A KILLER NOW. JEFF GRABBED DAVID, AND I SNAPPED...I CHANGED.
DAVID. HE AND ROCCO WENT LOOKING FOR CHARGERS AND FOOD. THEY FOUND OLD PIZZA--
--AND CORPSES, LOTS OF BODIES. ALSO, THE EDGE OF THE HUDSON RIVER, LAPPING GREENWICH STREET TO OUR RIGHT, THE WATER FAR TOO CLOSE AND FILLING STREETS.
NOT TO MENTION THE SILENT, BROKEN CARCASS OF A DOWNED EMPIRE STATE BUILDING--FELLED LIKE GOLIATH, LYING ACROSS THE ISLAND--AND OTHER SKYSCRAPERS, BROKEN AND CRUMBLING.
THE REST OF THE EMPIRE STATE BUILDING WAS OUT IN THE RIVER, THIRTY STORIES STILL SPEARING THE WATER AND THE TUNNEL BELOW, BACK WHERE WE'D LEFT MCNEIL.
WE SCAVENGED FOOD AND SEARCHED STREETS, HOPING TO FIND SIGNS OF LIFE. WE DIDN'T. OUR PHONES STILL DON'T WORK. ATTEMPTS TO ACCESS THE WEB RESULTED IN FRUSTRATION.
TIM FOUND ME THIS PAD. TO GET IT ALL DOWN BEFORE WE FORGET...WHAT HAPPENED. LIKE I'LL EVER FORGET.

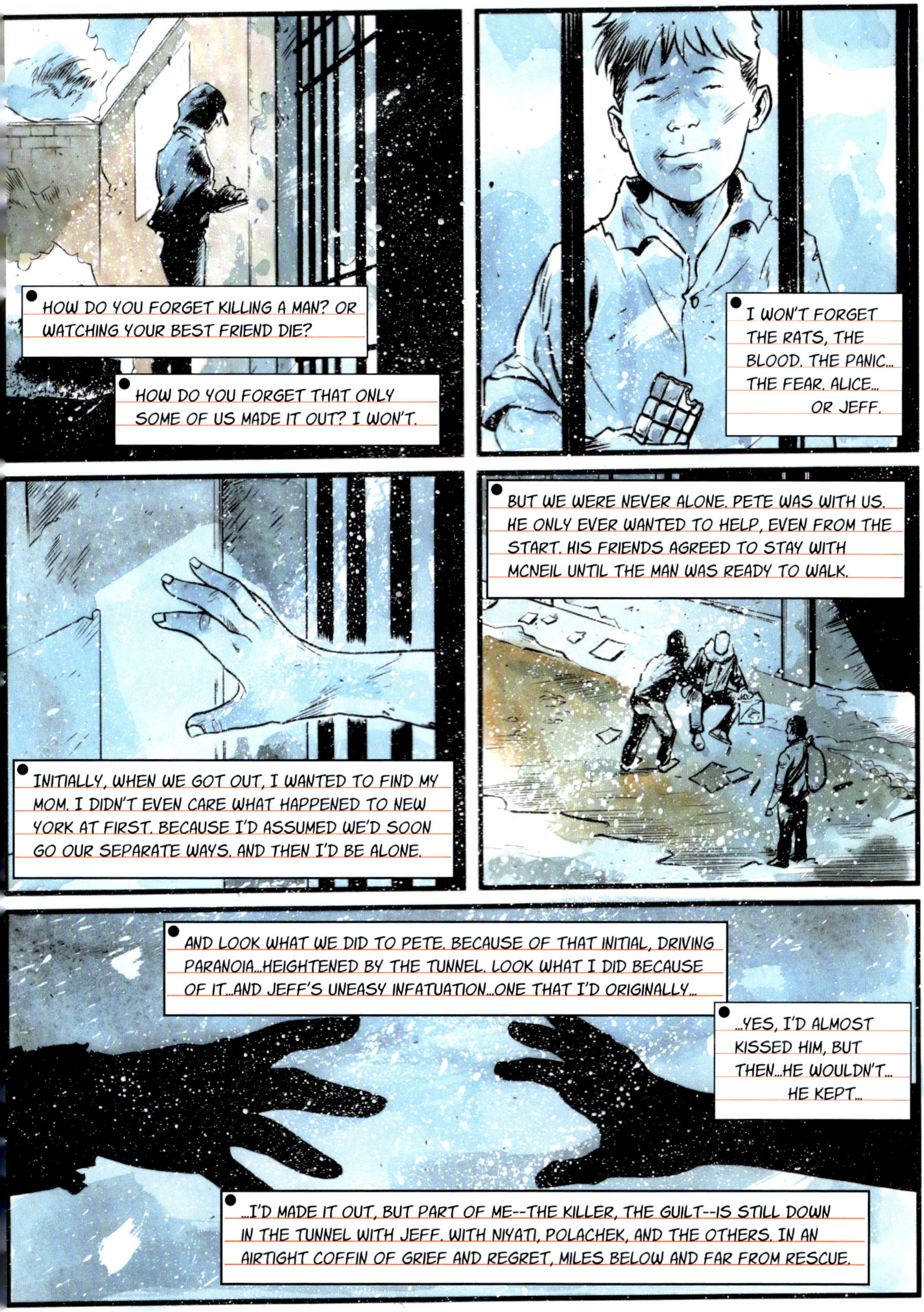
HOW DO YOU FORGET KILLING A MAN? OR WATCHING YOUR BEST FRIEND DIE?
HOW DO YOU FORGET THAT ONLY SOME OF US MADE IT OUT? I WON'T.
I WON'T FORGET THE RATS, THE BLOOD. THE PANIC... THE FEAR. ALICE... OR JEFF.
INITIALLY, WHEN WE GOT OUT, I WANTED TO FIND MY MOM. I DIDN'T EVEN CARE WHAT HAPPENED TO NEW YORK AT FIRST. BECAUSE I'D ASSUMED WE'D SOON GO OUR SEPARATE WAYS. AND THEN I'D BE ALONE.
BUT WE WERE NEVER ALONE. PETE WAS WITH US. HE ONLY EVER WANTED TO HELP, EVEN FROM THE START. HIS FRIENDS AGREED TO STAY WITH MCNEIL UNTIL THE MAN WAS READY TO WALK.
AND LOOK WHAT WE DID TO PETE. BECAUSE OF THAT INITIAL, DRIVING PARANOIA...HEIGHTENED BY THE TUNNEL. LOOK WHAT I DID BECAUSE OF IT...AND JEFF'S UNEASY INFATUATION...ONE THAT I'D ORIGINALLY...
...YES, I'D ALMOST KISSED HIM, BUT THEN...HE WOULDN'T... HE KEPT...
...I'D MADE IT OUT, BUT PART OF ME--THE KILLER, THE GUILT--IS STILL DOWN IN THE TUNNEL WITH JEFF. WITH NIYATI, POLACHEK, AND THE OTHERS. IN AN AIRTIGHT COFFIN OF GRIEF AND REGRET, MILES BELOW AND FAR FROM RESCUE.

WE ALL LIVE INSIDE PRIVATE COFFINS, RIGHT?
Annie? Are you okay?
HUMANS, THAT IS. LOCKED INSIDE OUR OWN COFFINS MADE OF GRIEF OR GUILT. BUT NOW AND AGAIN...
...SOMEBODY LIKE DAVID...OR A STRANGER ON A TRAIN...OFFERS TO HELP CARRY THE WEIGHT.
Not at all, pal.
But I *will* be.
How about Brooklyn? Some of us have family, and I know the area.
Who put *you* in charge?
TO HELP YOU SURVIVE YOUR CASKET OF ANGER.
C'mon, *still?* I'm wavin' the white flag over here, okay?
"*White,*" huh?
...we'll see. So, Brooklyn, then?
TO HELP SURVIVE BEING LOCKED IN WITH STUBBORN PRIDE OR SPECIFIC BELIEFS.
I'm just saying we should stick to bridges, stay above and out in the open.
If the bridges are still standing.
Well, all the people got off this island *somehow.*
Damn. Did they all evacuate, or...where the hell did everybody go?

My friends will try to recover all of the bodies below.
Meanwhile, I can help you see what's what, and maybe find safety.
"Safety." Right.
Annie...if you and David want to wait with McNeil...
Rest or mourn... *er*...we can always come *back?*
No, I'm just *hangry.* We stay **together.**
Time to stop dwelling and start *moving.*
Annie--
AND TO HELP SURVIVE THE SORROW, CHANGE, AND CRUSHING GUILT.
--here. It's my *last* candy.
Oh... David... thank you.
But next chance I get? *Hot. Coffee.*
Ha ha...! Okay.
Hey, David?
Yeah?
I *really* needed to hear that laugh.
EVEN IF, DESPITE THEIR HELP, THE BURDEN AND PANIC ARE YOURS ALONE.

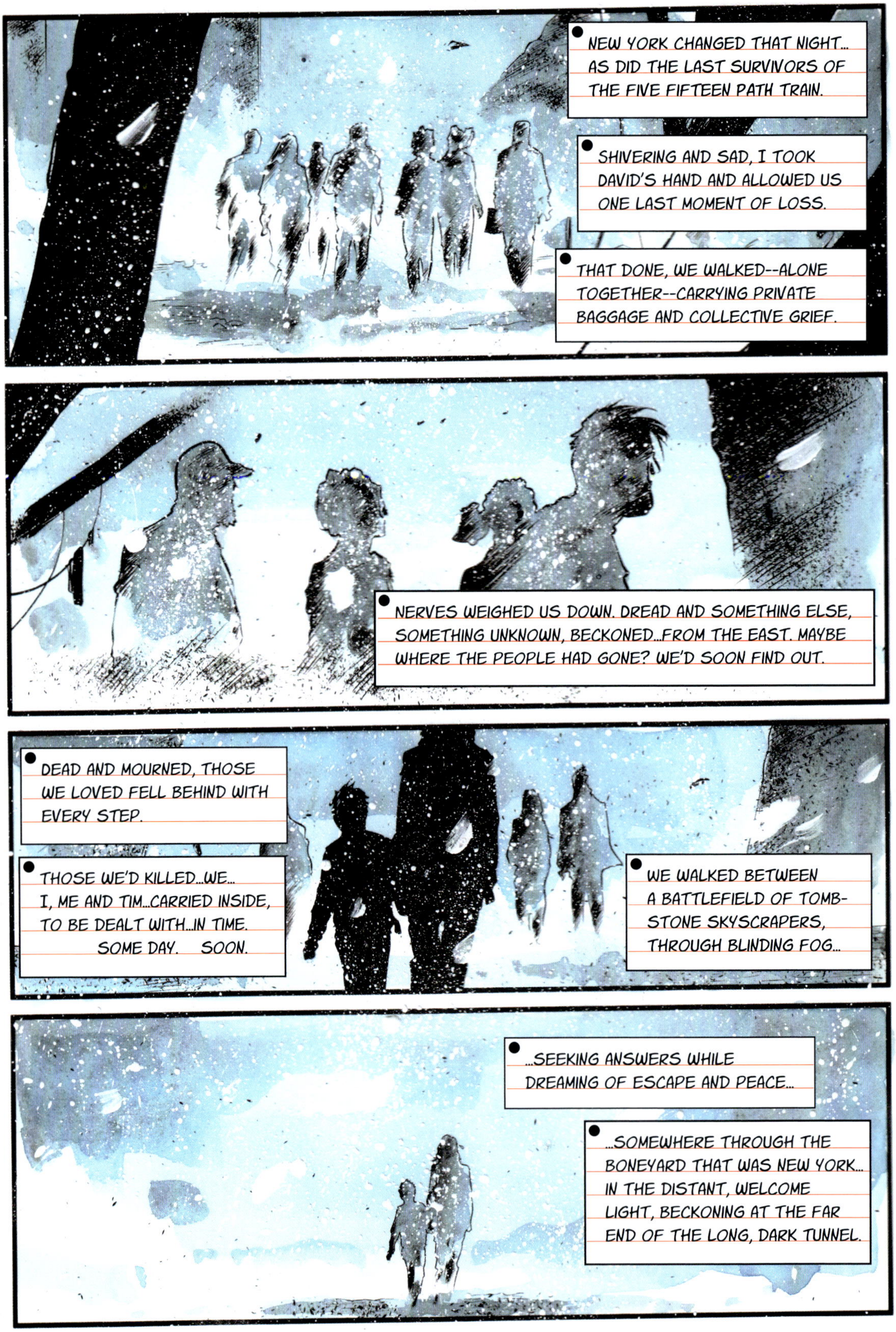
NEW YORK CHANGED THAT NIGHT... AS DID THE LAST SURVIVORS OF THE FIVE FIFTEEN PATH TRAIN.
SHIVERING AND SAD, I TOOK DAVID'S HAND AND ALLOWED US ONE LAST MOMENT OF LOSS.
THAT DONE, WE WALKED--ALONE TOGETHER--CARRYING PRIVATE BAGGAGE AND COLLECTIVE GRIEF.
NERVES WEIGHED US DOWN. DREAD AND SOMETHING ELSE, SOMETHING UNKNOWN, BECKONED...FROM THE EAST. MAYBE WHERE THE PEOPLE HAD GONE? WE'D SOON FIND OUT.
DEAD AND MOURNED, THOSE WE LOVED FELL BEHIND WITH EVERY STEP.
THOSE WE'D KILLED...WE... I, ME AND TIM...CARRIED INSIDE, TO BE DEALT WITH...IN TIME. SOME DAY. SOON.
WE WALKED BETWEEN A BATTLEFIELD OF TOMB-STONE SKYSCRAPERS, THROUGH BLINDING FOG...
...SEEKING ANSWERS WHILE DREAMING OF ESCAPE AND PEACE...
...SOMEWHERE THROUGH THE BONEYARD THAT WAS NEW YORK... IN THE DISTANT, WELCOME LIGHT, BECKONING AT THE FAR END OF THE LONG, DARK TUNNEL.

SO, WHY DID I WRITE *THE PANIC*?
by Neil Kleid

Truthfully, I've been writing *The Panic* for over a decade.

The book's original incarnation was a novel, *Coffin*, serialized in chapters online some time after 9/11/01. Originally, the story was about a group of diverse strangers coming together after a bomb derails their PATH train beneath the Hudson, influenced by New York's admirable resilience in the face of horror, tangentially colored by my, my family, and my friends' experiences after 9/11 and after suicide attacks on buses and restaurants throughout Jerusalem. *Coffin* was my way to deal with a post-9/11 world, optimistically noting that despite terrible things, the human spirit—particularly humans in New York for the weeks following the Trade Center attacks—brought us together as a community despite our many differences. Much more grounded, less speculative . . . somewhat jingoistic? I self-published *Coffin* via an early print-on-demand service, and that was that.

Eight years later, *Coffin* found its way into the hands of an editor at an imprint of Little, Brown, a well-known book publisher. Suddenly, there were plans to publish a trilogy of novels, rewritten to take advantage of the market's interest in genre fiction (influenced by the runaway success of *The Walking Dead*). The catalyst for our inciting incident was moved away from "terrorist attack" toward more scientific means and as a result, a more apocalyptic narrative. That shift changed the nature of not only the climax—adjusting to continue the story beyond its time beneath the Hudson, emerging to explore a changed society, eventually discovering what caused the crash—but the nature of the survivors themselves. Richer but different. Broader, but still about diverse strangers with unique fears and desires coming together to face sudden, unknown, gripping panic. And what that shift allowed me to do was turn *Coffin* from a standalone story about a handful of people in a tunnel into a sprawling, complex love letter to not only humanity's ability to thrive in the face of all kinds of adversity . . . but also to New York itself.

I wrote several drafts of that book. And then one of the editors left Little, Brown and the imprint's focus changed. And that, again, was that. For a bit.

SO, WHY DID I KEEP WRITING *THE PANIC*?

There had been so much development to *Coffin*, and I'd fallen in love with the world and these characters. I felt it could find new life as a comic book series, and thankfully others agreed. I developed it further with a number of intrigued editors, giving me the opportunity to keep inspecting my story with fresh eyes in a changing New York. The story kept getting distance from 9/11 with every year and iteration, but the nature of our rapidly shifting culture—social, political, and technological—also meant that the narrative was becoming less plot driven and more character driven. *Coffin* weathered the Occupy movement, Ferguson, the 2016 election, Charlottesville, #MeToo, George Floyd's death, a pandemic, a multitude of shootings and hate crimes, and . . . it evolved. America grew more divisive and tense, and as the book's coauthor I worried that our survivors might now be too politically and racially disconnected to come together when the lights went out.

At its heart, our book has always been about emotionally navigating the moment after something terrible happens, even (especially) if you don't know what caused it. The specifics of an inciting incident—why a train crashed, who is shooting, what exploded—became less important than the sinking feeling in the pit of one's belly, that sense of dread and unease when your personal world is upended and tossed into terrible conditions via unknown means . . . that . . . *panic* inside which has to drive all decisions to come, logical or ill advised. I'd always worried the script may have overdramatized specific reactions, particularly the ending—would the survivors just sit patiently for days, avoiding eye contact, waiting for help that would never come? Even after hours of stress, isolation, and pockets of frights, could someone like Annie (or me) be pushed far enough to take a life if she felt her life (or David's) was threatened or violated? Alone, hungry, and clueless for hours, would Alice really snap and start to feed? What are humans truly capable of when forced to stay alive? What happens when politically divided, previously isolated Americans have to work as a group in order to survive? That, to me, has always been this tale. Readers may not agree with the motivations, decisions, or conclusions drawn . . . but who *really* knows how humans will react after hours in the dark, facing driving, blinding, frightening *panic*? And so we had a new title.

I DIDN'T CREATE *THE PANIC* ALONE

Thankfully, I had others helping us arrive at said motivations, decisions, or conclusions. *The Panic* is the product of many influences and voices, some directly working on the series and some asking questions to shape its final form. First and foremost, enough thanks and goodwill cannot be sent to my incredible, talented, patient coauthor, **Andrea Mutti**. I've been privileged to be the first to see every thumbnail, every set of pencils, every color as they hit my inbox, as Andrea elevated my rambling vision into high art with each turn of the page. A gifted storyteller, he has been pivotal in making sure that not only fear, horror, sorrow, and creepiness bled from script to page, conveying our characters' motivations, guilt, the conclusions drawn as stated above . . . but he brainstormed the finer points, dedicated to ensuring that *The Panic* is the best damn comic you, our wonderful, good-looking readers, have ever read. Every conversation between us results in virtual high-fives and flame emojis, signed off as "brother." Andrea, thanks for letting me be your brother in panic, allowing me the privilege to coauthor this tale together with you.

Thanks to **Mariah McCourt** and **Felix Stringer Horne** for helping keep first the plot and then the ensuing narrative and dialogue on track. All authors should count themselves lucky enough to work with a fantastic editor; Andrea and I have been twice lucky. Thanks as well to **Amanda Stevens**, our diversity and inclusion consultant. As our characters evolved, ensuring they reflected a truly diverse set of New Yorkers, Amanda's voice has been crucial and welcome in making sure their stories have been told as authentically and as sensitively as possible. My gratitude to **Wes Miller**, **Mark Doyle**, and **Will Dennis** for helping *The Panic* out of its *Coffin* with every draft. Of course, Andrea and I are delighted to be partnered with the great **Chip Mosher**, **Bryce Gold**, **Nora Gomez**, **David Steinberger**, and everyone at Comixology who believed in *The Panic* and helped our team unleash this unnerving story. Finally and most importantly, Andrea would like to dedicate this book to his aunt Ornella, and Neil would like to thank **Laurie**, **Jack**, **Owen**, **Olivia**, and **Connor** for all of their support, even if it seems like Dad is always working. And thank YOU for reading and supporting *The Panic*, fellow survivor. Here's hoping we can venture together into the boneyard.

COVER CONCEPTS
by Andrea Mutti

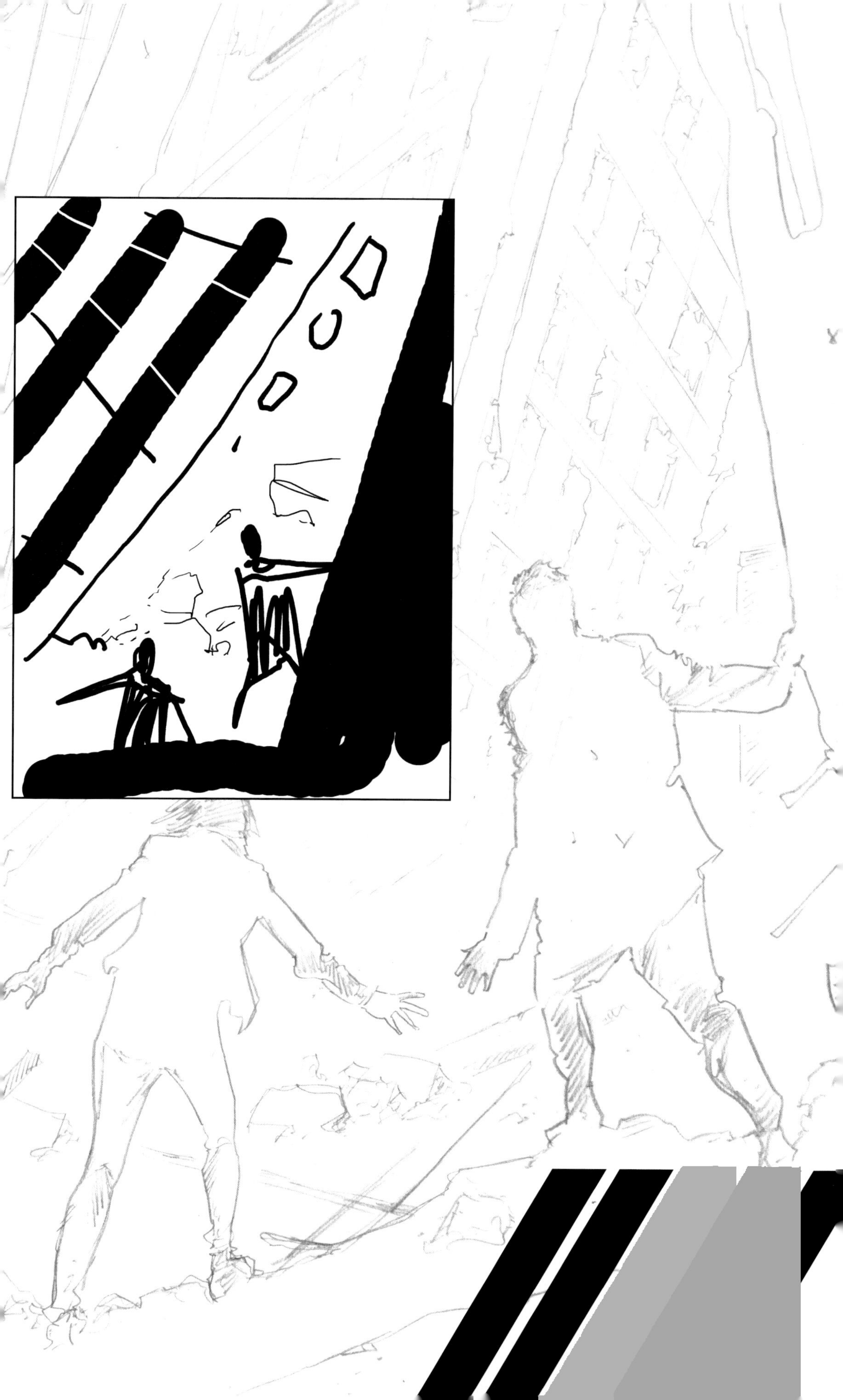

PAGE IN TRANSIT
by Neil and Andrea

Ever wonder how we build a page of *The Panic*, your favorite horror comic with a heart (and legs, arms, teeth, all somewhat bleeding and severed . . . sorry, I digress)?

01 First, Neil writes up all these awful words in a script:

Page 3 (4 PANELS)

PANEL ONE
Looking down at Tim sitting trapped in the cabin, staring at the door with the lighter flicked on, creating a small circle of light.

DOOR: You'll burn yourself, Tim. But that wouldn't surprise me at all.

TIM: Fuck you, door.

TIM: "This is your shot/"

PANEL TWO
EXT. CRASH SITE — NIGHT
Again, shot of the PATH train crash. Looking again at the first car, where Tim is trapped. Small fires and some dissipating smoke. Broken cars.

TIM (OP): "to get away/"

PANEL THREE
Moving further down the line of broken cars, we're now back at our compartment from issue #1, where the circle of survivors are trapped. We can maybe see their shadows inside…but we can't tell whether or not Pete is still there.

CAPTION: "Do you think Pete's still out there?"

CAPTION: "It's been a few hours now."

02 Then Andrea sketches up a fast layout for the action:

03 After Neil and Mariah stop salivating over the layout, Andrea draws a defined pencil stage:

04

The pencils are approved and high-fives go around! Now it's time for Andrea to apply visceral, brutal colors with astounding talent and violence.

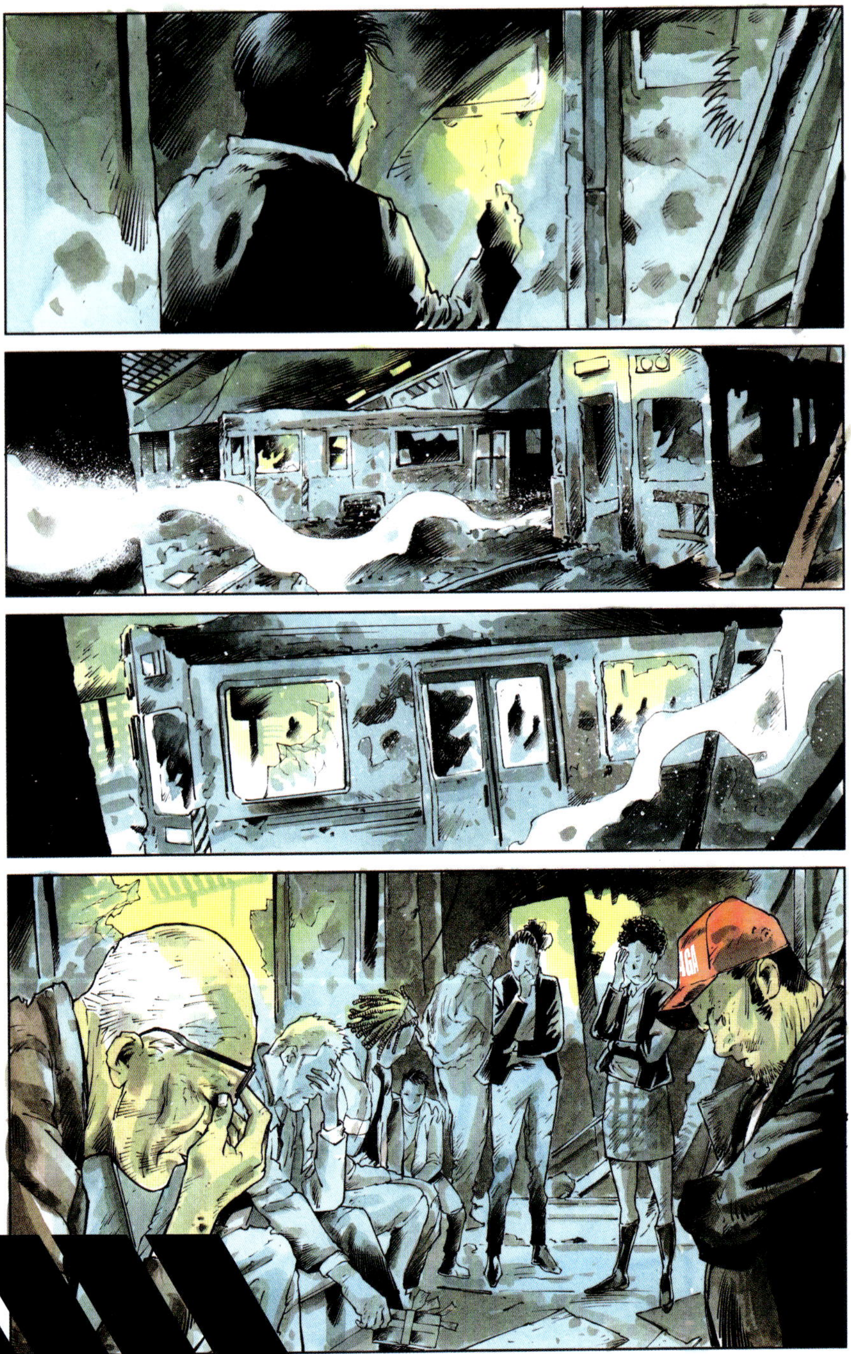

05 Now all that's left is for Neil to drop the final art into his favorite design software and apply the lettering (dialogue, captions, sound effects).

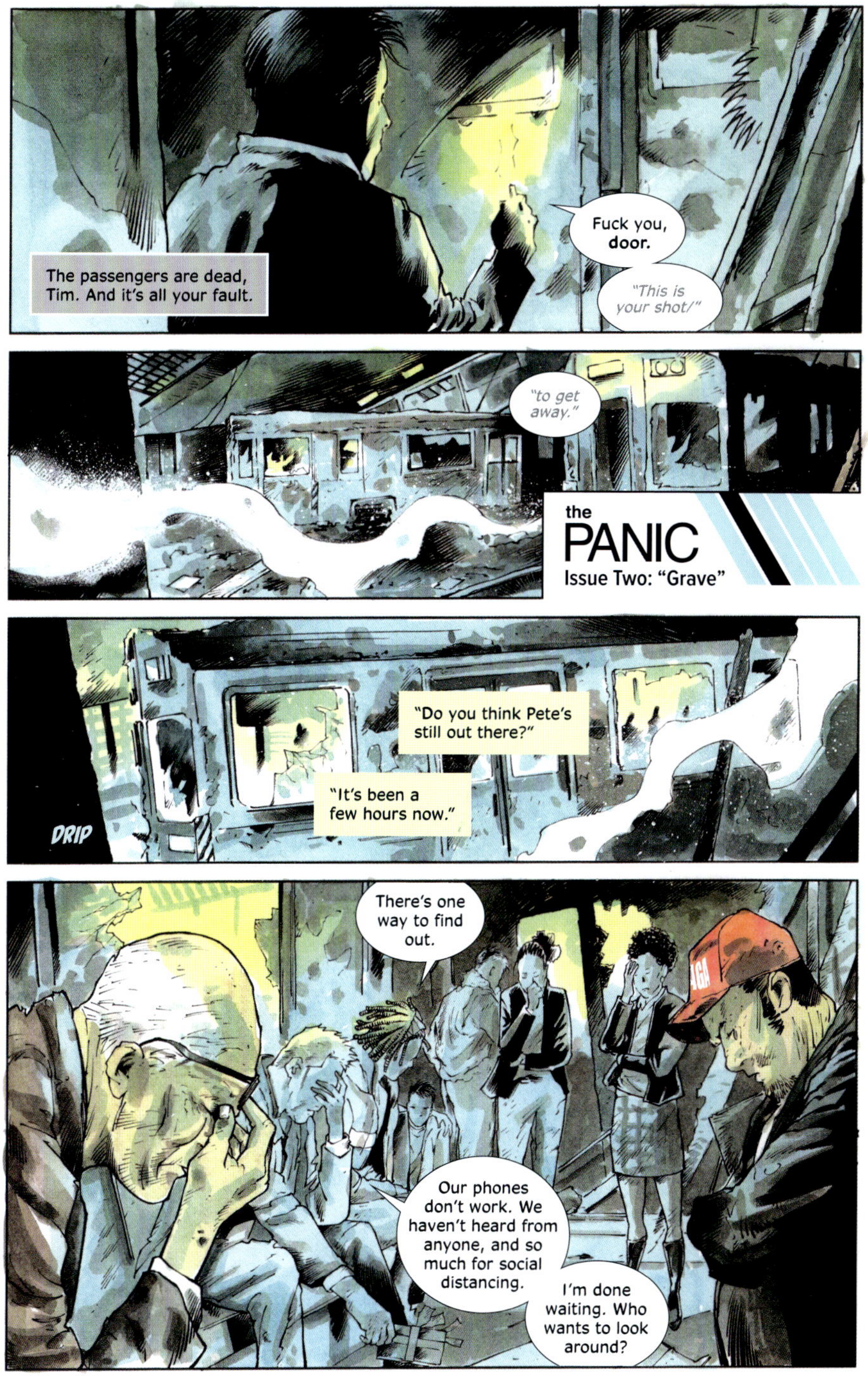
The passengers are dead, Tim. And it's all your fault.
Fuck you, **door.**
"This is your shot/"
"to get away."
the PANIC
Issue Two: "Grave"
"Do you think Pete's still out there?"
"It's been a few hours now."
DRIP
There's one way to find out.
Our phones don't work. We haven't heard from anyone, and so much for social distancing.
I'm done waiting. Who wants to look around?

BEHOLD. It is a comic book page. Welcome it to the world.

Now repeat that twenty-two times. For five issues.

(Sob.) (Kidding. We LOVE it.)

this has been
THE PANIC

Ten strangers, trapped beneath the Hudson, forced to depend on their fellow commuters in order to survive an apocalyptic event . . . that is, if they don't kill each other first.

THEMES

- Exploration of humans connecting as a group in an emergency vs. an individual's natural instinct to isolate.
- Being human helps overcome prejudices and divisions when left alone together in the dark.
- Never judge a book by a cover, because it may be the guidebook that saves your life.

OVERVIEW

The fallout of an incident that changes our world, narrowed to a group of survivors depending on one another to survive the unknown, claustrophobia, self-esteem issues, rats, emotional infatuation, despair, and death. What does humanity do to itself in the dark, forced to work together and find the end of a long, dangerous tunnel?

SO, OF COURSE THERE'S MORE.

Should we walk into a strange New York, we might ask ourselves what caused the PATH train to derail. What was the incident which trapped our survivors underground in the first place, and why is Manhattan empty (speaking as a New Yorker, I can say that only the worst scenario might give us an empty, silent Manhattan)? What could be so terrible that no one bothered to rescue the survivors of a train derailment or check on their whereabouts? What the heck is going on, and more to the point, will we find out?

Well, that's kind of up to you and others like you. Support of books like this—whether digitally or physically—via reading it (which you did, thanks!) or sales (thanks for buying) and most importantly, word of mouth, helps us tell more story. Your support and others' support translates into success, allowing us to do the next volume and the volume after that. This not only holds true for *The Panic*, but other creator-owned comics, as well. So if you've read something you like, and are vocal about it, tell others to do the same. Check out amazing books on Comixology and preorder them to your local comic shop.

You—our good-looking readers—are the most valuable part of ensuring the tale continues. Whatever may come, again, the coauthors thank you for your support.

THE COCREATORS

Neil Kleid \ The Writer

Xeric Award–winning graphic novelist Neil Kleid has authored *Ninety Candles*, a novella about life, death, legacy, and comics, as well as the acclaimed graphic novels *Brownsville* and *The Big Kahn*. He has written for nearly every publisher in the comic book industry; adapted Jack London's novel *The Call of the Wild* into comics for Penguin Books; did the opposite for the seminal Marvel Comics story line *Spider-Man: Kraven's Last Hunt*; and coauthored (with Brian Michael Bendis) *Powers: The Secret History of Deena Pilgrim* for MacMillan Books, the first-ever original prose novel based on the award-winning comic book. *Savor*, his new adventure graphic novel (with John Broglia and Frank Reynoso), debuted in 2021 from Dark Horse Comics. Neil is a trained product designer with twenty years of experience, having created experiences for clients such as Girl Scouts, Clarks Shoes, and the Topps Company. He lives in New Jersey with his wife, kids, dog, grill.

Andrea Mutti \ The Artist

After obtaining his degree in geometry, Andrea Mutti attended the Comics School in Brescia, Italy, led by Ruben Sosa. He began his career illustrating the superhero comic *DNAction* for Xenia Edizioni. He then illustrated horror comics for Fenix. He moved over to Star Comics, where he drew stories for *Lazarus Ledd* and some episodes of *Hammer*. Between 1993 and 2000, he was one of the artists for the Bonelli series *Nathan Never*. He has worked extensively for the French market, collaborating with Glénat, Dargaud, Soleil, Lombard, Ankama, Casterman, Dupuis, and many others. In 2001 Andrea landed in the US market, working for a wide range of publishers including DC/Vertigo (*The Executor* with Jon Evans, *DMZ*), Marvel (several *Iron Man* series), and IDW (*G.I. Joe: Origins*). Andrea won an award for best Italian artist in 2011. He lives in Sarasota with his family.

COMIXOLOGY COMES TO DARK HORSE BOOKS!

AFTERLIFT
Chip Zdarsky, Jason Loo, Paris Alleyne, Aditya Bidikar
US $19.99/CAN $25.99
ISBN: 978-1-50672-440-9

BREAKLANDS
Justin Jordan, Tyasseta, Sarah Stern
US $19.99/CAN $25.99
ISBN: 978-1-50672-441-6

YOUTH
Curt Pires, Alex Diotto, Dee Cunniffe
US $19.99/CAN $25.99
ISBN: 978-1-50672-461-4

THE BLACK GHOST
Monica Gallagher, Alex Segura, Marco Finnegan, George Kambadai, Ellie Wright
US $19.99/CAN $25.99
ISBN: 978-1-50672-446-1

THE PRIDE OMNIBUS
Joe Glass, Cem Iroz, Hector Barros, Jacopo Camagni, Ryan Cody, Mark Dale, and others
US $29.99/CAN $39.99
ISBN: 978-1-50672-447-8

STONE STAR VOLUME 1: FIGHT OR FLIGHT
Jim Zub, Max Dunbar, Espen Grundetjern
US $19.99/CAN $25.99
ISBN: 978-1-50672-458-4

LOST ON PLANET EARTH
Magdalene Visaggio, Claudia Aguirre
US $19.99/CAN $25.99
ISBN: 978-1-50672-456-0

DELVER
MK Reed, Spike C. Trotman, Clive Hawken
US $19.99/CAN $25.99
ISBN: 978-1-50672-452-2

DRACULA: SON OF THE DRAGON
Mark Sable, Salgood Sam
US $19.99/CAN $25.99
ISBN: 978-1-50672-442-3

TREMOR DOSE
Michael Conrad, Noah Bailey
US $19.99/CAN $25.99
ISBN: 978-1-50672-460-7

THE DARK
Mark Sable, Kristian Donaldson, Lee Loughridge
US $19.99/CAN $25.99
ISBN: 978-1-50672-459-1

CREMA
Johnnie Christmas, Dante Luiz, Ryan Ferrier
US $19.99/CAN $25.99
ISBN: 978-1-50672-603-8

SNOW ANGELS VOLUME 1
Jeff Lemire, Jock
US $19.99/CAN $25.99
ISBN: 978-1-50672-648-9

SNOW ANGELS VOLUME 2
Jeff Lemire, Jock
US $19.99/CAN $25.99
ISBN: 978-1-50672-649-6

THE ALL-NIGHTER
Chip Zdarsky, Jason Loo, Paris Aditya
US $19.99/CAN $25.99
ISBN: 978-1-50672-804-9

ADORA AND THE DISTANCE
Marc Bernardin, Ariela Kristantina, Jessica Kholinne
US $14.99/CAN $19.99
ISBN: 978-1-50672-450-8

WE ONLY KILL EACH OTHER
Stephanie Phillips, Peter Krause, Ellie Wright
US $19.99/CAN $25.99
ISBN: 978-1-50672-808-7

THE STONE KING
Kel McDonald, Tyler Crook
US $19.99/CAN $25.99
ISBN: 978-1-50672-448-5

LIEBESTRASSE
Greg Lockard, Tim Fish, Hector Barros
US $19.99/CAN $25.99
ISBN: 978-1-50672-455-3

EDEN
Matt Arnold, Riccardo Burchielli
US $22.99/CAN $29.99
ISBN: 978-1-50673-090-5

ASTONISHING TIMES
Frank Barbiere with Arris Quinones, Ruairi Coleman, Lauren Affe, Taylor Esposito
US $22.99/CAN $29.99
ISBN: 978-1-50673-083-7

WE HAVE DEMONS
Scott Snyder, Greg Capullo
US $19.99/CAN $25.99
ISBN: 978-1-50672-833-9

EDGEWORLD
Chuck Austen, Patrick Olliffe
US $19.99/CAN $25.99
ISBN: 978-1-50672-834-6

ISBN 978-1-50672-808-7 / $19.99

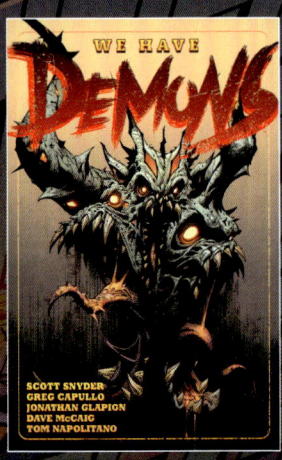

ISBN 978-1-50672-833-9 / $19.99

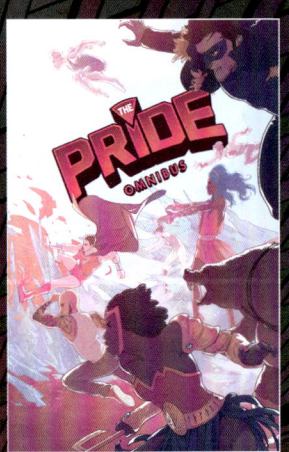

ISBN 978-1-50672-447-8 / $29.99

AVAILABLE AT YOUR LOCAL COMICS SHOP OR BOOKSTORE
To find a comics shop near you, visit comicshoplocator.com For more information or to order direct, visit darkhorse.com

COMIXOLOGY ORIGINALS

Afterlift™ © 2021 Zdarsco, Inc. & Jason Loo. The Black Ghost © 2021 Alex Segura, Monica Gallagher, and George Kambadais. Breaklands™ © 2021 Justin Jordan and Albertus Tyasseta. The Pride™ 2018, 2021 Joseph Glass, Gavin Mitchell and Cem Iroz. Stone Star™ © 2019, 2021 Jim Zub and Max Zunbar. Youth™ © 2021 Curt Pires, Alex Diotto, Dee Cunniffe. Dracula: Son of the Dragon™ © 2020, 2021 Mark Sable and Salgood Sam. Tremor Dose™ © 2019, 2021 Michael W. Conrad and Noah Bailey. The Dark™ © 2019, 2021 Mark Sable & Kristian Donaldson. Delver © 2019, 2021 C. Spike Trotman, MK Reed, and Clive Hawken. Lost on Planet Earth™ © 2020, 2021 Magdalene Visaggio and Claudia Aguirre. Crema™ © 2020, 2021 Johnnie Christmas. Snow Angels™ © 2021, 2022 Jeff Lemire and Jock. The Allnighter™ © 2020, 2022 Zdarsco, Inc. & Jason Loo. Adora and the Distance™ Volume One © 2021, 2022 Marc Bernardin and Ariela Kristantina. We Only Kill Each Other™ © 2021, 2022 Stephanie Phillips and Peter Krause. The Stone King © 2018, 2021, 2022 Kel McDonald and Tyler Crook. Liebestrasse™ © 2021, 2022 Greg Expectations, LLC, and Timothy Poisson. Eden © 2021, 2022 Matthew Arnold and Darkling Entertainment Inc. Astonishing Times™ © 2021, 2022 Barbiere, Quinones, and Coleman. We Have Demons™ © 2021, 2022 Scott Snyder and Greg Capullo. Edgeworld™ © 2021, 2022 Wimzi, Inc. "ComiXology" and the ComiXology logos are registered trademarks of ComiXology. Dark Horse Books® and the Dark Horse logo are registered trademarks of Dark Horse Comics LLC. All rights reserved. (BL5108)

DARK HORSE BOOKS